ABOUT THE AUTHOR

CW00395160

Stephen Baines was Yorks
ancestors who were mariners ot Whitby in the 18th and
19th Centuries, which has been the inspiration of all his
books.

After studying Theology at Cambridge University, Stephen
took a post-graduate year at Oxford. Then he studied at
the London Institute of Education where he met Susan
whom he married, after which they settled in East Anglia.
Stephen taught English at Philip Morant School in
Colchester for a dozen years, and then moved to the
Colchester Sixth Form College where he taught Religious
Studies, Philosophy (which involved making life easier for
his students by transcribing Descartes' Meditations into
rhyming couplets!), and Theory of Knowledge. He
introduced the International Baccalaureate (the College
being one of the first State Schools in the UK to do so).
After retiring from full-time teaching in 2006, he lectured
part-time on Ancient Greek Philosophy at the University
of Essex for two years.

Stephen Baines has had a range of articles published,
including Anglo-Norman sculpture, problem solving,
educating very able children, the sheep-breeder Jonas
Webb, and mediaeval drinking habits. He has been on
radio and television, and some of his poems have
appeared in print. His other interests include Geoffrey
Chaucer, ornithology, gardening, genealogy, croquet, and
playing the ukulele. His previous books are "*The Yorkshire*

Mary Rose, The General Carleton of Whitby" (Blackthorn Press. 2010) and "*Captain Cook's Merchant Ships: Freelove, Three Brothers, Mary, Friendship, Endeavour, Adventure, Resolution and Discovery*" (The History Press. 2015).

He has three daughters and four grandchildren.

ISBN 9781911266983

Williams & Whiting (Publishers)

15 Chestnut Grove, Hurstpierpoint,

West Sussex, BN6 9SS

FRIEND OR FOE

Stephen Baines

Williams & Whiting

Preface

This murder story is set mainly in Whitby. Most of the characters are my creation (though I have used local surnames) with the exception of the Quaker family of the Walkers, who are best known for their connections with Captain Cook.

The modern calendar is used for clarification, though in the period of this story England still used the Julian one. The post of Chief Constable of Whitby is fictional, created to simplify the rather confusing system of law and order at that time.

Chapter 1

Wednesday August 20th 1729

William Backas, Chief Constable of Whitby, and his wife Margaret, returned to their home in Skate Lane after a burial at the parish church. William hung up his formal coat and his tricorn hat, Margaret shed her trimmed bonnet and finely fringed black shawl. After asking Hilda, their maid, to fetch some tea, they slumped into the only two armchairs. It was noon and very hot.

For a time they were simply collapsed into silence.

William took off his wig, wiped his face and head with his neckerchief, and said –as much to himself as to his wife- "By all the gods, I'm broiled!"

"You have little to complain about, William. You didn't have to endure a laced-up bodice and layers of fabric, while pretending to be calm, cool and sad. I tell you, my dearest, coming down all those steps from the church was as painful as struggling up them. I imagined that at any moment I would tumble and roll, scattering the other mourners like skittles."

"That would have cheered the miserable onlookers."

They both laughed.

"I didn't want to go anyway; I still don't understand why you insisted."

"I had to go as a matter of duty, you came as my wife."

"Hm," she grunted, "I would have thought you could have gone without me holding your hand."

William smiled. "I always like to hold your hand, my dearest."

"Well, there are times, my dear, when I don't always want to hold your hand, and this funeral was one of them. Tell me more about him."

"Thomas Preston. A ship's carpenter. His was a terrible death, him being so young with a wife and three children to support. I spoke to her, but there are no words that will bring the dead back to life, or alleviate the grieving pain of a young widow."

"How exactly did he die?"

"It was during the turbulent weather of a few days ago. In that storm the pinnace had been damaged, and he was mending it. There was a sudden change of the wind, and he was struck by the boom. He died instantly. In a way it was a tragedy that the ship was so near Whitby, but also blessing that he could be buried in his home town, rather than at sea or washed ashore in some foreign shore. There are many sailors who die at sea."

"And also passengers; women and children - not just men."

"Indeed, and we must show our respect for such. The prosperity of Whitby is based on her seamen – this is why we went to the funeral. The vicar gave a sermon about the importance and fortitude of those 'that go down to the sea in ships, that do business in great waters.' A moving sermon in one sense, a stationary one in another, as it scarcely varies from one marine burial to another."

At this point Hilda brought in the tea, and poured it out. This raised their spirits and William and Margaret conversed merrily and briefly about the weather with Hilda, until the latter had to return to the ironing.

"However, Margaret, the service today was solely an opportunity to show our admiration to sailors in general, not for this particular sailor."

"Why is that so?"

"Do you not recall the name Thomas Preston?"

"No. How am I expected to know the names of all the seamen in Whitby?"

"He was one in that violent gang which was involved in the unpleasant incident on Coronation Day."

"Ah, yes. It comes back to me now. Thomas Preston. There would have been some who would have been willing to hasten his end; Jacob and Abigail were well thought of."

"I know, my dearest," William replied in a soft and gentle voice. There was a silence for a while as they sat quiet and still. Then William raised his teacup to his lips...

Suddenly there was a clatter of hoofs and banging on the door. Hilda abandoned the ironing and hurried across the hall shouting, "Patience, I am coming!" Sound of the door being opened, cautiously. "Hold your noise!" she cried, "What means you with all this furore?"

"I wish to see Mr Backas."

"Certainly, sir. If you come in quietly and take off your coat, I shall hang it up. Then if you would sit on this chair, I shall tell Mr Backas you are here. What name shall I say?"

"Mr Edward Hartley."

"And for what purpose is your visit?"

"It concerns a death."

"Thank you, sir."

Hilda came into the drawing room, and delivered the message.

Margaret muttered, "I hope it is not another fatal accident; I cannot cope with more than one a day!"

William asked Hilda to show him in. The visitor was a sturdy man, dressed as a workman in a leather coat and hat, but clearly of a higher status. He was in a full sweat, and his long hair was disordered with damp, shiny droplets clinging to his locks. His speech, hampered with breathlessness, spoke of urgency. "Master Backas, my apologies for this unruly entry, you must forgive me. My name is Edward Hartley, I am the supervisor of the Boulby Alum Works and something terrible has happened."

"An accident?"

"No, sir, a murder. You must come at once."

"But Boulby Alum Works is beyond my jurisdiction."

"The victim came from Whitby. By ship."

"And what makes you so sure that it is a murder rather than an accident?"

"No-one accidentally seals themself into a barrel."

William turned to Hilda, "Go down the road to Hargreaves and tell him to bring me the best horse he has for hire. Tell him it is an emergency."

"No," said Hartley, "Let me go, I shall be quicker; besides your maid is all a quiver and in no condition for such an errand."

"Thank you, sir. I accept your offer. Get me a horse firm of foot and speedy."

Hartley's departure was as sudden as his arrival.

"Hilda, Mr Hartley is right. I shall need to get dressed for out of doors, and to collect a few things, which I shall do myself. But you must go and lie down."

Hilda bobbed and said, "Yes, sir; thank you sir."

"And do not mention outside this house what has happened."

"Yes, sir."

"I mean it, Hilda!"

"Of course, sir."

The journey was nigh on twelve miles, and they travelled at a comparatively slow pace. Hartley's horse, though she had drunk a bucketful of water, had her ears tickled affectionately and had been treated to an apple, made it clear –as horses do- that she was not going to gallop all the way back. The horse which Hargreaves had provided, at a much higher price than was charged at The Flying Angel, was quite amenable to go at the same pace. Backas had asked for more details, but Hartley replied, "You must see for yourself, sir." After that not much was said, and neither felt the need to stop and eat.

A mile or so after Dalehouse they turned right onto a path. It was evident that horses, carts and boots travelled down the track with regularity; but what indicated that they were near the Alum Works was the shimmering effluvia of sulphurous acrid smoke and steam. Hartley was clearly habituated; but Backas covered his mouth and nose with his neckerchief. He coughed; and his eyes watered like those of the audience at a stage tragedy.

They dismounted outside a brick building, whose large door was guarded by two men. Backas looked around and it seemed like Dante's *Inferno* as the vast arena was surrounded with circles of pathways. All around were great burning pits whose covering of alum shale would sometimes split and bright flame would leap up. Crossing over this great Pandæmonium were men pushing wheelbarrows full of shale along the narrowest of planks. "No-one," thought William, "No-one has done sufficient wickedness to deserve this punishment. A terrible way to live; and a terrible way to die."

His musings were cut short by Hartley telling him to enter the building, and bring in the horse. The horses were tethered, and glad to be inside. The interior looked very large. There were all sorts of items scattered round the edges of this building; piles of stone, pickaxes, shovels, barrels, vats, sacks and mounds of unrecognisable substances. It looked as if all these things had been pushed against the walls to make a large space in the middle of the building, where there was a single, solitary item. It was a large cask; Backas reckoned that it was a butt of 126 gallons. It was standing on its end, some of the iron hoops at the top had been removed, and the lid had been removed and propped carefully by the side.

"Shall we go and look?" asked Hartley.

"Yes."

They walked slowly and quietly towards the barrel, hesitantly, almost reverentially. Once there, Mr Backas peered into the barrel. Inside there was a body with knees folded up almost to the chin. The head was bowed down and the body was squatting in some fluid which was suffused with blood. There was damage where the back of the head had been severely struck.

"Are you sure this is not one of yours?" asked Backas.

"No. The barrel came with seven other casks of lant in the ship from Whitby. This is a regular fortnightly delivery, so no-one had expected anything was amiss. All the butts contained lant, though in this one there was also a dead body".

"Drowned in urine?" Backas shuddered.

Hartley took the hair of the corpse and lifted the head; the throat had been cut.

Backas gasped, "I know this person!"

Chapter 2

Saturday 11 October 1727. Coronation Day.
(1 year, 10 months and 9 days earlier)

All day there had been riotous festivity: shouting, banging of drums, ringing of bells, singing – and much drinking. Now that it was dusk the noise was less, though in the streets and yards the smell of vomit and urine was stomach-churning. Wisely most of the inhabitants were indoors.

William Backas staggered home quite sober. He sat down in the hall and took off his boots. Margaret came out of the drawing room and kissed him. "Poor William, you look so weary. Has it been such a very bad day?"

"You have no idea, my love. My constable and the watchmen have done great work. Mainly they have been escorting drunks back to their home. Even so the lockup is full."

"At least the worst is over. I think it very inconsiderate of the king to allow people a holiday; they only cause trouble!"

"The king is not to blame, Margaret my dear. Besides, my time is largely dealing with trouble makers; if there weren't any troublesome drunks, I would not have a job."

"You are also in charge of organising the building of the workhouse."

"I prefer the drunks."

"You work too hard, William. At least you are home at last."

"Alas not, my dear. On coronations people put lit candles in their windows."

He was right. Anyone who looked down from the top of East Cliff would have seen the whole town of Whitby coruscating like the stars above, as nearly every house had lighted candles in their windows to show loyalty to their new king, crowned that morning as King George II.

"That is a pretty custom," said Margaret.

"Indeed. But some people, mainly Quakers, do not light a candle for the king. They think that all men are equal and that a king is just a man doing his job, as any others."

"He should come here and do your job; then he would know what work is!"

"At present I am worried about the Quakers who do not show a light. There could be trouble. The constable and his watchmen are already out there calming things down, I hope. I shall be going out to supervise and to ensure all the inhabitants of Whitby have a peaceful night." He pulled on his boots again.

"Can I get you some food before you go?"

"No thank you my dear, though it is a kind thought."

Not every house showed a light; and Jack Wheatear set out to ensure that all darkened houses were lit. Jack was 18; when he was 14 he had run away from his parents' rented smallholding, exchanging his life as an underpaid labourer for that of a sailor. He was sturdy with curly black hair — and he liked to be in charge. He had two colleagues, Thomas Preston and Simon Scott, who admired Jack's determination and feared his fists. Power is as simple as that.

On this evening Jack, armed with a thick staff, was flanked by Thomas and Simon, and in their wake was a mixed group of young men in varying degrees of sobriety. All were out to celebrate their day off work and to have a good time: drinking, singing, laughing, and hoping for a good fight or a good fuck. They swaggered and staggered from the Three Mariners in Haggersgate turning uphill into Flowergate.

Jacob Linskill, canvas weaver, cowered in his darkened house. He could hear them coming up the road long before Jack's entourage knew where he was leading them. Jacob knew. He remembered all too well the previous coronation when he had been beaten by just such a mob which had broken all the windows in the house, beaten him severely, and seriously damaged his loom. Fortunately, on that occasion thirteen years ago, his young wife and their daughter Abigail had taken refuge with her sister and brother-in-law in Pickering. Jacob's wife was now dead, and he had insisted that Abigail should once again stay with her aunt on this coronation day. He knew, as did Abigail, that a mob —even a drunken mob- might feel sympathy for a toddler, but an attractive 14-year-old girl might incite lust. But Abigail, his only child, was strong-willed as her mother had been; she refused to leave her father, though she had eventually promised to comply with his insistence that she should remain hidden in the back room.

The expected trouble had noised its ebullient way to the top of Flowergate, but when it reached the weaver's house it fell quiet. Jacob held his breath in the stillness, then came loud banging on the door and his skin tingled with fear. A silent prayer: *Give me strength, O Lord, give me strength*.

Jack thudded on the door once more with his heavy stick, and shouted "Open the door, in the name of the King, or we shall make a bonfire of your house!" Noise of bolts shot and the key turned; Jacob opened the door stepping back to allow his importunate guests to enter. Jack handed his wooden weapon to Thomas who was on his left, Simon was on his right and the rest instinctively formed a semi-circle behind them. A long, tense silence was ended by Jacob:

"You are guests in my house. What business do you have with me at this late hour?"

"You are a traitor!" shouted Jack, eliciting a rumble of "Traitor!", "Yes!", "Shame on you!" from behind him.

"I am no traitor, and thou art wrong to say so."

"Don't you 'thou' me with your Bible-talk. You are a Quaker and a traitor." More supportive shouts and mutters.

"I am indeed a member of the Religious Society of Friends; but I am no traitor."

"It is the coronation. All loyal subjects of the King have lit their windows this night."

"I doubt that. There must be some who cannot afford to light candles, and some who choose not to, as do I."

"You 'choose not to', villain, because you are not a loyal subject of the King."

"On the contrary, I have the greatest respect for George of Hanover. Ruling as king and governing with parliament must be a difficult task, and I wish him well. I wish all men well, especially when they are starting a new job of work; but I do not light candles for any of them, so why should I light one for the king? We are all equal in the eyes of God, and all people should be treated as friends. The king is my friend, and you are my friend."

Jack was aware that during this speech the comments behind him had diminished. He was losing support, and that angered him.

"But you have forgotten, Quaker, that you are no friend of mine!" And with these words he slapped Jacob fiercely on the side of his head. "And as a Quaker, you cannot retaliate!" Jack turned round to his audience with a self-satisfied grin and a wide-armed gesture of confidence. There was responsive laughter. He was in control again.

Jacob picked up his hat which had been knocked off by the blow, and straightened his wig which was awry. His head throbbed, his knees felt insubstantial, and his eyelids were twitching uncontrollably, but he tried to keep his voice calm.

"Thou wishest that I should light a candle?"

"Yes, you whoreson traitor! Surely I have made that clear, clodpole. But as you have been so disloyal in your speech, I shall also expect you to kneel down, beg forgiveness for insulting the King, and swear an oath that you will always be a loyal subject to the sovereign monarch George the Second."

"And if I do not?"

"If you do not I shall take that staff," pointing at Thomas who raised the weapon, "and break every window in this house, then I shall destroy your loom and beat you unconscious. Then I might set fire to this hovel of treachery."

Jacob: *Dear God, please protect my daughter Abigail and keep her from harm. And do not let him see how afeared I am, and save me from the shame of wetting my breeches.*

"I think, my friend, that thou wouldst be unwise to do that. There is no law in this land which maketh it a criminal offence not to light a candle on coronation night. However destroying property is certainly a crime. Also I kneel to no-one except God, and I beg to none but he. As a Quaker I do not swear oaths, as my word is true."

"Is that so, my smug 'friend'? You do not kneel? We shall see how true your word is, traitor! Thomas, Simon, seize him!"

Grinning with pleasure they obeyed his order. Jacob stood pinioned and helpless. Jack moved swiftly forward and punched the weaver hard in his belly. Jacob let forth an agonised moan, flopping like a marionette held up by his captors. "Make him kneel!" Jack commanded. They did.

"So now we know, lying Quaker, that you can kneel to me. Now beg and swear!"

Jacob hesitated, muttered: "I...I kneel...before thee...humbly..."

Jack turned to his audience and smirked. He had won. His conceit did not allow him to notice that his audience had diminished; several of his followers having secretively melted away. The situation had gone beyond a boisterous bit of fun.

Jacob began again, this time in a louder voice, "I kneel before thee humbly, O Lord, and beseech Thee to guide George in his office as monarch to rule justly and wisely. And I pray that all his subjects will live in love and harmony one with another, and that..."

Jack interrupted, his smugness boiled into rage: "Is this a joke? Do you dare to jest with me, Quaker scum?" He seized the staff which Thomas had dropped.

"It is not a joke, my friend; it is a prayer. I suggest that thou shouldst pray more often, and then perhaps..."

"You bastard! Son of a whore! Traitor! Who are you to tell me...?" Words failed him, and he turned to violence; viciously, repeatedly beating and kicking Jacob whose groans and cries of agony only stoked his fury.

"Papa! Papa!" Abigail came running from the back room, "Stop that! Thou art a wicked man to treat my good father so!"

For a fleeting moment all were frozen into silent immobility. Then, simultaneously:

Jacob: "Abigail, Run! Run!! Save thyself! Find help!"

Jack: "Thomas! Simon! Seize her!"

Abigail hesitated for two seconds – a second too long. Jack snapped a command to his minions: "Take her outside and hold her against the wall. I shall deal with her; you can have your turns after I have finished with her."

Jacob pleaded from the midst of his fallen agony, "I appeal to thee; leave her be. She has done no harm to thee. Let her go."

"So, weaver, you do beg after all, you hypocritical Quaker!" jeered Jack as he stamped heavily on Jacob's right hand, "Let's see how well you can weave with a warped hand."

"Do what thou wilt to me, but spare my daughter I beg thee. She is innocent, she is not yet fifteen years of age. Please...please."

"Old enough to be married is old enough to be fucked."

"No!" A new voice.

Jack looked round. It was Solomon King. Jack knew him by sight and reputation. He was of a respected nautical family, and was apprenticed to the master mariner John Walker. Solomon was taller and a year older than Jack. Six years at sea had made Solomon strong and resilient, and six winters ashore being trained by Master Walker had made him wise; but Jack's years before the mast in the unforgiving fo'c'sle had taught him to fight.

"Sol, you keep out of this. It is not your business."

"It is wrong to rape the girl. Your quarrel –if it is a quarrel- is with the father. The daughter is an innocent virgin. It would be more sensible to rape the weaver!"

"Who said anything about rape?" Jack smiled. "She'll enjoy it."

Solomon leapt forward, but not quick enough for Jack whose staff struck his opponent's head. Solomon dropped silently prone.

Jack strode out. He no longer thought of King George. He was the king, the victorious knight come to claim the spoils of war, the conqueror. He unbuttoned his breeches, oblivious to her screams; oblivious to all but pride and passion. A stiff cock has no conscience, as the adage goes.

Chapter 3

Solomon opened his eyes, instantly recalling the situation. Every part of him pained, but the girl's screams were piercing, desperate. He took up the staff, stumbled outside and, fogged with anger, summoned his available strength and struck Jack Wheatear behind his knees. The victorious knight yapped like a chastised puppy; his once proud prick drooped to a limp dribbling appendage as he fell to his knees and then slumped face-down to the unyielding ground, his breeches ludicrously encumbering his legs. He struggled to his feet, blood dripping from face and knees, vainly trying to regain his dignity.

The clatter of constables ended the scene. The spectators scattered. Preston and Scott ran, but Wheatear outran them even with the handicap of holding up his breeches. Only Jacob and his daughter remained to tell their truthful accounts of the event.

* * *

Solomon King's father was not only handsome and charming, but was also a well-respected businessman. He had started as an apprentice sailor and sped up the latitudes of promotion to master mariner owing to his talents and to the fact that his father was a wealthy ship-owner who had given his son a ship when he was 21. From then his ventures prospered and he soon had shares in a number of vessels. By 25 he had given up the life at sea and lived ashore acquiring properties, shops and manufactories, and ran money-lending businesses. Most who knew of him would have described him as an affluent gentleman who was highly respected.

But all was not well. Solomon's father was a strong believer in the hierarchies of the time, particularly with regard to the traditional family roles: a wife's duty was to support and obey her husband, to be in charge of the household and keep the servants in order, and to produce offspring – especially male ones who would also be taught their place.

Solomon was the first child and, although he was a large healthy baby, there were complications and the midwife advised them not to have any further children. Solomon's father took no notice of this advice, and his wife suffered what she had previously enjoyed.

Inevitably she became pregnant once more. She was fearful, and as time passed she was troubled by an intermittent dull ache. As her husband was away during the day, she spent much time with Solomon who was about five years old – they both found this was palliative. One day she was torn with a sudden pain and started bleeding, she cried out "It's too soon, too soon!" The midwife was sent for, but the father was not. After several hours the child was born; a little girl –a very little girl- who, in spite of all the skill of the midwife, lived outside the womb for only four hours. Solomon had witnessed all this, as everyone was so busy they didn't notice he was there.

His father came home shortly after his daughter died. He asked, "Why did no-one send for me? Is the child healthy? Is he a boy?" When told that the child was dead, and a girl, he became angry: "What have you done, woman, to bring this about? Have you eaten too much, or the wrong things?"

She could not reply. Still holding the child, with tears blinding her sight, she shook her head from side to side. In her own chasm of misery, she could say nothing.

The midwife said, "This is not her fault in any way, sir. You must not have any intimate intercourse with her. Another pregnancy would in all probability be her death."

"But what of her duty as a wife? And I want a boy."

"You already have a boy, sir. Count yourself lucky that your wife is alive. Treasure her, and forget about having another child."

He stormed out.

So she moved into a small bedroom next to Solomon's, and left the conjugal bed, which was from time to time occupied by the maid.

Time passed this way. His father thought it was not manly for a boy to be with his mother, and insisting that he learn male education and pastimes, but even so Solomon managed to spend much time with his mother who became more herself. The partition between their two bedrooms was fairly thin; every night they wished each other well. Solomon would say, "Sleep in peace, Mama" and she would reply, "May God protect you. I love you, Sol."

Years passed in this manner. Then one day, Solomon heard his father shouting as he came up the stairs, his words were blurred and somewhat jumbled; very drunk.

He burst into Alice's bedroom. "Bloody door!" he shouted.

Alice said, "Be calm. You are not yourself. Go to bed."

"Ish not your bed. Ish my bed; I paid for it!"

"Go in peace to your bed."

"Shurrup. You talk nonsensh, nonsush, nonsenses."

"I am the one who is talking sense. Go!"

"Don't you tell me I'm talking nons...Don't you tell me whattoo do. I own you! I bought you!"

Solomon could not hear her reply, but his father was shouting: "I wanna boy! An' I going to fuck you until you give me one!"

Then there were noises as if they were fighting. Then it went quiet.

Then his mother started screaming. Loud and shrill. And the screams of Abigail took him back to that night.

Although that never occurred again, Sol's mother was pregnant. Again she came early, though the symptoms were different, more like her monthly pains, and much less blood. The same midwife arrived. She looked at Francis as if he were a criminal which she knew he was, whatever the law said. She wouldn't let him stay in the room. She allowed Solomon to be there, as his mother had requested. The delivery was long and painful; she held her son's hand. She did not scream, but he knew when her pain became agony as she squeezed his hand so tight that her fingernails bit deep into his flesh.

He didn't know what to say; but he knew that words were needed: "Mama, I love you. Be brave! It will be all right. You have always been a wonderful mother to me.

You have helped me many a time. You have trusted me, you have been kind to me, when other mothers would not have done; and you could always know when I needed you."

She was too weak to talk, but she smiled. Then the crisis came; she did not scream, but her face was screaming, and her fingers clenched his hands with a firmness he did not know she could muster. The tiny baby was coaxed into a strange family in a strange world.

It was a boy and it cried, the midwife wrapped him up and took him out of the room for his father to see. The father's face softened into a smile, "What a lovely boy!" Then he turned to the little child and spoke to him in the universal voice that adults use when talking to new-born babies, "Shall we go to mama and to ask her to give you a name, little man?"

When they opened the door the baby's mother was lying on the bed as if sleeping, Sol was holding her hand. She was dead.

Her husband was desolate, and kissed her gently on her lips.

A week later the baby boy died.

*   *   *

William Backas was a tall man in his late twenties. He had been handsome when younger, but already worldly worry had lined his face. He was not a rich man, nor a pompous one. Indeed, he looked a trifle shabby and unkempt. His coat had seen some years of wear and his stockings were 'of two parishes' but his waistcoat was smart and had all its buttons. His wig was a few years out of fashion.

Paper, ink and his black tricorn hat were laid out in an orderly fashion on his desk, behind which he sat hoping to create a coherent account of what had happened in the house of Jacob Linskill the weaver from the words of the constable. Backas had to submit an accurate and succinct report to the magistrate concerning the disturbances on Saturday.

William pushed his wig aside, scratched his head and said. "So, I gather that you, together with two watchmen were patrolling the West Bank, and witnessed an affray." He dipped his pen into the inkwell and held it poised over the paper.

"Yes, sir, indeed we did. Or rather we did not, sir. There were me and the watchmen, and we set out, as you did say just now, sir. But it were difficult to know what was going on, sir, what with all the singing and the shouting, the banging of drums and the playing of fiddles. Well, now, sir, to be brief..."

William sighed and put down his pen.

"...There was much talk of the gangs going abouts, sir, insulting those who showed no light – as has been the custom since time out of mind. We were told that there might be aggravation as you might say, sir, in Cliff Lane. But, as it happened, the affray was at the top of Flowergate, so by the time we got there it was all but over."

"In Cliff Lane? That must surely be one of the most peaceable parts of the West Bank."

"Aye, sir, and so it were that night."

"And even when it was so quiet, you stayed in Cliff Lane?"

"That is so, sir, because we had been reliably informed there would be much trouble there."

"And who was it who gave you this information?"

"A gentleman, sir." The constable looked William Backas up and down appraisingly. "A proper gentleman, sir. If you knows what I mean."

"And did this 'gentleman' give you his name?"

"Oh no, sir. That would not be right, sir."

William sighed again; "What made you think he was a gentleman?"

"He seemed agin he was a gentleman, sir. His clothes, his speech…"

"Can you describe him?"

"Medium height, about 30 years old. Well maybe more like 35. Though from the side we thought perhaps he was nearer 25."

"And his clothes?"

"Wearing a fine blue jacket, with lace cuffs. And a fancy waistcoat, with a gold watch chain. And he wore a clean white neckerchief." The constable sat back in his chair with a smile of satisfaction, adding, "That is as fine and as true an image of the man, as we would swear to it on Bible oath."

"Where did you meet him?" asked William.

"In Haggersgate, sir."

"Where in Haggersgate?"

"In the Three Mariners, sir"

"Did you have a drink there?"

"Just a glass of ale, sir, none of your strong Hum Cap. Just to wet our throats before a night's hard work."

"Did the 'gentleman' pay for your drinks?"

"Purely out of courtesy, sir. As one Whitby townsman who wishes to keep the King's peace to another."

"Did he give you any money?"

This question elicited much visible outrage. The constable grunted and shook his head.

"I are much offended, sir, that you would even think us capable of taking a bribe!"

"So you would be willing to take a Bible oath that you did not take a bribe?"

"The Bible is a sacred book, sir, and it would surely be sacrilege to use it on every little question, as I am sure any parson would agree."

William Backas reflectively chewed the feather-end of his pen and then wrote a few lines on his paper, before returning to his interrogation:

"What made you leave Cliff Lane and go to Flowergate?"

"We did hear screaming sir, and fighting."

"And what did you find when you got to the top end of Flowergate?"

"We saw some young men running away from Jacob Linskill. The knuckles on the weaver's right hand were bruised and bleeding, and a wooden stave was lying on the ground with bloodstains on it. We cautioned him and went our way, sir, as by statute we could not do more: no arrest if the affray is over before we arrive."

"I know that," retorted William, somewhat petulantly.

"Did you say that you thought that Jacob Linskill had attacked those who ran away?"

"That were our judgement, sir, after considering the situation."

"Jacob Linskill is a Quaker?"

"Yes, sir."

"But Quakers are pacifists."

"Which only shows how devious they can be, sir."

*   *   *

The collier ship *Freelove*, of which John Walker junior was the master and owner, was on her first season of voyages. She had sailed between Shields where she was loaded with coal which was taken to sell in London, a profitable trade. She had docked at Whitby on Friday 10 October to purchase provisions, to make some minor repairs, and to allow the crew to have the chance to celebrate the coronation. Walker had kept her in port over Sunday, allowing the men to have Sunday off for worship in church, chapel or meeting-house and/or sobering up. Among the crew on board was Solomon King, one of Walker's apprentices, working out his last few months of service after which he would be qualified as an able seaman- the next rung on the ratlines of advancement in a maritime career. She sailed with the morning tide the next day, with a full crew; but how many of them were spiritually uplifted was debateable, as many seemed still to be suffering from barrel fever. Monday morning had been beautiful, the sun burning away the morning mist and a mild north-easterly wind carried the ship steadily and easily past Filey Brig, Flamborough Head and Burlington Bay. Then the sky was obscured with ever-thickening grey clouds which whirled in a vortex of wind and ice-cold rain. "All hands!" was called, and the crew swiftly obeyed the mate's reiterations of Walker's commands, the experienced ones knowing exactly what had to be done: the top sails were furled, to avoid the danger of their being shredded by the wind or capsizing the vessel. Taking soundings was difficult but crucial as the ship was in the area of that large ever-shifting sandbank known as 'Dreadful' near the Humber estuary. Fortunately within three hours the storm had subsided, and Solomon and others who had missed their rest watch retired below. Solomon climbed into his bunk, weary but invigorated because he had done his job well and successfully. He slid gently into sleep.

Then he saw the young red-haired girl running out of the darkness, shouting, "Papa! Papa!", and heard the screaming, the terrible screaming. He lurched, trembling, into wakefulness.

Chapter 4

William Backas had been appointed as Chief Constable of Whitby in 1723. Although he had only been in post for four years, he knew his law-and-order team well; almost as well as they knew him. His interview on 13 October had concealed much, and he knew there would be nothing gained in pressing any further. But also some information had been given: the 'gentleman' had given beer and probably money to the constable and the watchmen in The Three Mariners. This man, aged between 25 and 35, was something of a dandy wearing expensive fashionable clothes, with a gold watch-chain. The details may be unreliable; but the overall picture, William conjectured, was probably sound, and therefore of interest.

The Three Mariners was a rather seedy pub, where mainly sailors and fishermen drank away their earnings in a fug of cheap tobacco, which struggled to overpower the smells of stale ale, fish, sweat and tar. Sailors and fishermen were very different groups of men and they socialised and married within their own traditional work families. The Three Mariners was therefore a rather unusual inn; but unsurprisingly the fishermen and the sailors congregated at different ends of the pub, usually swapping insults, or with loud delivery of their different ballads each group attempting to out-sing the other in boastful competition which only rarely ended in a serious fight.

One thing was certain: no real gentleman would visit this pub. But it seemed likely that the person in question visited The Three Mariners often, and was accepted at least by some of regulars. William was intrigued.

After much thought he realised that he should frequent this bar; but, as his job meant that he was well-known in the town, he must go in disguise. He would need to take on a new persona. He could not pass as a fisherman, as fishing was largely restricted to a handful of families, who would also know the families in the neighbouring fishing ports such as Staithes, Robin Hood's Bay and, indeed, all along the coast. However, sailors stopping off or overwintering at Whitby could be from a range of ports – even those from overseas. He decided that he would pretend to be a ship's carpenter, as they often did shore work, especially in winter which would account for his face not being so ruddy and his imitation of a seaman's gait was not exactly right. On the evening of Wednesday 29 October, dressed appropriately, William Backas set forth as David Strother of Deptford and went to The Three Mariners. It was with some trepidation, but also with the exciting frisson of a child playing a game that he knows his parents would disapprove of.

As he opened the door, he was aware of a lull in the chatter as several faces turned to look at him. He paused for a moment, and a voice called out, "Shut t' door! You're lettin' in t' cold air, tha knows!" He did, and most of the customers turned back to what they were doing before; but he felt very self-conscious as he made his way to the bar. The innkeeper, with his trade-mark blue apron, welcomed him without a smile and asked what he wanted. William said, "I'm told that your best beer is drinkable."

"All our beer's drinkable."

"No offence. I'll have a tankard of your best."

The publican leaned forward, placing his large hands firmly on the bar; his arms were massive, as befits a man who is used to heaving barrels, stopping brawls and throwing out unwanted customers. He said, "Is that a quart? Or were you thinking of just having a pint?"

Backas looked into his steely, unblinking eyes and said, "A quart, of course."

"Of course," the publican replied, reaching for a quart tankard, and filling it carefully. "You're not from Whitby. You a foreigner?"

"I'm from Deptford."

"A foreigner, then. Sailor?"

"Ship's carpenter. Looking for winter work."

"That'll be one penny three farthings."

Backas placed tuppence on the bar.

"Looking for work, eh?" said the innkeeper, taking up the coins and replacing them with a farthing, as change. "I'll tell thee summat."

They both looked at the farthing. Eventually Backas put his forefinger on it and slid it over the counter.

"Thankee, sir."

Backas smiled in response.

"The mates of some ships come in here. They're the ones as decides."

"And you will point them out to me?"

"Happen."

The difficult part was done. But no sign of the 'gentleman'.

When William Backas was free of an evening, he went down for a jar or two at The Three Mariners as David Strother. He was pleased to be accepted and to join in seamen's conversations. He spent some time with James Boyes who also came to the inn by himself. Boyes had worked his way up to be the master and main owner of the collier vessel *Dolphin*. Boyes didn't spend the evenings joining in the bawdy and noisy chatter of the sailors, so was pleased to converse with the more civilised David Strother.

William had been beginning to enjoy this charade purely as recreation when on 8 November he was startled by the entry of the 'gentleman', almost exactly as his constable had described him. William's mind was so far from thinking about him that it was a surprise, and it took him a few moments to realise what had happened. He turned to John Boyes and said,

"Who in Hades is that?"

"Pay no attention to him. He likes to make a display of himself."

"What does he do? He's no shipman!"

James laughed. "Certainly not. I doubt he's even been in a boat, let alone a ship."

"No-one else seems to be surprised to see a man dressed like that in an inn like this. Is he a regular?"

"As regular as the tides. He is always here on the second Friday of the month."

"What's his name? What does he do?"

"No idea what his name is, and who cares? He's known as 'The Provider', some even call him 'Divine Providence'. If you want some brandy, or canvas, or playing cards, or an anchor, anything, he will get it for you – usually at a bargain price."

"No wonder he's so popular!" William had noticed how people had clustered round The Provider as soon as he had reached the bar.

James Boyes looked at him, his expression suddenly serious. "Take my advice, Strother. Have nothing to do with him. Providence, divine or otherwise, punishes as well as rewards. Keep clear. Once in his clutches you are there for good. Doing business with The Provider is as if you'd sold your soul to Satan."

"He looks rather jovial and pleasant to me."

James slammed down his jug of ale. "You think the Devil appears as hideous and nasty as he is painted in churches? How do you think he catches the souls of the unwary? You have been warned. Goodnight." Having said this he departed.

William stayed until The Provider left the inn, and he discretely followed him. The Provider walked along Haggersgate and then over the river and into Church Street where he entered a building. He had tracked The Provider to his lair. William went home very pleased with himself.

When he opened his front door, he was confronted by his angry wife Margaret.

"What are you doing, William? On several occasions you secretly dress in strange clothes and creep out of this house, imagining that I do not see what you do. Then some hours later you return smelling of beer and tobacco smoke, imagining that my sense of smell has deserted me. If you visit a woman, then she is a common slut. If you go gambling you do so in dubious and dangerous company. You are risking your reputation and mine. Are you mad? It is time you told me what is going on!"

"It is part of my work, Margaret. Not any of those vile things you imagine. I have been in disguise to track down someone who may be a criminal."

"And who would that be?" There was a clear edge to her question.

"I don't as yet know his name; he is known as The Provider."

"The Provider? I thought everyone knew him. He's easy to find; he's in the Market on Saturdays. Really, William, you are such a fool! You could have saved yourself a lot of trouble if only you'd asked me."

And indeed the proud man who had recently entered his home, confident in his cleverness, now felt like a buffle-headed ninny. He needed to regain his self-esteem.

"I know where he lives: on the far side of the baker's shop in Church Street. All I have to do is to check the Poor Rate Assessments, and I shall have his name."

"The far side of baker's shop in Church Street? Why, that's rented out! It'll be the landlord's name that'll appear on your Poor Rate list."

"Do you happen to know who the tenant is, Margaret?"

"Lawks, William! 'Tis the Provider, as you say. 'Tis Ralph Theaker."

Chapter 5

In a calm sea *Freelove* had anchored off Whitby and had sent a boat ashore for fresh water and provisions. Not only were these cheaper in Whitby than in London or Shields, but also the pier renovation toll was less if the ship did not come into the harbour. Among those who went ashore –at his own request- was Solomon King.

The tide was out so the boat was beached on the sand. Solomon was first out, hurrying to the Crag while the others were still discussing the best way to fulfil their orders. In Haggersgate he passed a rather eccentric figure, flamboyantly dressed and with a gold watch-chain who was making for the beach; but Solomon did not notice him. Past St Ann's Staith, cutting through St Ann's Lane to Flowergate, up the incline he went, passing the house of John Walker senior to whom Sol was apprenticed and where he lived, when ashore, in the attic with other 'servants'. John Walker junior, captain of *Freelove*, also lived there. Solomon gave it but a fleeting glance as he passed onward. Near the top of the road was the house of Jacob Linskill, and Sol paused. The events that occurred there on coronation day had stalked his subconscious ever since. He desperately wanted, and desperately feared, to know what he would find.

After much dithering outside Jacob Linskill's house, Solomon King eventually knocked on the door. The wait before it was opened seemed eternal.

It was Abigail who opened the door, but Solomon at first didn't recognise her. He expected a frightened girl, instead there was a mature, confident and sensible girl. She was beautiful. She smiled. He gulped.

"Good morrow, Miss Linskill, I am Solomon King."

"I know who you are. You are welcome here. Come in, and meet my father."

He entered, as Jacob rose from his loom holding out his left hand to Solomon; the awkward handshake was forgotten when Jacob smiled and spoke words of welcome.

"You are looking well, Mister Linskill," said Solomon, once they were all seated, "Your hand is mended more than I had surmised."

"Indeed it has. I feared I might never weave again, but now I can - though I have to go slowly and carefully."

"The physician said it would get even better, and might be as sound as it was before. We are very grateful to have a physician, are we not, Father?"

Solomon smiled to himself: *No longer 'Papa', but 'Father'.*

"Yes, Abigail we are very pleased with him."

"And he comes sometimes twice a week! Of course we cannot afford such a thing, Master King, but it is all paid for by an anonymous donor. I think he might be..."

Her father interrupted. "Come now, child, do not rattle on so. We do not need our private family matters spread to any outsiders, with the risk of our becoming the subjects of gossip."

Abigail's smile deserted her for a moment; but whether it was the content of his speech or his calling her 'child' which annoyed her the more, was indiscernible.

"Oh Father," she said, "Mr King is no stranger. He did a good thing for us."

Jacob's expression fixed as an image of annoyance; but he was silent. She continued, "We have many kind people who have helped us. For example, Mr Cornelius pays Father the same wage every week, even though he cannot weave the same amount as before. He says, 'Jacob, thou hast always done well with me; every week you produced the right amount of canvas of the right quality. And I know thou wouldst continue to do so if you could, and that in time you will be able to do so once more. I do not imagine your expenses have become less when your hand was damaged.' Is that not a true Christian deed, Solomon?"

"Indeed it is, Miss Linskill". He smiled and nodded; he had noticed how she had called him by his Christian name. Her father had also noticed.

"Would you care to take some refreshment?" she asked.

"I think, Abigail, that Master King must have many duties to perform. An apprentice's time is not his own, you know, he cannot squander the time in a working day making social calls."

Solomon, who would have liked to stay in her presence above all things, rose to his feet.

"Indeed, Sir. Much as I would have wished to stay and discuss with you many matters, such as the war with Spain; but my duty —as you have rightly said- lies elsewhere." He took Jacob's left hand and gave him a brief slight bow. Jacob, who remained seated, grunted a brief acknowledgement.

His daughter escorted him out of the house. Momentarily they were facing each other outside. Each knew that the other felt some kind of affection for them. She whispered, "Solomon, please come again" and he retorted, "I shall, Abigail, soon. When my apprenticeship is finished."

They grinned at each other, not knowing what else to do or say, when Jacob's shout of "Come in, child, and shut the door!" decided the matter.

Once she was inside, her father rose, put his good hand firmly on her shoulder and looked into her eyes with unblinking seriousness. Firmly and clearly he commanded: "You must never meet him again!"

"Why, Father?" She was puzzled.

"He has seen our shame."

*   *   *

As the sailors rowed back to *Freelove* Solomon continued to smile, as he had done since he left the Linskill home. Sol did not notice that the others were also grinning; they had bought all they needed at a cheap price from an entrepreneur, who was colourfully attired and had a fine gold watch-chain. He had also written them a receipt for a greater amount; the difference they shared between themselves. They thought they would not include Solomon, as he seemed to be happy enough already.

*   *   *

Michael Cornelius, a wealthy canvas merchant in his early 30s, met his friend and colleague Elisha Root, shoemaker, in the Whitby Meeting House in Church Street, on a surprisingly warm and sunny autumn morning. They were both leaders of the Quaker Meeting but were very different in behaviour, values and beliefs. Michael, although at least a dozen years younger than Elisha, was generally accepted as the chief leader because of his wisdom, good sense and business success. Although both Michael and Elisha were dressed in sober black coats and breeches as was the Quaker manner, their appearances were very different. Elisha's clothes were of woollen homespun; his black jacket -fading in places to a musty green- was tied with thread. His plain cotton neckerchief had clearly served many other uses. His shoes, as might be expected from a cobbler, were well-made but fastened with pewter buckles. Michael's jacket was made from finest cloth professionally cut and pressed, and provided with smart but understated and unused buttons; his jacket ajar to display an equally splendid and undecorated waistcoat. His stockings were of silk, as was his clean neckerchief, the corner of it peeping out of one of his jacket pockets. His shoe buckles were of plain silver.

Michael spoke first.

"Good morrow, Elisha. I hope I find you in good health."

"And may the good Lord shine on thee, too, Friend Michael, and guide our actions this day."

"Remember, Elisha, our purpose today is to 'admonish in love and tenderness', ascertaining the actual situation and the reasons thereof. After which we shall make a decision, to be ratified at the next meeting."

"Friend Michael, as ever I shall be guided in all my works in accordance with the true Inner Light which is granted by the Lord God in spite of his servant's unworthiness."

"Of course," replied Michael, somewhat tersely. "I think we should go now."

The two set off together down Grope Lane and Sandgate, across the river bridge, and up past the Golden Lion to Flowergate. They walked in silence, apart from the puffing and grunting of Elisha who found it difficult to keep apace with Michael on the road's steep incline. When they reached Jacob Linskill's house Elisha was sweating, mopping his brow with his neckerchief. His face somewhat reddened by his exertions. Michael waited until his companion had regained his composure, before knocking on the door. It was opened by Abigail, her blank expression unreadable.

"We are come to see your father, Abigail."

Abigail stepped aside, saying not a word, letting them in.

Jacob was sitting at his loom. He stood up and welcomed his visitors, offering them refreshments which they declined. He invited them to sit down, which Michael declined, though Elisha looked as if he would have been happy to accept.

Abigail vanished into the back room.

Elisha said, "Friend Jacob, we have come to admonish thee for trespass against the guidance of the Society of Friends which has been given us by the wisdom of God."

Jacob simply said "Oh?" and then looked at Michael.

"Friend Jacob," said Michael, "your absence from the Meeting yesterday was noted. Can you give us your reason for so doing?"

The weaver lifted up his right hand which was swollen, distorted and blotched with purple. "I can work but slowly at the loom now. I need all the time to produce sufficient canvas."

"I see; it is much damaged. I hope you are having treatment for it. Indeed it was your hand and the circumstances that caused it to be in that state that we have come to learn more about."

"Thou hast struck a man!" cried Elisha, "And God has punished thee!"

"Did you strike a man?"

"Yes, Friend Michael. I did."

"Why did you so?"

"He raped my daughter."

"He raped your daughter? That is a terrible sin and crime. Is what you say true?"

"He would have raped her had I not intervened. I prevented a sin and a crime. I saved my daughter; what father would not do so? I did a good thing, and should be praised, Friend Elisha, and not condemned."

"Out of thine own mouth thou hast condemned thyself! The Society of Friends holds firm to be peaceable, and violence of any kind for any reason must be condemned because the world is wicked, and our fellowship does not permit us to act likewise. Thou art now disowned by the Society of Friends, and art no longer a member of our Meeting."

"Friend Elisha," said Michael, "It is for the Meeting to make the final decision, not either of us. However, Friend Jacob, it is clear that you have contravened a basic tenet (and there are few) of the Society of Friends, which is a sin against God, who wishes us to live in harmony. You have shown no signs of regret or repentance for your wicked deed, nor sought forgiveness for your transgressions. Therefore I must say that there will be little doubt that the Meeting will disown you with 'love and tenderness'."

"This is cruel work," replied Jacob. "Dost thine inner light not show thee that a man must protect his family, especially a young daughter brought into this sinful world? Is it I that is to be punished and the villains go free? What kind of love and justice is that? What kind of tenderness is this? What kind of Friendship?"

Michael was somewhat abashed, so Elisha responded: "Thou hast sinned, Friend Jacob, taking punishment into thine own hands. It is writ in Holy Scripture: 'Vengeance is mine saith the Lord'. Think that thou, a sinner, shouldst be a god to punish sinners?"

"You are not my Friends!" cried Jacob. "Leave my house! My inner light is clearer that your tickle-texting. I disown *you*! Go! Now! Go!"

They went.

Abigail, who had of course been listening behind the door, came rushing in and put her arms round him. "Papa, we have each other. Together we shall prosper, shall we not, Papa?"

"Yes, my dear daughter, my Abigail. We shall be happy together for ever. We shall look after each other, and God will look after us both." He held her close, his eyes wet with tears.

*　　　*　　　*

Jack Wheatear told himself that his life was good, since he left Whitby. He enjoyed the life at sea, and he had become a skilful thief. Whenever he was paid and discharged from a ship in London, he would find accommodation at an inn where he was not known, and there were plenty of such places in Deptford and Wapping. Many sailors chose such inns, taking the cheap option of sharing a room; and the money they saved on accommodation was spent on ale and whoring. Jack did neither. Then, sleepy with indulgence, they randomly cast aside their clothes before climbing into bed. The ale, numbing their awareness of the fleas, ensured they slept soundly. Jack slipped into bed fully clothed, and pretended to asleep. Once his room-fellow was deep in slumber, Jack would rummage quietly through all his things, stealing anything of value – often including his clothes. He knew who would buy them off him, and the booty would often be sold on before the victim was aware of their absence.

On this day, Jack was feeling lucky. His target sailor had fallen asleep quickly and soundly, gently snoring. Jack had noticed earlier that he had some fine shoe buckles; saleable if made of pewter but very rewarding if they were of silver. Sailors sometimes bought silver shoe buckles as an easy way of carrying cash value. Jack silently slipped out of his bed and crawled on all fours across to the room, his hands deftly searching the floor. He found the shoes and removed the buckle of one of them. In the gloom feeling for an assay mark, his finger delicately identified a lion. He was shivering with excitement, almost shouting out in pleasure. Suddenly a noise. Before he knew what was happening he felt a strong arm round his neck, almost choking him. The arm pulled his head painfully backwards, and a knife blade was pressed against his throat.

"Do exactly what I say, or I shall kill you. Understand?"

"Yes," gasped Jack.

"Remove your neckerchief."

He did.

"Lie flat on your face."

He did that as well. Jack's wrists were tightly tied behind him with his own scarf and then he was rolled over. His captor stood up, fumbled for his tinder box and lit one of the candles.

Then he sat down, looking at the helpless Jack.

"What is your name?"

"William Johnson," stuttered Jack.

"Do you think I'm an idiot? Reflect a while: you do not have much time left in this world. I might kill you now, or maybe later. I might hand you over to the constable for a trial at the Old Bailey. Stealing a pair of silver buckles is a capital offence, for which you might hang. Have you ever imagined what that must be like? After the cart is moved and you are left hanging by the neck it takes a long time choking and writhing before you die. Fat men die more quickly than someone of your physique. It must be very painful. Your life is not in your tied hands. So do not waste my time, and in the little time you have left, be honest with me. So, let us start again. What is your name?"

"Jack Wheatear."

"Good. For how many years have you been stealing?"

"Not long."

"Do you have a wife and family to support?"

"No."

"Robin Hood, as you must know, robbed the rich to give to the poor. How much have you given to the poor?"

"Well, erm..."

"I assume that means you have given nothing."

Jack did not answer.

"So, Jack Wheatear, you rob the poor and keep the money yourself?"

"I have to say that is what I do."

"And you, a sailor, rob other sailors?"

"Yes, mainly."

"Are you proud of yourself?"

"No." His answer surprised himself.

"Have you done other wickednesses?"

Jack grunted agreement.

"What do you think happens when you die?"

"They say that the wicked are judged, and are sent to Hell eternally."

"Do you believe that?"

"I don't know. How can anyone know?"

"The Last Judgement. Imagine that you are not judged by God; imagine all the people you have cheated, robbed, impoverished or harmed in any way come together to judge you, to make known to everyone what kind of a man you are, and you are shown the consequences of all the wicked things you have done? How would you feel?"

"I would feel ashamed."

"Shall I kill you now?"

Chapter 6

This whole conversation seemed to Jack to be very strange; but this last question was the least expected. He could think of nothing to say.

His captor finished dressing and collecting his possessions. Then he grasped his knife and cut Jack free.

The stranger said, "I shall not take you to the constables. You are a man; you know what is wrong and what is right. Go, and sin no more." He walked towards the door and opened it.

Then he turned to Jack once more and tossed a florin to him. "This is to pay for a new neckerchief. But remember, when I say 'Sin no more' it is an order, not a suggestion. I know your name, and the sailors' world is a close one. If I hear that you have been wicked, Jack Wheatear, I shall hunt you down and I shall kill you, and I shall kill you in a very unpleasant way, but in a way that will be as nothing after you are dead and in Hell in agonising, relentless suffering to the end of time."

He left the room, closing the door quietly behind him.

*　　　　*　　　　*

"It seems," said William Backas, as the maid Hilda placed a fairly substantial breakfast of bread, butter, smoked herring and tea upon the table, "that the weather will stay fine for the rest of the day. What think you, Mrs Backas?"

"I do certainly hope so, Mr Backas, rain at this stage would severely hinder the breaming of *Freelove*."

"She is but newly launched, Mrs Backas, and I doubt she will need much attention."

"The process has to be done thoroughly, clean or not, Mr Backas. The crew need regular and consistent training."

Hilda took out the tray. Mrs Backas watched her until she was out of the room. Mr Backas envied her youthfuless, and gave an inaudible sigh. Neither noticed her expression. Hilda, daughter of Caroline Norrison, had not been in service for long, so William and Margaret talked only of mundane matters when she was in the room. Once she had gone they turned to more interesting topics.

"Tell me, William, are you still pursuing Ralph Theaker, the Provider?"

"No, I am not. I had a word with Mr Woods, the Collector of Customs, a few weeks back. He is aware of the Provider and knows what he does, but is unable to find any proof against him. Why do you ask, Margaret?"

"There is quite a lot of gossip concerning him. Nothing specific, but it might indicate that something unusual is going on, or is about to happen."

"You are a mine of information, Margaret; but Theaker is not my responsibility. However, I would dearly like to know why he bribed my night-watchmen, and what exactly happened at Linskill the weaver's house that night."

"I thought that there was no doubt about what happened."

"It is true that the watchmen saw three men running from the scene, and recognised them; they were Jack Wheatear, Thomas Preston and Simon Scott. It took three days for my men to find them, but when questioned they all agreed with what Mr Linskill had said, namely that they had insulted him and his daughter, and that the weaver had hit Wheatear very firmly in the face, and then my men came and all three ran away."

"If they all agreed about what happened then surely, William, it is like to be true, is it not? Especially if the offender is a Quaker. Are not Quakers bound to tell the truth?"

"Everyone tell lies at one time or another, for one reason or another."

"You doubt the truth of the account that all four agreed upon?"

"They say that the weaver hit Wheatear so hard that his hand was damaged to such an extent that he has been rendered unable to continue his work effectively. Yet Wheatear himself bore no marks at all of an assault."

"Then clearly they are all lying; but why? What really happened that night?"

"I wish I knew, Margaret. I wish I knew. The doubt troubles my mind."

"Yet there must have been other witnesses. I heard that there was quite a mob going up Flowergate that night."

"Maybe; but finding any of them would be difficult. And would any member of a violent mob tell the honest truth?"

"Has it occurred to you, William, that the two events that night may not be connected?"

"How do you mean?"

"That perhaps Theaker's bribery of the night-watchmen had nothing to do with the fight at the weaver's. Maybe he wanted them to remain specifically in Cliff Lane for his own purposes; maybe he wanted them away from any road that was far enough from where he was involved in some illegal act."

"Perhaps, maybe; but it is mere speculation. But, as I say, it is no longer my business, and therefore nothing for us to worry about."

"But still, one cannot help wondering…"

*   *   *

John Walker Senior was in the attic of his home in Flowergate, he was sitting in the only chair in the room, which the apprentices were not allowed to use, and he was testing Solomon King on his knowledge of seamanship, which he would have to internalise if he were to progress in his career. After an hour of questions and answers, Walker was impressed.

"Well done, Solomon! Thou progressest well."

"Thank you, Master."

"As thou knowest, your indenture expires on the second day of the twelfth month – the month you would call February, and the day Candlemas. Then thou willst be a servant no longer, and no longer live with us here. No longer shall I be responsible for feeding and clothing thee; thou willst have to pay for all that thyself. But you will be a real seaman. We shall truly miss thee, Solomon.

However, I have arranged with my eldest son that he shall take thee on board his ship as an Able Seaman. I doubt that she shall sail on the day after thine indenture expires, so we shall be happy for you to stay here until thou art entered as one of the crew. I hope thou likest this plan?"

"I thank you, Master. Your kindness is much appreciated."

"And should thy year as a seaman be successful, I hope that we shall be able to find a place for thee on one of the Walker-owned ships as a Mate."

"I, too, would wish for that, Master, and shall strive to achieve it."

"Much rides on how thou farest next year, Solomon; but I am impressed by both thy knowledge and thy practise of true seamanship. I hope that in time thou shalt sail as Master on a ship owned by the Walker family."

"I dream of that, Master; and I thank you from my heart for all you and your family have done for me over the past years of my apprenticeship."

"A good servant is a joy to his master, Solomon."

They sat smiling at each other, a silent mutual tribute to their achievements.

"Are there any questions thou wouldst ask of me?"

Solomon responded, but hesitantly: "There is something, Master; but it is nothing about a sailor's life."

"Ask me."

"It is rather... personal."

"Fear not. Are we not friends?"

"It is about Friends that I wish to talk. I mean Quakers, Master."

"Indeed? And why is this?"

"I wish to learn about it, and to understand the Quaker life and beliefs."

"I shall be happy to help thee so to do. But thou sayest that it was personal?"

Embarrassed, Solomon blushed and stared at his shoe buckles.

Walker continued, "One of the first things Quakers must do is always to tell the truth."

"There is someone –a Quaker- whom I have met..."

"A girl?"

"Yes."

"You like her?"

"Very much."

"And she liketh thee too?"

"So I believe, Master."

"How old is she?"

"Fifteen, I think."

"That is very young. Are her parents respectable?"

"Her mother has died; her father is a weaver."

"I believe I know whom thou meanst. Does her father approve of thy friendship with his daughter?"

"I think not, Master."

"My advice then, Solomon, is that thou waitest until thou art at least a mate. Then call again and see how you both feel. Fathers can be won over; but –if he is whom I think you mean- he is having a difficult time at the moment. Mayhap –if God willeth it so- all will be good in another year."

*　　　　*　　　　*

Michael Cornelius and Elisha Root were tidying up after the members of the Quaker Meeting. It was an occasion when they were together without anyone else, so Cornelius took advantage to raise an issue which had worried him enormously.

"Friend Elisha, I am deeply concerned about Jacob Linskill. Since he was unfriended he has refused any medical help which I had been paying for him and consequently his hand is becoming worse."

"He hath raised the same hand in an act of violence, Friend Michael. And he hath showed no repentance."

"I think we all know that he did not commit an act of violence, and that it was Wheatear who destroyed his hand."

"So he told us all a lie."

"He was a victim, not a villain. We, the Quakers of Whitby, should support him and not condemn him."

"But still he hath lied, and telling the truth —no matter what the circumstances- is fundamental to Quakerism. That is what I spake unto the Meeting and that is why they agreed that he should be unfriended."

"He lied because he was ashamed that he did not defend his daughter."

"Still he lied, and he lied because he did not want people to know that he did not fight to defend his daughter and himself. He did not want people to think he was a coward. He died because of his sin of pride, one of the seven deadly sins."

"The 'sin of pride' is not in the Commandments, is not mentioned in the Bible; and the sort of pride Friend Jacob revealed is not to be greatly condemned. Can you not see that his daughter was violated *because* he was a good Quaker? We should praise him, not condemn him."

"At present he is a bad Quaker, he lied, he was proud, and he hath shown no signs of condemning his acts. Refusing your medical help is another example of his arrogant pride. He stays unfriended until he repents."

"Friend Jacob showed pride. But our response, as members of The Religious Society of Friends, was simply that we spurned him. Did we help him? Did we show that we loved our neighbour, or did we simply wash our hands of him? And if his infected hand results in him being unable to work, unable to support his daughter, can we say we are not guilty? If he dies, can we say we are not responsible? Are we the Pharisees or the Good Samaritan?"

The conversation collapsed into silence.

As Elisha Root left the building he thought: *He hath made me angry, which showeth how wicked he is. 'The devil can cite Scripture for his purpose'. He is trying to destroy our Quaker Meeting. How can I remove him and his poisonous ideas? If I were not a Quaker, I would kill him for the preservation of The Society of Friends.*

Michael Cornelius locked the door of the Friends' Meeting House. He felt depressed, and thought: *I can do nothing. If Jacob becomes incapable or even dies of putrefaction, I shall feel guilty. What can I do to help Jacob and his daughter? Certainly it looks as if Elisha continues in his stubborn self-righteousness and if he infects the Whitby Quakers with it, the result would be disastrous. I think at times a bad deed is needed for a good result.*

Chapter 7

Solomon's time as a seaman in 1728 had started dramatically with heavy rain and floods. The collier run between Shields and London, always difficult and unpredictable, was even more dangerously tumultuous. However, although the ship was much damaged and was at times tossed helplessly by vast relentless waves, none of the crew were killed or even seriously wounded. She even managed to complete several successful voyages carrying coal from Newcastle to London in the furious weather, making a profit for the ship's owners.

Summer was better and dryer, with the sea reverting to its usual troublesome normality. Whatever the crew felt in those struggling months, once the worst was past they felt brave heroes, proud of surviving –even conquering– the fierce dragonlike German Ocean. In many inns in London they told many tales, re-vamped with the telling, to eager landlubbers prepared to buy them strong ale.

When the collier sailed into Whitby to over-winter, Solomon felt like a real seaman. He rented a room in one of the many rather dilapidated buildings on Gaskin Bank which sprawled up from the east side of the River Esk. As he walked the streets he nodded at acquaintances, he had conversations after church on Sundays; but he was lonely. Although he had some money, he had the tedious task of shopping. But the soggy spring had damaged crops; and the price of wheat had soared. Solomon found himself moaning about prices of food with women in the market.

Sol's room was cheap; he had only intended to rent a place which provided a roof over his head, and the means to keep warm. Unfortunately when it rained a little snake of water slithered down his north-facing wall, enough to be distressing, but not enough to fill a kettle. The days of Christmas passed with little joy.

In January the trickle of water ceased, but that was simply because it had frozen. There was not a day in the whole of the month January that was not below freezing. Solomon spent his time either shivering in front of his meagre fire rubbing his hands to keep them warm, or spending time and money in a warm pub.

It was therefore with much pleasure that he had accepted an invitation to dine on February 2nd with John Walker senior and his wife at their recently acquired home in Grope Lane. As Quakers, the Walker family did not celebrate Christmas with all its pagan rituals, festive gluttony and excessive consumption of alcohol; but had taken the opportunity to use the season to gather together in friendship before the next sailing season began.

Solomon wore his coat and scarf indoors, so to go visiting all he had to do was to wrap them more closely around him. Everywhere was bleak: most days the ground was covered with fresh snow that crunched underfoot, and icicles glittered in the pale sun. The scenery might have been delightful if it were not so vicious and relentless. Sol found no pleasure in it, even though the journey from his room to the Walker's house was not long, it seemed endless. He had to walk up Church Street struggling against a slicing northerly wind which was funnelled between the cliffs on either side of the river. Past the Quaker meeting house he turned into Grope Lane which was narrow and gracefully curved which reduced the ferocity of the weather.

He was shown into the drawing room which was tastefully but moderately arranged, and there was a fine view over the harbour, now crammed with huddled vessels, etched with rime, awaiting the sailing season. Solomon was the only guest, which was a great honour, and he appreciated it; when he was an apprentice in Flowergate he had not been allowed into any of the family rooms. The conversation was mostly about the weather and shipping; and Solomon was surprised that Walker's wife was so knowledgeable of merchant ships and trading.

When it was announced that dinner was ready, they walked into the dining room informally. When all were seated John said a grace, too lengthy to Solomon's mind. The meal was simple: ham and mutton with turnips and cardoons, millet pudding and custard pudding, and ale to drink. The conversation was interesting but somewhat subdued. When the table was cleared, the sole lady withdrew, and John Walker and Solomon settled down for man talk.

"How didst thou enjoy thy first year as a seaman?" asked John.

Solomon pondered:

He had at first been apprehensive about signing on as an Able Seaman. For all its indignities, the life of an apprentice with a kind and knowledgeable master had been something of a cosy existence - at times more like a family than his own had been. But when his apprenticeship was over he had become a free man, who earned money and could go where he liked. It was a liberation.

The captain was efficient and knowledgeable in seamanship, which was valuable in the stormy weather. He regularly patrolled the ship but said little to the men; mainly he spoke to the mate and to the apprentices. Sleeping before the mast was a new experience too, but he found most of the other sailors were supportive. There had been some rough initiations and humiliating practical jests; but it was clear that his seven other seamen accepted him into a group and considered him as a colleague. They patronised the mere apprentices and resented, but admired, the captain. The mate was grudgingly respected by the seamen. It was traditional for the sailors to moan about their mate; but they knew of this mate's reputation and had to admit, albeit rather reluctantly, that they had one of the best mates on the East Coast collier trade. Solomon had learnt much from him.

Solomon's colleagues in the fo'c'sle were a mixed bunch; proud of their skills, knowing they were what made the ship sail, and that if there was a disaster it was they who would have to look after each other. They might quarrel, fight, and swear at each other, and laugh at their failings; but they were a group of men thrown together largely by chance, and they, of necessity, were –ideally– a team.

When the wind was steady and the ship driving calmly then one of the crew would get out his fiddle and play tunes: *The Jolly Town Rakes*, or some of the ruder ones, *Oh Mother* or *A Soldier, A Sailor* - the others singing along with them and roaring out the vulgar lines, such as when the sailor "let fly at her a Shot 'twixt Wind and Water". They sang and foot-danced in the cramped fo'c'sle momentarily happy, lively and free. Once he had played *Would ye have a young Virgin of fifteen Years?* He noticed that it seemed to affect Solomon badly, it was never played again, and no-one asked.

"Well, sir," Solomon replied to Walker's question, "It taught me a lot."

This was clearly a sufficient response. John Walker nodded several times. Then he asked, "Well, Solomon, how wouldst thou like to be mate on *Freelove*?"

"Very much, sir."

"Consider it done. Report to my son John at his premises in Haggersgate tomorrow morning at eight of the clock. He shall be expecting thee.

"Yes, sir. I shall."

They shook hands, and went their ways in satisfied silence. Sol, hardly noticing the freezing wind, thought that soon he would be a mate. Then he could go and see Abigail again, and her father could have no objection to their meeting, to their getting to know each other, to their kissing and cuddling, to their getting married. He would even be prepared to become a Quaker, a way of life that was appealing – he had learnt much about the Society of Friends from his master John Walker.

Chapter 8

William and Margaret Backas, after a supper of beef pie and a blancmange with some fine Portuguese red wine, had settled themselves comfortably round the coal fire. William was perusing the laws which needs must be enforced by a constable; while Margaret, with her workbox and a pile of damaged clothes beside her and needle and thread in hand, was busy darning. The conversation was sporadic.

"I think that Hilda did well tonight," said Margaret.

"Yes, a good meal."

The clock pendulum slowly measured the passing of time.

"Margaret, listen to this. 'By the Statute of the third year of Edward II c.4: where a man or any living creature escapes alive out of a ship cast away, the same shall not be adjudged a wreck but the goods shall be saved and kept by the sheriff for a year and a day for the owner'. What rubbish! 'Any living creature'? That would include the master's dog. Even the ship's cat, or the chickens."

"Or the ship's rats."

By now they were laughing.

"Or nits."

"Or even the Barghest hound?

"Or *teredo navalis*, the ship worm."

"Typical man."

"A typical lawyer, you mean, my darling?"

"All lawyers are men. No woman would have compiled that rubbish."

The laughter drained away, and the conversation ceased.

Many evenings had the similar routine. Margaret knew their pattern well: while she stitched, darned and patched, William would read civil law books. After a while his eyes would flicker and close, his head slump into slumber. Some minutes later he would shudder himself awake; his eyes would open and he would momentarily look around as if he had entered an unfamiliar room. Then he would return to his book. This would sometimes last for several cycles.

Margaret caught him on an attending moment between dozes:

"Is it true that that Jacob Linskill has refused medical aid?"

"Yes. Michael Cornelius, one of the leaders of Quaker congregation, who is also Jacob's employer, paid for a physician to heal his damaged hand. Later Jacob refused it."

"Why was that?"

"The Quakers unfriended him, because he had hit Wheatear so violently that his hand received the damage. Quakers are pacifists, he should not have hit Wheatear."

"If that is what he did."

"Indeed, Margaret. My belief is that he did not. It seems more likely that Wheatear did the damage to Linskill's hand. But so long as Linskill sticks to his version, the Quakers will stick to their position."

"And he rejects the Quakers' charity out of stubbornness?"

"He sees it as hypocrisy: on the one hand they reject him, on the other they offer help."

"Hypocrisy or not, refusing the offer of paying for a physician could be very dangerous, surely."

"Indeed, Margaret. The hand –his right hand- could become useless. It may have to be amputated. Worse, the whole arm might become gangrenous; if nothing is done he could die."

*   *   *

Freelove, anchored in Whitby Roads, had sailed from Shields. The sea was placid so the voyage was of few days. Solomon and some members of the crew were rowed ashore. His outwardly dignified exterior barely confined his tangle of hopes and anxieties. Seeing Abigail once more would be a delight; but would she still have feelings for him? Would they kiss? Would her father accept him more favourably now he was a ship's mate? Would she one day ever be his mate - Mistress Abigail King?

But Solomon was sent ashore not to fill his imagination with pleasurable romance, but to complain about the standard of meat which had been loaded onto the ship at the beginning of the season. He strode firmly towards the market practising his bluff face of determined dissatisfaction. There were three butchers' shops in fairly close proximity, each with a similar sign of a cow hanging outside. The shop with the most ancient and weather-pealed of these was that of George Hill, the rather tawdry exterior proudly indicating several generations of the Hill family maintaining a sound reputation for butchery. Solomon opened the door and entered. He liked butchers' shops, with the suspended carcasses and the sawdust on the floor; even the massive slab of timber and the rather formidable collection of knives and chopping cleavers displayed upon it. In the far corner a young man was sweeping, but when Solomon entered he put his brush aside, smiled, gave a brief nod, and said, "Good day, sir. What is it you wish for?"

"I am Solomon King, mate in *Freelove*."

This information elicited a formal bow, and a tone that showed he was impressed, "*Freelove?* Young Master Walker's ship."

"Indeed. I wish to speak with Mr George Hill."

"He is away on business, sir; but I am his son Mark, and I shall be honoured to serve you."

"Mrs Hill?"

"Alas, my mother died several years ago."

Sol mumbled some kind of sympathy.

"Can I help, sir? I am quite competent."

"I have a complaint. The meat you provided last year was inadequate. And when this year's beef barrel was opened it was much the same: too much fat and gristle, added bone to make up the weight, and already smelling of putrefaction. I demand recompense and replacement; and if I do not receive adequate satisfaction we shall never purchase meat from you again."

While Solomon was spouting his tirade, Mark was looking increasingly perplexed. And when the mate stopped the butcher's boy was rendered speechless. For what seemed like an aeon both stared at each other in surprised silence. Eventually Mark found words:

"But, sir, we have never provided any meat for *Freelove*."

"You have. It is recorded in the ship's accounts. Do not make me angry, with such subterfuge."

"I shall check, sir, in our book, if it so please you; but I am certain sure no beef -or any meat- has been sold to *Freelove*. When a new ship is launched here there is much competition to gain contracts for business, and a large vessel such as *Freelove* does not escape notice."

Mark disappeared into the back room, leaving Solomon irritated and frustrated; he thought this task should have been a small matter quickly concluded so he would have more time with Abigail. Instead this mere boy was denying that any meat was sold, let alone explain its poor quality.

Mark returned with the book; there were no entries for any meat being sold for the *Freelove.*

"There must be some error here," growled Solomon.

"It must be as I said, sir. I swear by all the devils in Hell that no meat has been sold for your ship. However, I shall make up a barrel of best meat, and have it ready for you on St Ann's Staith, tomorrow at dawn, properly sealed and labelled. It shall be free of charge, and I guarantee that it will be the best beef you have ever tasted."

"I accept your offer. There has clearly been some error."

Solomon left all this behind him as he hurried across the river, past the Golden Lion Inn and up steep Flowergate, past the Presbyterian Chapel, up to the Linskill house. For a while he stood outside, catching his breath and controlling his emotions, before he knocked (too loudly?) on the door. It seemed an age before the door rattled with bolts and was opened. Solomon frowned; the young man who stood in the doorway was a total stranger.

Solomon said, "I have come to visit Mr Linskill."

"I am Mr Linskill," came the reply, "Mr Esau Linskill."

"Where is Mr Jacob Linskill, the weaver?"

"Alas he died."

"How?"

"Some festering wound. People did say that he spurned treatment, and hastened his end." Mr Linskill realised that this sounded rather abrupt, so he added, "Great tragedy, very sad; such a loss..."

"And his daughter Abigail?"

"Also dead."

Both fell silent. Then Esau continued:

"She went to see her aunt at Pickering, where she caught smallpox and died."

Another pause; neither could think what to say. Eventually Esau muttered, "Is there anything else?"

Solomon was full of misery and supressed rage. *Is there anything else? No, without Abigail there is nothing else!*

What he said was, "No, I thank you for your time, sir".

Out in the street he stood stunned into statue. His rage turned inwards: *Maybe if I had come earlier she might still be alive?*

Two hours later he realised he was on the ship; but he had no recollection of what had happened in all that time.

He knew he had to continue in his work, showing no weakness, no sorrow. He owed this to the master and to the crew. And to the owners of the ship, one of which was John Walker senior his erstwhile master – and the man who had told him to wait until he was a mate before seeing Abigail again. *Bad advice. If I had not listened to your advice, Master, I could have saved Abigail's life. Why did I take your advice? Why did I keep away from Abigail for so long? Lovely Abigail, I killed you...*

Chapter 9

Margaret Backas finished her last mouthful of cold pie and dabbed at her lips with a napkin. "Tell me, William," she said, "If Jacob Linskill, the weaver, died of a much festered wound which became fatal because he refused to accept medical help, would that make his death suicide?"

William was speechless for a moment, struggling to chew and swallow a rather overfull portion of pie; his accompanying grunts and circling hand gestures were intended to indicate this predicament. A bit of coughing and spluttering and a mouthful of ale eventually rendered him capable of speech. "In the eyes of God, maybe, Margaret; but in the law not so. He died of a surfeit of pride, I believe; and pride is indeed a sin, but not a criminal one, I think."

"I think he was being very selfish! As if the poor girl hadn't suffered enough. And there she was trying to keep up the weaving quota while her father sat there feeling sorry for himself."

"A tragedy indeed. Help was offered; but spurned. What was the girl's name? Angel?"

"Abigail. And I hear that when he became very ill Jacob Linskill sent her to stay with her aunt in Pickering where they both caught smallpox and died. But for his selfishness, his daughter might still be alive."

"Innocent children often suffer for the iniquity of their fathers."

"I am told that the house has been sold to a young Quaker from Fishlake."

"Not sold, but given. Jacob's grandfather set up his loom in that house and made a lot of money in trading sailcloth. His will revealed he had entailed the premises to go to his nearest of kin on condition that they carried on the weaving trade, that they were a Quaker, and that their name was Linskill. The entail was to continue for twelve generations."

"What happened to the money?"

"I know not. Jacob Linskill died in debt."

"The talk in the town is that the Whitby Quakers paid some of Jacob's debts, and the new young tenant has already paid off the rest. But opinion is divided about the motives: guilt, greed or generosity."

"Margaret, I don't suppose your horde of local gossips can give him a name?"

"Oh yes; he is called 'Esau'."

"Hmm. I hope he proves better than his biblical namesake."

*   *   *

When George Hill returned to his shop he was confronted by his son Mark with the anomaly which had been revealed in Solomon King's visit. George confessed that many years ago he had taken some contraband liquor from Ralph Theaker to sell on to some of his friends. After that he had been put under increasing pressure to deal with Theaker's criminal activities, including selling inferior meat to ships. The cook, or purser, on board a ship would be given a false receipt from a reputable butcher -in this case George Hill- when in fact it was an inadequate provision which had been compiled from low grade meat and many bones which had been delivered by a man employed by Ralph Theaker, the Provider. The further George was involved in this illegal trade, the more he was forced to go further.

"But what can we do, Father?" said Mark.

"I am in too far; but you must not be implicated. When I am gone you must live to run this shop and to restore its reputation for good meat. Stay honest, do good, and live in the ways of the Lord. Make your mother proud of you."

"Father, you speak as if you are about to die, are you ill?"

"No, son, not ill. I hope providence will let me live long; but I do have an ailment caused by the Provider, who has blighted my life. I suspect Theaker will already know what happened this morning with the mate of *Freelove*, and rumours will already be circulating in the town. Theaker will not like that, it puts him in an embarrassing situation and he will seek to punish me."

"What might that be?"

"I know not, Son; but the important thing is that you are not involved. Do not try to save me. Promise?"

"I promise not to endanger the reputation of the firm; but I cannot promise not to try to save you, Papa."

*   *   *

Jack Wheatear had been deeply moved by his strange experience when he tried to steal a sailor's silver buckles. For several days he had been in a mood of mental suspension during which he was unable to make sense of his thoughts and feelings. The phrase 'sin no more' echoed and re-echoed in his brain.

Jack had signed on to the next ship sailing to Whitby, turning his back on his London life. When he was paid off and disembarked at Whitby, Jack felt he was coming home. He found a lodging house in the north end of Church Street run by a rather old-fashioned widow who had been married to a master mariner. She tended to be particular about how her residents behaved, but this was oddly reassuring for Jack. She was in some ways like a mother to him, and she could cook excellent pies.

Jack had done many bad things, which troubled him. He hoped that by putting his wicked self behind him, he could eradicate them; but he did not know how he could ensure that such a life would be sufficient to keep him from punishment after death.

On Sunday 13 March Jack climbed all the wooden stairs up to the parish church in the hope of finding order and guidance, of learning how to sin no more. This was the first time he had been to church since he was baptized— and he only had his mother's word for that. He was embarrassed about not knowing where to sit and was brusquely guided to the benches by the west wall. Some of the prayers he did not understand and the language was old-fashioned, but some words made sense, such as "God pardons and absolveth all them that truly repent", and a prayer for corn to be of "cheapness and plenty".

However the Litany seemed endless, and the long drawn out moaning of the metrical psalms was bizarre.

The vicar preached a sermon of tedious length and which for Jack was totally incomprehensible; there were several mentions of Arianism and Sabellianism and it seemed at times that he was encouraging his congregation to worship three gods, all of which meant nothing to Jack – and certainly provided no guide to how to 'sin no more'. Also he had not anticipated that the service would take so long, and by the time it all ended, his bladder was urgently in need of release. To his dismay after the vicar had left, the congregation filed out in order of social rank led by the Lord and Lady of the Manor, and they processed out very slowly. So, as he was near the door he dashed out, causing a degree of tut-tutting among the finely dressed ladies and their merchant husbands, and pissed behind the nearest headstone.

The only thing that meant anything to him was the readings from the Bible. He did not know which books were being read from, and indeed he could not remember any of the words; but what he had heard was for him overwhelmingly beautiful and shrewdly wise. As he went down the Church Steps to his lodgings, he was determined to own a copy of the Bible and to improve his reading to be able to understand it.

*　　　　　*　　　　　*

Thomas Norrison had been born in Shields, the son of a master mariner and a daughter of a ship owner. From as far back as he could remember his life revolved about shipping. His first toy (and so far as he could recall, his only toy) was a model ship, and his mother would tell him stories woven round this ship. Sometimes it was a trading ship sailing to far distant parts to bring back exotic fabrics and spices, sometimes it was a man-of-war fighting the Dutch in fierce sea battles, at times it was a pirate ship pillaging in the Caribbean, at times it was a collier braving the perils of the German Ocean bringing sea-coal to London.

His mother would take him down to the wharf to watch the collier ships, she taught him the names of all the sails and types of vessels, and explained the functions of keelmen and hostmen. Thomas was apprenticed to his uncle for seven years, after which he moved to Whitby where the air was fresher and the prospects more promising. He was a mate by the time he was twenty-five and two years later he became a master of a collier. Within a few years he had accrued sufficient money to buy a property in Atty's Yard in Whitby; not a luxurious messuage but it suited his purposes. It was adjacent to the gateway into Baxtergate and had a storehouse on the ground floor which not only had double doors opening into the yard, but also had a more discreet portal at the side which led into a small ginnel. Above both was an apartment of several rooms which suited his purposes. One of which was marriage to Caroline, another daughter of the sea; and in 1714, he married her. She was pragmatic, knowledgeable, kind, thorough, hard-working, witty and beautiful –all that he could want in a wife– and a perfect mother for all the boys that would follow in their father's footprints. Their first child was to be called Alfred, but was a girl. She was named Hilda, and her father –when he was not at sea– doted on her, twining his roughened fingers through her curly brown hair and singing gentle songs that made her slide into slumber.

Two years later Caroline gave birth to twin girls; the delivery was difficult and but for the help from the midwife, they would probably not have survived; though she was told she would be unable to have any more children. Thomas wanted to call them Amphitrite and Thetis, but Caroline rejected these names, suggesting that they would admirably suit his first two ships. Eventually they agreed on Elizabeth and Sophia - though they always called them Lizzie and Sophie.

Of course the three girls were initiated into the maritime world, they were taught about the rigging and the sails of a ship, how to use a quadrant, a logline, a lead line, how to guide a ship at night by the constellations, and how to use a chart to plot a voyage.

Hilda loved her little sisters and tried hard to be the grown-up daughter. She showed Lizzie and Sophie how to make a boat out of paper, and they floated their fragile craft down Bagdale Beck to see which of them sank the last. But much of the time the twins just wanted to play together and share jokes together, and Hilda felt excluded. As they grew up Hilda came to believe that Mama and Papa loved her sisters more than her. Hilda thought this was partly because it was something of a miracle that they were born alive, and partly because they were so vivacious; but worst of all they were growing up to be very pretty with iridescent blue eyes, delicate fingers, and long shiny honey-coloured hair hanging naturally into gentle wavy curls. When Hilda stood in front of the mirror what she saw was a podgy figure and a boringly plain face with red blotches, topped with dull brown frizzy hair which looked like the twisted stalks of heather on the moors after the burning. Her parents, of course, did not see any of that.

When Hilda was eight her father took her aboard the ship of which he was captain to London and back, and she felt special and grown up; it was the most wonderful experience of her childhood. But her little sisters were very jealous, and Thomas promised that he would take them to Shields and London as soon as they were seven, and they giggled with delight at the prospect, chattering like nestling chicks eager to be fed.

It was not to be. A collier, captained by Thomas Norrison, foundered on the shifting sand banks of the coast of Norfolk in a rising storm. The inadequacy of the lighthouse flames ensured the he had little knowledge as to where they were. The pinnace was lowered in an attempt to pull the ship off the sandbank which seemed to be successful, but then the tumultuous wind and the rain drove the ship back on the sandbank with greater ferocity, splintering a hole in the ship, causing her to roll over on her side. Norrison remained in the ship, but ordered all the crew into the boat which was provisioned and the nautical devices were given to the mate. The crew were able to reach the shore at Mundersley two days later, but the ship left no trace. The body of Thomas Norrison was washed ashore near Palling, where he was interred. For many weeks there was a plethora of wooden planks washed up on the Norfolk shore.

Caroline petitioned Trinity House which provided a small pension; but the death of Thomas Norrison changed the family. It made them tougher, but also more vulnerable. Whitby was prospering, and the population was expanding, but there was a housing problem. Atty's Yard became more populous, with many families living together in rooms intended for one. The earlier inhabitants, whom the Norrisons knew well, left to find better accommodation elsewhere. The yard suffered from the overcrowding; the single water pump and the necessary house were overdemanded, and the sound of quarrelling, fights and unseemly language were common. Many of the new inhabitants were metaphorically as well as actually fish wives, and on many occasions Caroline, drawn to the window by the noisy clatter, saw two such, arms akimbo, shouting abuse each to the other calling them with offensive insults such as *trollop, gobble-prick* and *wagtail*. Naturally there were such occasions as when Lizzie innocently asked, "Mama, how can someone pray with her knees upwards?"

Laundry hanging out to dry disappeared, and accusations of theft were made – which was probably more likely than blaming the traditional targets the kites, as these birds were diminishing in number. The rats in the yard increased in number.

Chapter 10

Solomon King was getting used to being a mate. He had worried at first that the crew would not consider him worthy, or would not respond to his commands. He need not have worried; it was soon clear to the crew that he knew more than they did, knew exactly how to sail a ship efficiently, appropriately and without unnecessary danger. They admired him as he admired them. His commands were accepted as they knew they were right, indeed they knew the appropriate orders word for word, as they know the words of sea shanties. Solomon did neither attempt to make friends with the crew nor to bully them, and consequently they liked him. It did not mean that those in the fo'c'sle did not make fun of him, imitate his way of talking, and give him an unflattering nickname. That was what sailors did.

Solomon was busy most of the time, particularly at noon –the beginning of the ship's day– when he ensured that he had all the appropriate information of the ship's speed, direction, latitude, and approximate position; the speed and direction of the wind; the weather; the depth of the sea; and any significant sightings of birds, fish and seaweeds; and any sightings and conversations with other ships. All this had to be available for the master to enter in the ship's log.

But sometimes life was dull if the sea was calm and there was a moderate following wind. Then the mate's job was to find work for the crew, such as making spun yarns, plaits, gaskets and grummets. And once the crew was busy, and happily chatting amongst themselves, Solomon had little to do. At such times he thought of Abigail Linskill buried unloved in the muddy churchyard at Pickering. He wished to know more about her last few months, and to be able to put flowers on her grave; but most he imagined what might have been had she lived.

Freelove docked for a few days in May 1729 at Whitby for repairs, and Solomon was granted two days absence. Solomon wasted no time and was up before the sun. He was rowed ashore in the jolly-boat by the youngest apprentice, who was told to return to collect him at 6.00pm on the following day.

Solomon first went to the house of Esau Linskill to find out more information about Abigail's death. He said he had little information except that Jacob's wife was a sister to the wife of a lawyer in Pickering, and that Abigail had spent her last days there. After being given directions to the lawyer's house, Solomon walked on to The Flying Angel at Ruswarp which was not only an inn, but also had a stock of horses for hire. The inn-holder was sitting outside his establishment enjoying the bright sunny morning; he watched King approaching and realised four things about him. First, that he had come to hire a horse - as few would come to his inn to consume ale that early in the day. Secondly, that he was a mariner; even though he was not dressed in seamen's short jacket and trousers, his ruddy complexion and his loping walk were decisive. Thirdly, as he was neatly dressed and not wearing sea-faring clothes, so he was probably a comparatively wealthy sailor. Fourthly, because he would be at sea for most of the year he would not be very experienced with riding and how to treat a horse.

The innkeeper rose to his feet and greeted King politely with a slight bow of his head, "Sir, are you here to hire a horse to ride?"

"Indeed, that is my wish."

"At your service. Where are you riding to, sir, if I may ask?"

"To Pickering and back."

"Returning?"

"Tomorrow."

"Ah, sir. That is a fair distance and the road is rough, cartwheel tracks that were soft and muddy a few days ago are now toughened in this sunny weather, as hard as stone. It will put extra strain on an ordinary beast, but I think I have just the horse for you."

They went into the stables, and Solomon was shown a sturdy gelding.

"He is called Incitatus after the Emperor Caligula's horse."

"Which he made a senator?"

"Indeed, sir. I can see you a man of good education. Far be it my place, sir, to say such things but I rate my Incitatus as cleverer than many men in our House of Parliament."

They both laughed.

"Of course, sir, because your journey will be hard for a lesser horse, I think it a wise choice to settle on Incitatus. Naturally, the cost will be slightly higher, but you will not regret the decision."

The deal was struck, and Incitatus was led out into the yard. While he was being saddled and harnessed, the gelding looked Solomon up and down and snorted contemptuously.

"Easy boy," said his owner, and patted him on the neck. Then he fetched a mounting block and helped Solomon into the saddle.

Once settled on Incitatus, Solomon kicked his sides, and called "Go on!" The horse did not move until the innkeeper gave the gelding a sharp smack on his buttock, which made him move forward at an easy pace.

As the sun rose in the sky the day grew more and more hot and sweltering. Solomon was aware of the inchoate nature of his horsemanship, and this was not enhanced by the fact that it had soon become clear to Solomon that this horse was not the best in the stable: he travelled slowly, occasionally stumbling over the rutted road across Goathland Moor which seemed endless. Solomon kicked the horse's sides to encourage him to go faster, but that seemed to have a negative effect. Occasionally Incitatus would wander off the barren road to walk on the heath and the heather, not yet in bloom, but clearly the horse seemed to prefer to walk on twiggy stems than on the road. Solomon would get him back on the road by pulling the reigns tight; the horse reluctantly obeyed but he snorted and stamped with his front feet, with his ears sharply and angrily pricked. Even Solomon realised that the horse disliked him, and he certainly disliked the horse. The journey was going to be an ordeal for both of them.

They met the occasional waggon and Solomon was embarrassed to see how their horses were struggling but seemed willing to work as hard as their attendant carters. Several riders passed Incitatus. A light two-wheeled one-horse cart came past with a young man driving and a young lady by his side. The man doffed his hat in mockery and called out words which Solomon pretended he neither heard nor understood. The young lady was also amused but was having difficulty in keeping her bonnet on her head. When they were about a hundred yards ahead, Solomon had the pleasure of seeing her hat fly off and get entangled in a gorse bush. The man did not stop the cart.

Solomon's amusement was short lived. Just as they were approaching the abandoned lady's bonnet a gust of wind filled it making it flap hither and thither, billowing out like a ship's sail with sudden snapping noises. Incitatus reared up in panic, galloping in the opposite direction. Solomon tried to make him stop by pulling on the reins and shouting, but this increased the horse's terror. Leaping and stamping the horse threw Solomon to the ground. Incitatus then calmed down of his own accord, and slowly walked over to where Solomon lay immobile, he nosed him, pawing the ground in frustration. Solomon recovered from the shock of his fall, and unsteadily stood up. He patted Incitatus on his neck and stroked his forehead, then in a calm voice he said, "I am sorry, Incitatus. I have not treated you well. I am not a good rider." The horse nodded his head up and down as if agreeing. "We are near Eller Beck; you can see it over there fifty yards away or so. Come." He walked towards the stream and after a brief hesitation Incitatus joined him. Solomon leaned over from the bank and filled up his water bottle in the swift-running stream. Incitatus stood on the edge of the beck, drinking water from the stream and eating the fresh grass on the bank. Then Solomon waded into the water and the horse followed him. Like a child he splashed in the water, till both man and horse were soaked. Then they both clambered out of the stream and onto the road. Solomon gently held Incitatus' face and said, "All right, Incitatus. You know this business better than me. Let's go to Pickering." With some difficulty he got into the saddle, holding the reins slightly, and patting his neck. "Go, Inkie, go," and he did. The man, the horse, the saddle, everything was wet; but horse and man were happy, each respecting the other. Incitatus set off in a steady trot and soon they arrived at Pickering. With a gentle use of the reins Solomon guided Incitatus to The White Swan on Market Place. He dismounted, still somewhat damp and dishevelled, but that did not bother him. The innkeeper came out to greet him and asked if he was staying the night. "Yes," replied Solomon, "Just the one night. I must be back in Ruswarp tomorrow evening. But I want you to look after my fine steed. Wash him, brush him, give him water. If, when I am ready to return, I see a handsome and happy horse you will be well rewarded. If I do not you will regret the day you were born." The last comment was the sort of language he had learnt since being a mate.

"Certainly, sir, your wish will be completed in full."

Solomon King walked to the house of the lawyer, and knocked on the door which was opened by a male servant who looked at him with a dubious aspect, but in due course Solomon was shown into the office.

After some minutes, the lawyer came in, and -after the usual formalities- he asked, "How can I help you?"

"I wish to know more about your niece, Abigail Linskill."

"Is this a legal matter?"

"No, sir, it is a personal request."

"If it is not a legal matter, I cannot do much for you. The girl in question was sent to live with us while she had smallpox, she infected my wife. Indeed she killed my wife. Both are dead to me now." He rose to his feet, and said, "This discussion in now concluded." He rang a bell and his servant appeared surprisingly quickly – almost as if he had been listening at the door. "See Mr King out."

Solomon gave the attorney the briefest of nods, and left the house. He was angry; he had come all this way to be told nothing at all. And he was hungry.

Chapter 11

Back at The White Swan, he summoned the patron and ordered a jug of ale and a partridge pie. As there were few people there, he got talking to the innkeeper who asked whether it was business or pleasure that brought him to Pickering.

"Neither, really. I wished to find out more about the young Abigail Linskill whom I knew some time back. She came to Pickering to stay with her uncle and aunt. The uncle is the attorney."

"In Burgate?"

"Yes, I came to visit him to get more information, but he was unhelpful. Indeed I was virtually thrown out of his house."

"I don't mix with attorneys if I can help it, sir; but I do recall that there was quite a bit of gossip in the town about it at the time."

"Why was there so much gossip?"

"Because his wife had the smallpox, and then he took the girl into his house as a servant. Being so young and of necessity being in regular contact with her aunt it was no surprise that she caught it too."

"Are you sure it was like that? Abigail caught the smallpox from her aunt?"

"Oh, yes, sir. There was much talk about it at the time. It is a shame that they have both gone, and the attorney lives on in his house. There were plenty of people who would prefer that it was the lawyer who died."

FRIEND OR FOE

In the afternoon, Solomon walked to the parish church with its impressive steeple. In the churchyard he found Abigail's aunt's headstone, there were only a few lines about her, leaving ample space for a fuller eulogy when her husband came to share her grave.

Solomon had an early breakfast, after which he set out to find the Quaker Meeting House which was in Undercliffe, with their burial ground adjoining it. Though misty, the sun was slowly clearing the morning into a bright day. Solomon thought Pickering looked beautiful as he walked along the road which meandered beside Pickering Beck, and on his right the impressive but rather sinister castle towered above the fog, secure on its cliff.

The Meeting House was unobtrusive, similar to many of its neighbouring houses, but Solomon had been well briefed and he entered the wicket gate of the adjoining area which was the Quaker burial ground. Quakers eschewed tombstones as they were only for those who could afford them, and they were often pomposity engraved in stone. The cemetery therefore looked very like an ordinary fallow field. There was a bench so one could look over the ground to the beck and the rising bank beyond, and there was indeed a man sitting there. Solomon was surprised to see anyone, as in his mind he had imagined that he would hold a silent vigil in the field where Abigail, his first and only love, lay. He thought of the funeral words, "I shall see for myself, and mine eyes shall behold, and not another". However he assumed that this man was grieving as was he, so he did not wish to

85

disturbed him. The man, without looking, shuffled along on the bench to make way.

"Thank you," muttered Solomon.

The other man tuned his head and looked. He said, "Solomon King?"

"By all that's blue, it's Jack Wheatear!"

"It is I."

"There was a time when I would happily have killed you, Jack Wheatear."

"There was a time when I would happily have killed you, Solomon King. But I am a reformed man. 'I abhor myself and repent in dust and ashes', Lamentations chapter 42 verse 6."

"I am pleased. And, by the way, your quotation was from Job."

"Sometimes I think I might take some work on land, far away from Whitby which has too many memories."

"You have shown that you are a good man and a good sailor, Jack. You have put your hand to the plough, don't look back."

"Good advice, Solomon the wise, and a reference to St Luke's Gospel, chapter 9, verse 62."

"Correct."

Although the conversation seemed pleasant there was a deep tension, perhaps even re-stirred hate, which both sought to hide – whether that was out of kindness or cowardice neither was willing to examine.

A supercilious magpie strutted past. Aware that it was ignored, it flicked its tail and nonchalantly flew away.

So involved were they in maintaining a civilised conversation that not only did they fail to notice the magpie but also were not aware that a woman was coming towards them until she spoke.

"Good day, friends, can I help you in any way?"

Solomon was the first to recover sufficiently to answer.

"Good day, madam. We are not Quakers, but both of us are from Whitby, and were close to a young Quaker girl who lived there. However, due to a series of sad events in her life, she came to Pickering, but caught smallpox and died. We assume she is buried here, and we have come to mourn her loss."

The woman looked perplexed. She said, "She may not be buried here. I think I know her. Canst thou give me more information, my friend?"

"Certainly. Her name was Abigail Linskill, daughter of Jacob. When her father died she came to live here with her aunt, wife of the attorney."

Whatever Solomon and Jack thought she would say or do, her response was startlingly unexpected: she burst into spasms of laughter.

Solomon and Jack were speechless, and could do nothing until the laughter subsided.

"I am sorry, my friends, to laugh at what you think is a sad event; but the news is good. Abigail indeed caught smallpox, and was ejected from the attorney's house after her aunt had died. She came here, and did live in this house, the Quaker Meeting House. She had to be looked after, but in return she did what work she could as a kind of caretaker. She recovered from the smallpox which was comparatively mild, and her face was only slightly scarred. She is a good and strong woman, independently minded as befits a Quaker woman."

"Are you saying that she is alive?" asked Solomon.

"Yes, yes. Abigail is alive."

"Where is she now?"

"She stayed here until she was strong enough to travel and then she set off for Shields where she hath kin."

"So she is well and thriving in Shields? You are sure?"

"Indeed, my friend. The Quaker network is excellent in passing on information. 'Twas but last week when I heard news of her. She keepeth busy weaving, at which she is well skilled. Fear not, friends, Abigail Linskill is living in Shields with her cousins, Henry and Jonathan Dunn. She is well-employed weaving there. She is in very good health. And so is the baby."

Chapter 12

Solomon ate early at The White Swan. After which he summoned the innkeeper and said, "I am returning to Whitby now. Thank you for a splendid meal. Fetch my horse, please."

When Incitatus was brought round his coat was gleaming, and when he recognised Solomon he let out a soft snort, his ears pointing forward.

After settling the bill, Solomon pressed a florin into the innkeeper's hand and thanked him for looking after the horse so well. The gratitude was returned in words and in helping Solomon into the saddle.

Solomon was a quick learner, and had understood at last exactly what was meant in the old adage "A happy horse makes a happy rider, and a happy rider makes a happy horse." Incitatus seemed more content with a slight chill in the air than he had with the hot weather on Thursday. Solomon relaxed and generally let Incitatus lead the way, and nothing eventful happened as the horse walked and trotted as the mood took him.

Then suddenly Incitatus stopped. Solomon gave him a little prod with his feet, a kind but firm "Go! Go!" even a little touch with the crop. But the horse stood still, shaking his head up and down and sniffing. Then Solomon realised. He dismounted and went round to Incitatus' face and smiled, gently patting and stroking him. Then he said, "You remembered this place, don't you? You can smell Eller Beck. Come on, you silly beast, let's go." He took the reins and set off towards the stream, Incitatus followed.

Both were eager to enjoy the cool water. Standing ankle deep in the water, they —in their different ways- drank the refreshing draught. They stayed there barely ten minutes and then the horse turned, moved towards the road a few paces then stopped. Solomon surprised himself by managing to mount the horse in a single movement, even though he had to do a bit of shuffling to get comfortably seated. Then back to the road and an eventless journey to The Flying Angel.

Solomon felt quite sad parting with Incitatus at The Flying Angel; but he was a sailor and when he saw *Freelove* in the bay he felt true joy. He was even more joyful when he saw an apprentice on the shore with the jolly-boat.

It was shortly after the second bell of the afternoon watch that the anchor was raised and *Freelove* sailed out into the German Ocean. The journey between Whitby and Shields was comparatively short in nautical miles and could be swift, but even in spring a change of wind could whip into a squall with the heavy breathing of the sea.

*   *   *

Caroline Norrison stood looking out of the window at the yard, vague in the gloom of night:

I am so lonely. Thomas I miss you so much: your cuddles and kisses, your way of talking, your humour, your strength, your refusal to give in, your smiles. Most of all I miss you just being here: being a husband, lover and friend.

The children are wonderful, but they are children. They knew you only as Papa who played with them, taught them, told them bed-time stories - and their memories are good. But when they grow older, they will miss knowing you as a grown man. My memories are not so good; already I forget things about you, Thomas. Will you forgive me? I have nothing that still smells of you. I will keep your sea possessions for ever: your telescope, compass, pistol and quadrant. Sometimes I take them out of the case and feel them, caress them. Is that silly, Thomas? Sophia loves them; if she had been a boy she would be a captain one day. I cannot bring myself to sell them. Maybe if I had, we would not be so poor. At least you have left us our fairly spacious accommodation; but income is small. It was a great wrench when Hilda went as a servant in the house of William and Margaret Backas. So young. Such a separation. I miss her, she misses us all. She gives me the money she gets; though it is but poor addlings.

Can you remember me? Do you remember our cat called Ninetails, which was made much of, particularly as it kept the rats out of our apartment? There are two rats now in the storeroom; typically the girls have given them crumbs and names. How they manage to make fun out of nothing is a pleasing puzzle.

This Yard was once lovely to me, when we were both young and the children tiny. Now I hate it; it is full now of the wicked world that I have tried to shield our daughters from. I have tried to bring our daughters up well and shield them from the sordid vulgarity which surrounds them. I try. I try, Thomas. But that is as possible as shielding them from the smell of fish guts and shit. It is the money. Our financial problems meant that we were in debt and I was caught in the web of The Provider – at first a friend and then a fiend. For a small income our storeroom is used to hold some of his unlawful commodities. He sends his minions to move in or take out smuggled, maybe stolen, goods. I worry. I do not like to be involved in crime. Sometimes The Provider himself has been round in lecherous mood hoping to have his sexual pleasure. I hate him. How I wish you were here Thomas.

Do you remember Captain James Boyes? You and he were friends. I keep in touch with him. His manners are acceptable, and he knows how to treat a lady. Also he makes me laugh, and tells me stories of the seas; sometimes the same stories as you did. It is useful to have a man who knows about things I cannot cope with; I am quite reliant upon him for advice. But don't be jealous Thomas – he is not the sort of man I would want to marry! Though sometimes I wish there was one. I am so lost without you.

Chapter 13

When dusk seeped into dark, a middle-aged man moved stealthily through the streets of Whitby, pleased that the warmth of spring evenings seemed to have set in at last. He had a brown jacket and brown breeches, a brown shirt, a brown neckerchief and brown shoes. Even his face was brown from many years at sea. He must have had a name once, but he was known by the rather unsophisticated sobriquet of 'that brown thing'. He sidled into Atty's Yard from Baxtergate.

Up a familiar brick staircase climbed the brown thing. He thudded his fist on the stolid door, scattering flakes of paint which time had robbed of identifiable colour. The door was opened by Caroline Norrison. He saw her as a woman worn by poverty, but whose demeanour was dignified and whose beauty had not yet been erased by hardship. But this appraisal was irrelevant – he was there on business.

"Oh, it's you," she said with a weary sigh, "What now?"

"Tomorrow at this time of the day, some more goods will be brought to be kept in your warehouse. You understand? You will ask no questions, and observe complete secrecy."

The woman nodded agreement, and shut the door. The man left the yard by the other entrance, being careful where he put his feet.

He walked down beside Bagdale Beck, turned left and passed the Angel Hotel whose windows were brightly lit, and from which dance music was clearly audible. He noted this, as he passed along the quay and over the bridge. Some ships were moored in mid-stream, their lights casting ever-moving scattered yellow reflections on the water which was dark as sea-coal. These ships were silent apart from the creak of oak, hemp and pine. In contrast the outer harbour was bustle as the fishermen prepared their boats for their early morning voyages.

Once over the Esk, the brown thing walked down Sandgate and into the Market Square, to knock on another door, which was opened by Mark Hill.

"Can I help you?"

"Tell your father that he must take all the goods which he is storing on our behalf, except the four ankers of Burgundian wine, and take them to Mrs Norrison's abode in Atty's Yard at this time of the day tomorrow. Make sure you exactly repeat this order to your father. Ask no questions, and observe complete secrecy. Understand?"

"I understand." Mark shut the door, and the brown thing gradually faded into the gloom.

*   *   *

As the light waned, Caroline Norrison sent Elizabeth and Sophia to their room. She explained that someone was coming to put things in the storeroom below and they need not be worried by the noises. They wanted to know if their little rat friends would be upset, but Caroline assured them everything would be all right as she would be there as well.

There was quite a noise in the ginnel, followed by footsteps up the stairs and a knock on the door. Caroline opened the door.

"Good evening Mrs Norrison. My name is Mark Hill, I am come to deliver some boxes and barrels."

"I know who you are. Your father was kind enough to give us a joint of mutton recently; he knew my husband."

"He sends his regards."

"It is a pity he did not come with you."

"He did help me unload the items from our cart and stack them in the ginnel. He did not wish to come in as he is ashamed. He was caught in the snare of the Provider."

"Your father is a good man," she said. After a pause adding: "I shall fetch the keys and we shall get to work."

There were sacks, casks of various sizes, and boxes with rope handles. Mark had envisaged he would have to do their moving; but Caroline insisted on helping. Within the hour all was neatly stored and stacked, including four ankers of Burgundian wine. Despite a slight chill of the evening they were both sweating after their heavy work. They sat side by side on a crate, breathing heavily.

Caroline took his hands in hers, and said, "Poor Mark, you have done good work but your hands are chafed. I thank you."

"There is no need to thank me, Mrs Norrison. I think none of us had much choice in this matter."

"We are friends are we not, Mark? You must call me Caroline."

"Certainly I shall, Caroline." He looked at her. Properly looked, not the cursory glance that most people grant most people most of the time. Her hair was charmingly tousled, her forehead –though wrinkled with grief– was firm and beaded with perspiration, her eyes were sparkly and vivacious. He freed his hands and clasped hers. "Caroline," he said, "You are beautiful." She looked at him with penetrating eyes and smiled a smile that made the world vanish and caused a sharp tingle flash through his body – a feeling he was not sure was pain or delight.

"Thank you, Mark, every woman likes to be told she is beautiful. But we are friends are we not?" She withdrew her hands from his and held his head, kissing him gently on his forehead. "Maybe, in a few years, you will say such things to one of my daughters. That would be good. I would make a fine mother-in-law." She laughed. "Come in now and we shall have a cup of tea."

Mark had been told that one must not refuse a gift from someone poorer than oneself.

"Yes," he said, "I would like that very much indeed, mother-in-law." *But I would prefer you to be my wife.*

Once in the house the twins came running out of their room to see who this night visitor might be, and their mother introduced him. Then she made a special facial expression which the girls instantly recognised as preface to some jest or whimsy. "This young man," she said, "is going to marry one of you when you are older. Which of you do you think he will marry? I shall tell you that he is a butcher, and he is kind. I think that you, Lizzie, should have first say, as you are the elder."

"But she's only five minutes older, Mama!" said Sophie, grinning.

Lizzie ignored this remark, and said, "Mark has a good trade; after all, everyone eats meat from time to time so his wife shall be provided for. Kindness, I have observed, is not a virtue which is common amongst men, but it is a glue which binds husband and wife together in happy matrimony. So I would certainly consider him."

"Now it is your turn, Sophie."

"He is very handsome, is he not, Mama?

Caroline blushed.

Mark retorted, "And you, Miss Sophie, are beautiful beyond poor words."

Sophie blushed. Then she smiled and said, "Dear sir, I hope that in time you will be able to find sufficient words to describe my beauty." In jest, she made a curtsy. "But, I have two questions to ask my suitor."

Mark laughed and said, "Ask whatever you will, Miss Sophie."

"Do you like cats?"

"Yes, we have one in the shop – to keep the mice at bay."

"Do you dance?"

"Not as well as you can, I imagine."

"Do you like the sea?"

"That's three questions! But, yes, I like the sea – provided I do not have to sail in a ship when in a fierce gale."

Sophie turned to her mother, "I am not sure that his answers are sufficient. However he is very handsome which outweighs his shortcomings. After all, anyone can learn to dance well enough. He is reassurably sensible, but also can make me laugh. And, best of all, he called me beautiful, for which I absolve him of all his sins and I shall certainly be his wife, provided he flatters me twenty times a day and turns his pork chops and sausages into beautiful dresses."

Caroline turned to Mark and said, "You will have to make the Judgement of Paris." Mark smiled, but had no idea what she was talking about. Caroline continued, "You must choose which of these young maidens you will marry." This was greeted by the two maidens calling out "Choose me! Choose me!"

Mark turned to Caroline and said, "I may marry your eldest daughter, Hilda." *I may marry you, Caroline.*

"Of course, Mark, but in this game you have only two to choose from."

"Then it shall be Sophie."

"Why is that?"

"Because she called me handsome, of course."

There was much laughter and teasing, and then Mark said he must leave, which he was eventually allowed to do. After which the girls were sent to their room, and it was some time before sleep lured them to silence.

Caroline looked in the mirror, adjusting her hair and practicing a variety of expressions from the cheerful to the seductive. She also found it difficult to sleep.

So did Mark.

And no-one had any tea.

Chapter 14

The Saturday market at Whitby drew people in from numerous small villages and homesteads in the vicinity. The worst of the winter months were over, and frost was unlikely (though not impossible). Robins and blackbirds sang their early morning magic from twisted winter-blasted trees which were plumed with fresh green leaves and already beginning to show blossom.

George and Mark Hill were busy preparing for the market; they planned to bid at auction for some sheep and maybe a cow if the quality and price were right. These would be taken round the back of the shop where they would be slaughtered and butchered. Rabbits, hares and game were brought to the front door by the keepers of large estates; and sometimes were brought round the back with no questions asked. They also hoped to make many sales. While they were setting out their wares, George seemed very excited. His son asked what there was to be so merry about.

"I expected you to ask sooner, Mark. There is going to be a bit of drama today."

"What kind of drama?"

"You recall that when the brown thing came round and told you to take all the goods of the Provider which we held in our premises to Mrs Norrison with the exception of the four ankers of Burgundian wine, but I told you to take the ankers as well?"

"Yes, I wondered why you said that. I assumed that you wanted to have nothing further to do with the Provider."

"It is not that easy to remove the Provider from one's life, Mark. Why did you think that he wanted us to keep the Burgundian wine?"

"I know not; but clearly not as a present!"

"No, it is a punishment for our refusing to sell any more of his fraudulent bad meat to merchant ships."

"I don't understand."

"I suspect that the revenue men will pay a visit, tipped off by one of the Provider's men. And the Provider will probably come as well to see me being arrested for handling smuggled goods. But there will not be any smuggled goods!"

*   *   *

In the early afternoon Ralph Theaker, the Provider, appeared in the Market Square with a man who on first glance could have passed for a gentleman, albeit as a gentleman who had been involved in a duel as he had a cut on his right cheek. A second glance would take in his muscular physique, his dispassionate expression, and the pistol tucked into waistband; he was a bodyguard. His name was Charles Legge, which was appropriate as the rumour was that he had broken more legs than there were inns in Whitby.

Theaker mingled among the crowded fair with a smile here a nod there, occasionally a bow and a doffed hat, exuding charm - though his eyes flicked surreptitiously around the square as if expecting visitors.

And they came, parting the crowd Moses-like. Mr Woods, the Collector of Customs, followed by William Backas and the constable with his night watchmen. They went straight to George Hill's butcher's shop, which Theaker and his man had already reached. George Hill was outside, pretending he was unaware of both groups, nonchalantly chatting with one of his regular customers - an act he could no longer maintain as the man he was talking to had seen who had appeared and was transformed into a trembling idiot mumbling incoherently. Hill turned, and raised a querying eyebrow.

Mr Woods spoke loud and clear. "Do I have the honour of addressing George Hill, butcher, of this town?"

"You do."

"I have here a warrant signed by a Justice of the Peace to search your premises for illegal goods, and if we find any such, to hold you under arrest."

Hill smiled, stood aside and with a gesture of his right hand and a bow that was so low that it was clearly sarcastic, he said "You are welcome".

The two watchmen stood by the door, but the rest of the group walked in, followed by the butcher.

The crowd outside forgot their buying, but huddled round the entrance to the shop, buzzing like a colony of bees.

After twenty minutes Mr Woods emerged with his entourage. He looked very cross.

Theaker was surprised. He asked, "What smuggled goods did you find?"

"None," was the curt reply. "These premises contain no unlawful goods".

"Are you sure?" asked Theaker.

Mr Woods did not deign to reply.

Then Legge burst out, "But what about the four ankers of Burgundian wine?"

There was a frightening silence.

Mr Woods turned to Legge, "What do you mean?"

Legge paled and then blushed.

Theaker, smiling, intervened. "Pay no heed, sir, it is just gossipy rumour. We are glad that it is false."

Mr Woods grunted and swept out with his entourage.

Theaker's smile vanished, and the look he gave George Hill was full of anger and menace.

Chapter 15

William Backas, as on most mornings, had been working since eight o'clock, ensuring the worst of his paperwork was finished in the two hours before breakfast. Margaret also had work to do, though the addition of Hilda, who started her working day from 5 o'clock made life easier for her. Hilda was a quick learner, and Margaret sometimes felt she was teaching an apprentice, but cramming all the seven years' training into a handful of months.

It was a cool morning, and once Hilda had cleared the breakfast table, William and Margaret sat in the fireless and rather chilly drawing room. William only wore his wig outside or in formal occasions, otherwise to keep his shaved head warm he wore his home cap, which the richer and more pretentious inhabitants of the town would call 'un bonnet d'interieur'.

William said, "A strange thing happened on Saturday in the market."

"What was that, dear?"

"I am not entirely sure. We were all summoned because a man had told Mr Woods that the butcher Hill was hiding contraband in his shop. He would not give any further details, but he swore on the Bible that this was so. Mr Woods thought that this was sufficient to go to a Justice of the Peace for a search warrant. We all went to the Market Square but noticed that the Provider, that is Ralph Theaker..." He paused and gave a little bow to Margaret to acknowledge her informing him of the name, "was loitering around the butcher's shop attended by a ruffian. We went into the shop and searched thoroughly, but found nothing, which was annoying; but as we came out it was clear that Theaker expected us to find smuggled goods, which was suspicious. And then his thug blurted out that there were four barrels of wine in there. Mr Woods was momently interested, but Theaker passed it off as a foolish hearsay."

"So the whole event was to humiliate both the Collector of Customs, possibly you, the Justice of the Peace, and the Provider? Is the man who swore the oath known?"

"No. He gave a false name."

"It seems a lot of trouble just for a cheap joke. Therefore it must be the case that the perpetrator of this event was certain that the smuggled wine would be in the shop. The only person I can think of who had the money to arrange this trap was the Provider, who ensured he was there to enjoy his would-be triumph."

"Yes. So either the wine was going to be taken there but there was a change of mind or a delay. Or they had been removed."

"But the Provider would surely have ensured the wine was in the butcher's shop before he set the event in motion. So its removal must have been recent."

"And the only person who would do this would be the butcher Hill, though he may have had help from his son Mark or his friends."

"I cannot imagine the Provider being made a fool of without seeking retaliation."

"You are right, Margaret. I shall go and warn Hill, and warn him now."

Margaret thought that Hill would be well aware of the danger he was in; but said nothing.

William discarded his home cap for his wig, and putting on his hat and coat, he stepped out into Skate Lane which was slightly warmer than his parlour.

*   *   *

George Hill was in his shop cutting chops on his butcher's block, when he noticed someone had entered by the back door. His first thought was that it might be a poacher come to sell some rabbits, but as the visitor came closer he could see that it was Charles Legge, the Provider's bodyguard, but this time he was alone.

Hill put the chops aside, and said, "What do you want with me?"

"I want to teach you a lesson about your place in life, you clubber-de-gullion. The Provider is the boss, you are his slave and you will do what he orders you to do. And as you have been very disobedient it is going to be a very nasty lesson and it will not be a short one; when I have finished with you, you will be shitting your teeth out through your arsehole." He then grabbed Hill by his neckerchief with his left hand and punched Hill in his face and then in his stomach with surprising speed, letting him collapse on the floor bleeding and breathless. Legge then kicked his victim, sneering, "Now, on all fours like the creature you are, go and lock the front door. We don't want any spectators, do we?"

Pretending that he was damaged more than Legge had actually achieved, Hill crawled slowly towards the door, gasping and grunting. Then he suddenly sprung up and seized his butcher's knife from the block – it was sharp enough to slit open a cow, and it was ten inches long. He said, "You bring your fists anywhere near me again and I shall sever them from your wrists, and I might give you a cut on your other cheek for my amusement. Who's the nigmenog now?"

For a moment Legge was fazed, but then he moved toward Hill who backed away towards the open door. Legge sneered as he withdrew his pistol from his belt, "You're the nigmenog now! That little penknife is useless against this." He waved his weapon menacingly.

Hill by now was in the doorway. He brandished his knife and taunted his opponent, "I don't suppose you know how to use that thing; I bet you couldn't shoot a pumpkin at three inches, you useless, futile son of a whore!"

George Hill heard the click as the pistol was cocked. He threw his knife aside, and backed out of the shop and into the bright sunlight. He made four steady backsteps still facing Legge, then he stopped and spread out his arms. Legge burst out of the doorway, his face red with rage, and fired the gun. His aim was good, the ball smashed into George's chest which spurted out splintered bone and much blood. George momentarily remained standing, swaying, and then fell backwards on the cobbled market square. Some witnesses later reported that he seemed to be smiling.

It took Legge a moment to realise what had happened: he had killed a defenceless man in front of many witnesses. He ran across the square seeking to escape, but a hue and cry had been raised and he did not even reach Sandgate. When the constables came they saw a dead man, badly bruised and lying on the ground, and there were several witnesses. Charles Legge was taken to the lockup, where he would stay until Monday when he would be safely transferred to York Castle Prison awaiting trial. No-one doubted that he would be hanged.

Chapter 16

Once in captivity, Legge was eager to tell all he knew, possibly to make his peace with God -though he never asked for a cleric- and possibly in the vain hope that he would not be hanged. From what he said to William Backas when he was in the lockup there was sufficient evidence for a Justice of the Peace to grant him permission to search the premises in Church Street which was rented by Ralph Theaker.

The house was thoroughly searched; but nothing incriminating was found. Interestingly Mr Backas found in the main bedroom two lace-trimmed blue jackets, five very fancy waistcoats, and a gold chain from which several gold pendants were attached. In another bedroom, neatly piled, were a jacket, waistcoat, breeches, shirts, neckerchiefs, stockings and hat – all brown. The owners of these clothes had ridden out of the town as soon as the murder in the market square was known; unrecognised and unnoticed.

*   *   *

Michael Cornelius knocked on the door of the weaver Esau Linskill, and was received cordially. Michael made it clear that his visit was two-fold: primarily to thank Esau on behalf of himself, Elisha Root his co-leader, and all the members of the Whitby Quaker Meeting for the generous donation he had made for the poor and needy among the Friends.

The other reason he was there was a matter of business. As soon as Esau had inherited the house of his second cousin he had wished to renew the contract to provide woven canvas which Jacob had made for Michael, but which in his latter months neither Jacob nor his daughter Abigail had been able to fulfil. Michael had come to say that he had closely looked at the sample sailcloth Esau had submitted and that he was satisfied.

"Indeed," continued Michael, "the quality was, if anything, finer than your cousin had woven even at his peak."

"I am glad you are pleased. Would you be interested in buying a greater quantity?"

"While the Whitby master-builders keep on making ships, there will always be a demand for canvas, and sails have a fairly short life before they have to be replaced. I envisage growing the business, as there is also money to be made in government contracts."

"In that case, Friend Michael, come with me."

Esau led him out of the backdoor into the yard where there was a sizeable newly-built shed. The noisy and repetitive clunk-clunk made explanation unnecessary. Esau was forced to speak louder to be heard above the looms, "I have two apprentices whom I have taken on from a weaver in Newcastle whose business failed". Then pointing to each in turn, continued: "Over there is a really talented weaver. He in his fifth year of his apprenticeship. He can weave up to number seven grade. The other is a year behind, but is also slower and can, so far, weave only numbers one to four grades. But the lower grades are cheaper, as you know, and there is much demand for them."

They went outside.

"I shall be happy to do business with you, Esau." They shook hands.

*   *   *

James Boyes ran up the stairs and knocked frantically on the door of Caroline Norrison's apartment. As soon as she opened it he burbled, "You are in great danger! Legge has been arrested for murder, Theaker's house has been searched and he and his right-hand man are on the run. The authorities will almost certainly visit you as you have helped the Provider, so it is important that all the illegal goods you have stored below must be moved. Some of Theaker's cronies may think it was you that betrayed him, and seek to punish you – even to kill you."

"But what can I do?"

"I have a cart on Baxtergate, and have brought my mate Samuel Suggett, a trustworthy man. He will help me load up the goods and we can take them to a safe place we know in Fylingdales. Then I shall return to collect you and your twin girls and we shall escape on *Dolphin* which is in the harbour. So go and pack up all your essential property, but first write a note to Hilda explaining the situation, which I shall deliver for you. Give me the key to the cellar and we can get started."

She did.

Before he left, he looked back at her and said, "Of course we shall have to get married. I can get a licence."

Then he hurried down the stairs.

Caroline could scarcely take all this in it was all so hurried and confused. *And what was that about marriage?*

She sat down at her table, tried to control herself, trimmed her pen, and on a sheet of paper wrote a letter beginning "My dearest and much beloved daughter Hilda..."

When her letter was finished, she folded it up, sealed it and addressed it to Hilda Norrison, c/o William Backas, Skate Lane.

She heard the noise below of the storehouse being emptied. Somehow she did not feel like helping them, and she remembered the evening when she helped Mark Hill fill the same storehouse and they both felt so at ease with each other. She dipped her pen into the ink and on a new sheet of paper she wrote, "Dear Master Mark Hill, it is with great sorrow that I heard of the terrible murder of your father. I regret that circumstances will prevent me from attending his funeral tomorrow..." This too was sealed and addressed. Then she took the letters downstairs and gave them to James Boyes, who promised to deal with them as swiftly as possible. She thanked him with a feeble smile, before returning up the stairs to start the packing.

All the illicit goods had been cleared out of Caroline's warehouse using the discrete door to the ginnel, and were stacked on the waggon which was waiting in Baxtergate. The single window which overlooked the ginnel was in the bedroom of the twins; while Lizzie was busy deciding what to take, Sophie watched the goods being removed. Samuel Suggett was doing nearly all the work. He was a wiry, muscular man, tough, but somewhat shorter than one would expect. He had light brown hair and a ruddy, beardless face. His eyes were small and deep set, so it was difficult to judge his feelings. Suggett was sufficiently strong to have done most of the loading onto the cart, but at the cost of profuse perspiration, and heavy breathing. He was probably in his thirties. As soon as he could recover his breath, he said, "God's beard! That was a heavy cartload!" It was not clear whether this comment was of relief or complaint.

Then Suggett locked the door, and carried a large canvas sheet. Knowing that there would be nothing else to see, Sophie did her packing.

Suggett threw the canvas sheet over this profitable cargo, and secured it firmly with rope before climbing into the driving seat. James Boyes swung up beside him. At the end of Baxtergate by the Bagdale Estate, where the stream tumbled haphazardly towards the Esk, Boyes screwed up the two letters and tossed them into water.

Chapter 17

It was the custom that on Sundays Hilda attended Mattins at the Church with William and Margaret Backas, but walking a few steps behind. Mr Backas had an ex officio box pew which fitted them nicely. After the service Hilda was free to go to spend the rest of the day with her family; much as she liked her employers, home was the highlight of her week. When the vicar said the words that ended the service: "The grace of our Lord Jesus Christ, and the fellowship of the holy Ghost, be with us evermore" it meant nothing to her except that she would soon be in fellowship with her family, the only place where she was loved.

Hilda normally spent much time when in church, especially during the sermon, looking around for her family. Then she would catch the eye of one of her sisters, usually that of Sophie, the more mischievous of the two, who would nudge Elizabeth and they both smiled at her. But on this occasion, March 20th, she could not see them, which was hardly surprising because this service was to be followed immediately by the burial of George Hill the butcher, whose murder had caused much excitement, gossip and anger. Usually burials were later in the afternoon, but the vicar deemed it would be better to bring it forward. So the church was packed with more than twice the number who usually attended Sunday services. Taking this opportunity the vicar had preached a fearsome sermon full of the wickedness of the human heart, and the importance of turning away from sin and seeking the good. This might have incited a few to turn away from sin, but many had turned away from good manners and as soon as the priest had left the church there was a frenzied unseemly rush to follow him out into the graveyard. So pressing was the crowd that William and Margaret Backas, helped by Hilda, were unable to push open their pew door until the church was almost empty.

Outside, the coffin was nearing the top of the donkey road. It was being carried by six shopkeepers, three of whom were butchers. It was a strenuous business as the road was steep, so there was a reserve group to take over when the initial six were exhausted. However it was clear that the original pall bearers, red-faced and sweating into their best clothes, were not going to surrender their office out of respect and pride. Behind the coffin a single mourner, George's son Mark, whose face was fixed and unreadable. The mob made way for this procession as it slowly moved to the grave on the north side of the church, but as soon as it had passed the crowd swarmed together again. At last, with much grunting and panting, George Hill was lowered into the earth. As soon as the vicar started the service those by the grave became quiet, and this reverential silence rippled out through the crowd until all were soundless, apart from the occasional cough and shuffle. Even so few heard much, the occasional phrases drifting audibly on the breeze over the bowed heads:

"And though after my skin worms destroy this body...Behold, thou hast made my days as it were a span long...make me not a rebuke unto the foolish...I am a stranger as all my fathers were...it hath pleased thee to deliver this our brother out of the miseries of this sinful world..."

As soon as it was clear that it was all over, the crowd melted away at first quietly but growing more noisy the further from the grave; and once they were at the bottom of the steps the assembly could have been mistaken for the happy visitors at St Hilda's Fair.

At the grave a small group of men, who knew George well, lingered in embarrassed grief, some shaking Mark's hand, some just nodding in his direction, but each mumbling well-meant phrases such as "Your father was a grand man, tha knows", "Ee up, be strong, lad", "If there's aut I can do..."

The last to go was the vicar who said, "A great tragedy; but he is in a better place now, I'm sure of that."

Mark was left all alone, the only living person in the graveyard. He felt miserable and alone. "Too many men," he muttered, "Why are men unable to bring solace on such occasions? I shall visit Caroline Norrison, she will know what to say."

Hilda's panic increased. She had lost Mr and Mrs Backas nor could she see her family among the pressing crowd. Barging her way out, she hurried down the steps, over the bridge and ran to Atty's Yard, which was eerily quiet. She went up the steps and knocked on the door; her home seemed dead. As she had feared there was no response. Sitting on the bottom step she waited, telling herself that they had been caught up in the funeral crowd, but knowing that was not so. *Where have they gone? Why is there no note? Have they abandoned me?*

The sound of shoes on cobbles, someone was entering the Yard. It was Mark Hill. She was disappointed but pleased.

"Oh, Mark, they have all gone without thinking about me!"

He sat down beside her and put his arm around her. All he could think of to say was, "Ee up, Hilda."

After a long pause she said, "I wonder if they took the cat."

*   *   *

Even though it was a Sunday, William Backas had documents to read concerning the murder of George Hill, and then to visit the Lockup and transcribe more of the useful information that Charles Legge was revealing. So William was tired when he returned home.

He had no longer settled himself in his chair when his wife came bursting into the room and said, "Hilda is upstairs worried and crying; she thinks she has been abandoned. She is uncontrollable. Do something!"

"All right my dear," he replied easing himself from comfort, "She's a good girl, and I'll go up and see if there's anything I can do to help." Up the stairs to the attic he went, and knocked on the door, saying "Can I come in, Hilda, please? It is Mr Backas." The response from inside was something between a groan, a sob and a mumble which he took for a yes, and he opened the door.

Hilda was sprawled face down on the bed, all tears and misery.

William perched on the side of the bed and said nothing. After a long while Hilda became more quiet. William spoke quietly as if he was just talking to himself, "It has been a busy day for me; but I was glad I was able to see the interment of George Hill. He was a good man. For all the Spring sun, it was a rather chilly morning. He would have been surprised at the number who attended his burial. I suppose that some were there out of curiosity, but most were there to show solidarity and friendship. He made a mistake and was shot when he tried to undo it. A good person who made a mistake; we can all see that in ourselves. Which is perhaps why there were so many at his funeral. And death can come at any time, the old, the young, parents who lose their children when young, children who lose their parents when young. Mark must be devastated. Did you know him?"

A voice that emanated from the pillow said, "Yes, a bit."

"How was that?"

She turned and sat up on the bed. "He has worked with my mother, they got on well."

"He must have enjoyed that. His own mother died when he was very young."

"He came to Atty's Yard after the funeral."

"I suppose that, having lost his father, that he wanted to talk to the only person who was anything like a mother to him."

"I hadn't thought of that."

"Did you try to console him?"

Hilda did not answer that question, but said, "I have lost a parent, and two sisters."

"Do you think they are all dead?" William's voice was so gentle that, although she wanted to cry, the tears no longer came. She said, "I hope not; I suppose I think they have just gone away – but have gone away without me."

"Your mother loves all her daughters. Would she have taken you if she was going somewhere nice?"

"I don't know; she would usually have discussed it with all of us."

"Think."

"I don't know."

"Think harder."

"I suppose there wasn't time to find me."

"A good thought. Can you think of any other reason?"

"That she didn't want me to go with them?"

"Why might she not want you to go with them?"

"That they were going somewhere nice and she decided to leave me out."

"Is that why you were crying?"

"Yes. I am always left out, it's not fair!"

"Has it occurred to you that they may have had to go somewhere nasty, and wished to save you from it?"

Hilda furrowed her brows but said nothing.

After a pause William changed tack and asked, "What was kept in your warehouse?"

"Nothing of ours. I think she rented it out."

"Have you heard of the Provider?"

"Yes, I think he is a smuggler."

"Indeed. A smuggler on a large scale. Your mother rented the storehouse to him, and in that sense she worked for him. The items in the storehouse were contraband goods owned by the Provider."

"By Satan's horns!"

"Some might have thought that she had, therefore, committed a crime."

"But you won't arrest her, will you, Mr Backas?"

"Not if I can help it, Hilda." Then he changed tack, "Do you know a man called James Boyes?"

"Yes, he often came to our home of late. He is a master-mariner and ship-owner, and knew my father. He has been very kind to Mama recently. Sophie said that Mr Boyes will be our new Papa."

"Do you think so?"

"No, Sophie and Lizzie can be very silly. Mama is not."

"At first light this morning Mr Boyes' ship *Dolphin* sailed out of the harbour. Do you think that your mother, Sophia and Elizabeth might have sailed in her?"

"That is certainly a possibility, sir. Sophie and Lizzie would enjoy it, and in the light of what you have said it would have been wise perhaps for Mama to be out of the town for a while."

"There is nothing to fear, Hilda, all will be well. Soon your family will all be together again."

"Thank you, sir."

"You can stay up here if you wish. Mrs Backas will be happy to prepare the supper."

"That is kind of her, sir; but I would prefer to have something to do."

Chapter 18

On 16 June in a cloudless mid-morning, *Freelove*, master John Walker junior, mate Solomon King, furled her topmast sails as she veered into the Tagus River.

Freelove sailed slowly up the estuary. She went past the Belem Tower in the middle of the river, and gradually the magnificent panorama of Lisbon came into view: the Jerónimos Monastery, the ropery and Ribeira das Naus shipyard, the Royal Palace and the Terreiro do Paço Square near which the ship moored for customs clearance. The fine new town spread away northwards amid myriad steeples of churches and convents. Towering to west was the castle, below which was the twin-towered cathedral, solidly rooted in the old town of narrow streets, many steps and much poverty.

Although England had a treaty of mutual trade with Portugal, it still took a long time for the goods to be unloaded and the wine to be bought and stowed below in the ship, with all the appropriate documents. Walker knew that if sailors were discharged in the city there would be great difficulty in reassembling them, so he had agreed with them to pay them more, but the first instalment would not be paid until the ship left Lisbon. Otherwise they were free to wander in the town when they were not needed on board. Their lack of ready money certainly reduced, if not totally prevented, visits to the brothels.

One of the sailors on board *Freelove* was Jack Wheatear, no longer a candidate for the whore houses.

He had bought his own copy of the Bible, which was not cheap, and his landlady had helped him to improve his reading, which she felt was her moral duty so to do. Unfortunately she had not taught him to read silently, and some of the other sailors who were on the same watch as Jack were annoyed when he read his morning and evening passages. Jack's original plan was to read the whole Bible from *In the beginning* to *Amen*, but his inner voice guided him to pick books at random. Although he often misattributed his Bible extracts, generally his memory for quotations was good.

Solomon King and Jack Wheatear treated each other professionally on board the ship, though both found the other's presence an embarrassment. Jack had applied to sail on *Freelove*, and Solomon could not find any reason why he should not accept him.

John Walker had not heard of Jack Wheatear before; but he had come to be quite impressed with his Bible devotion. On one of those rare occasions when the wind and waves in the Bay of Biscay were tamely helpful to the ship, and the sky was a bright woad-blue tent stretched taut from horizon to horizon with an occasional smear of cirrus, Walker had seen Wheatear leaning over the side of the ship staring out to sea, and went over to speak to him. "You are Wheatear are you not?"

Jack came to attention. "Yes, sir!"

"Were you looking at anything in particular?"

"I was looking at the effect the sun has on the sea, sir, and was reminded of the words of the prophet Hosea who wrote of the sun that it 'treadeth upon the waves of the sea'.

This was not the sort of answer the master would have expected; but he had been at sea long enough to know that ordinary seamen were far from being ordinary. The conversation lasted some time, until Walker felt he should continue on his business of inspecting the ship. The parting left both men feeling (maybe reluctantly) a degree of respect for the other.

What Wheatear's fellow sailors thought of him were mixed. He was clearly not a tub thumper or prating parson, but for many his constant reading aloud had come to be increasingly irritating day by day as the voyage was long. There had been complaints to the mate, which had been passed on to the captain. But the crew had to admit that as a sailor he was skilful.

*   *   *

Some yards down the quay from *Freelove* was James Boyes' ship *Dolphin*. The latter was preparing to leave in a few days' time. Out of courtesy Boyes invited Walker to dine with him on the following day, which he accepted. He was welcomed aboard by Samuel Suggett, the ship's mate who, in Walker's first impression, would be someone whom it was better to have as a friend than a foe. Suggett led the visitor to the great cabin where he was greeted by the captain, who introduced Walker to three women whom were only referred as Caroline, Sophia and Elizabeth. Walker was rather nonplussed, though he followed the conventional introduction ritual. The great cabin was not very great, so everyone was speedily seated with Boyes at the head, Walker at the other end of the table, Caroline on Boyes' right and the girls opposite their mother.

The food was served by the cook, an old seaman who had difficulty walking and was troubled with an occasional disconcerting twitch. He had been appointed cook as a kind of pension, and not for his culinary skill. The dishes that he had cooked were mediocre at best, which was impressive as most of their ingredients had been freshly purchased in the town. Out of politeness Walker ate a little of all the dishes; but favoured the fruit and wine.

At first the talk was of nautical matters: the route, the weather, the average speed, etc which, Walker noticed, seemed to interest the women as much as the men. Then the conversation moved to cargoes, which inevitably lead to political issues, especially the peace between Spain and Britain which had still not yet been officially concluded. The two captains agreed that, after Britain's disastrous blockading of Portobello and Spain's failure to capture Gibraltar, neither country wanted the war to continue, and that a signed treaty would be a matter of months. James Boyes confided that he was going to take a chance and trade with Spain, where he would buy goods that would sell for a good profit in England. All this time the women said nothing, but continued to follow all this man-talk with mute enthusiasm.

John Walker decided to find out exactly who these females were. As the only women on merchant ships were usually either paying passengers (which seemed unlikely in this case) or the family of the captain, he felt that it would only be polite to draw them into the conversation.

"Captain Boyes, I did not catch your introduction of these three charming ladies. Am I to assume that Caroline is your wife, and these are your beautiful daughters?"

There was the briefest of pauses before the reply, but long enough for Walker to realise he had strayed into embarrassing territory.

"Elizabeth and Sophia are not my daughters. Not yet. They are the daughters of Caroline who is the widow of Thomas Norrison, master mariner. Caroline and I are engaged, and will be married soon." Before the conventional congratulations could be expressed, Caroline with calm assertiveness intervened:

"Captain Walker, Captain Boyes has misled you. We are not engaged."

Boyes turned to her with a face twisted with rage; and then turned and addressed Walker calmly and covered in smiles:

"Officially not yet, but we are to be married here in the Protestant Church, in the next few days."

Caroline said nothing, but when Boyes turned to the cook ordering him to bring some more wine, she caught Walker's attention: she shook her head and displayed her left hand to show the absence of any token of affection. Her daughters' expressions betrayed nothing.

Time to change the conversation.

"Mrs Norrison, was not your late husband a master of one of my father's ships?"

"Indeed, sir, he did tell me of that. He sailed as mate and then master, and he did say they were happy days. He died on a ship."

"I did hear of that, Mrs Norrison. A tragedy, but he nobly saved his crew at the cost of his own life. Such men are few. You chose well, madam."

"Captain Walker," said Boyes, "I would like your advice. I plan to sail on Thursday, and I told the crew to be back on board ship by noon today. Three of them have not returned. I do not wish to delay departure for a day. Besides that, the crew say the others are not intending to return. They say that life is cheaper here; that even the whores are cheaper and better, and the weather here is better than in the north-east ports of England."

"Well, they are probably right about goods being cheaper here– after all that is how we make our living. They are certainly right about the weather, though storms can be as violent here as there. As to the whores, I cannot comment."

"It may be indecent for a woman to comment on such matter," interposed Caroline, "but my husband used to say that the French pox is freely given in any port, and that mercury cannot cure it. It is prescribed simply to enrich physicians."

"I have heard tell," said Walker, "that English seamen believe they cannot contract the French pox in Lisbon, as the brothels are overlooked by the Castle of St George, the English patron saint. If your recalcitrant crewmen, Captain, believe such nonsensical superstition they will fit in well in a Catholic town!"

"Maybe, Captain Walker, but it does not solve my problem of being three men short. I don't suppose you have any spare sailors?"

"No captain sails with surplus seamen; the owners would not like it," retorted Walker, but then an interesting idea struck him. "As it happens, though, I can possibly offer you one man, if he is happy to agree. He is a well-trained, thoughtful and moral man; he won't run at whim but will fulfil his contract, and he certainly will not squander his money in bawdy houses. That is as much as I can spare, but two seamen short is better than three, and the man in question will do the work of two lazy and recalcitrant ones."

"Thank you, that is much appreciated, sir."

"If he agrees, I shall send him to you tomorrow afore the fourth bell of third watch. It will inconvenience him, so you must recompense his trouble before the agreement is made. If you do not do so, I shall tell him to return to my ship. Agreed?"

"Agreed."

On that note the party broke up. John Walker said his farewell to James Boyes. Then he turned to Caroline, made a bow, and said, "It has been a delight to meet you Mrs Norrison. May your future, and that of your charming daughters, be happy. When you are next at Whitby I would be pleased and flattered if you would visit me."

After that Samuel Suggett saw him off the vessel. He had listened at the door of the great cabin, of course, and his thoughts were about what should be done with the three women on the ship. He muttered to himself that it would have been better if the three missing sailors were aboard, and that the superfluous females in the ship had been left in the brothel.

Chapter 19

Dolphin sailed from Lisbon on the Wednesday afternoon. Even with the addition of Jack Wheatear, the crew was two men short. Apart from the first mate Samuel Suggett, the rest of the crew involved: the second mate (Alexander McDaniel), the carpenter, the cook, three seamen (the young Matthew Willson, the recently-acquired Jack Wheatear, and Joseph who -though his father was a freed slave in America- was still known by a single name and treated as a slave by Captain Boyes) and Hans Nielsen of Norway who was still an apprentice.

Caroline, Sophia and Elizabeth lived in the mate's cabin. Sam Suggett was not pleased with this arrangement as he had to bunk up with the cook in his kitchen. Caroline supped with Boyes, but her children were fed in their room with the same food as the crew ate.

James Boyes and Caroline Norrison had sat silently over supper. The mood was tense and frigid.

"Why did you say to Captain Walker that we are engaged to be married?"

"Because you need to marry me, and so you will."

"It is not my will to marry you. I have told you many times recently."

"Who will protect you, and your children, if you have no husband?"

"I am quite capable of looking after my family."

"So why are you here and not back in Atty's Yard being arrested for being in possession of stolen goods?"

"You cajoled me onto this ship, sir. On reflection, I think if I had told the truth, I would have been exonerated."

"Have you not come with me because you like me and wish me to be your husband and protector? A man who can bring your family into respectability and out of poverty?"

"There was a time, James, when I thought those things. I liked you much; maybe even loved you."

"And now you don't?"

"I still regard you as a friend; but recently –since we boarded this ship- I have had my doubts."

"Doubts?"

"It has crossed my mind, just as a fleeting thought, that you might be eager to marry me so you can have our premises in Atty's Yard."

"Nonsense!" retorted Boyes, but for a moment there was a quaver in his voice, and his eyes would not meet hers. He recovered, and continued:

"You and your useless children live in this ship and eat our food. If you are not my wife-to-be then you must be a paying passenger. So pay me your fare!"

"You know I cannot. I am here because you offered me friendship and security."

"Conditional upon you marrying me."

"Not so. As I have several times told you. You performed an act of friendship, an act of kindness for which we are grateful. But kindness is not conditional."

Boyes stood up suddenly, knocking his chair over and thumping his fists on the table. His face crimsoned with frustrated rage, "The crew already think you are my whore. Don't you see you have to marry me, whether you love me or not?"

Caroline remained externally calm. She dabbed her lips with her napkin, and rose slowly to her full impressive height.

"If, Captain, you ever love a woman, I suggest you do not use those words as a proposal for marriage." She gave an exaggerated bow and curtsy, turned and

*   *   *

Caroline Norrison was deeply worried about her situation; but her children were not, even though they were already twelve years old. When their mother had told them to hurriedly pack a sack of things they needed on the voyage, in addition to clothing, combs and other essentials, Elizabeth had included Ninetails the cat, and Sophia had included her father's case of nautical items.

The cat proved useful in reducing the number of rodents aboard, and ensuring that the mate's cabin where she slept with the family was pest-free. The girls made friends with many of the crew, showing off their skills in using a quadrant and in tying knots. Some of the sailors had never held a quadrant before, and were very pleased to be shown how to work it.

Sophia's favourite crew member was Joseph who had many tales that his father had told about his life as a slave in America.

Elizabeth was drawn to Hans Nielsen who was strong and handsome. Most of the time he looked rather severe, but in conversation he became lively and smiled much. He told her stories of frozen rivers and of fierce creatures of the night who hid in the cliffs during the day, which she only half believed; he also told stories of the Norwegians long ago who were fierce fighting sailors and who had ruled England, which she certainly knew was not true.

When Jack Wheatear, the Bible reader who never went to church, joined the crew both of the girls were attracted; mainly because he was not like any man they had met before. He was eloquent, sincere and kind. He called them Miss Elizabeth and Miss Sophia, and treated them as adults.

In spite of their mother who seemed despondent (Sophia explained to Elizabeth that all women got like that regularly when they became grown up. Hilda had told her), those days on board *Dolphin* were full of fun and delight for the girls.

On Thursday evening, the 19th of June, the weather was perfect with a gentle northerly wind. For sailors there was little to do, so Matthew Willson came up from the fo'c'sle, sat on the for'ard hatch-cover and magicked lively tunes from his fiddle; the available crew members and the girls leapt and whirled about in time to his music.

They were wholly unaware that at noon on the following day the lives of all those aboard would be changed forever.

Chapter 20

Sophia and Elizabeth ate their banal breakfast with little enthusiasm. The sun was drilling down with heat, so they decided to stay in their cabin, which was unusually cool. They sat on their bunks; Elizabeth read stories from the *Fables of Pilpay* to Sophia who was cuddling the cat.

It was not until five bells on the forenoon watch that they came on deck, Sophia clutching the quadrant and Elizabeth with the telescope. They both sensed that something wasn't right: previously they were sailing down the Portuguese coast, keeping in sight of the land, but no land was now visible even with the telescope.

"Did you feel a veering to starboard in the night, Lizzie?"

"No I didn't, Sophie. And as we are sailing due south, there would have to have been two adjustments: to the east and then to the south again. Surely one of us must have been aware of one of these changes of direction."

"And what would be the reason so to do? If there had been danger from a privateer there would have been much shouting, which certainly would have woken us both."

It was the Master's watch, but as shipmasters had to be available at all times, the command of the Master's watch fell to the second mate, Alexander McDaniel, whom the girls found leaning on the waist-rails.

"Mister McDaniel, sir, why are we no longer in sight of land?" asked Sophia.

"Why, lassie, the Portuguese coast is just over the horizon yonder."

"The ship must be travelling more slowly than we thought if we are still off the Portuguese Coast."

"Dinna fash yourself, we shall soon round Cape Saint Vincent. Leave the business to us seamen, a ship is manned, ye ken, not womanned. Now off you go. I have work to do. Noon is nigh." He stood up, picked up the ship's quadrant case, and climbed up to the poop deck.

The girls found a place on the deck where they were out of the way of the crew, crouching behind casks and coils of rope. McDaniel and Sophie both waited for eight bells, so they could use their quadrants to determine the ship's latitude north.

Then eight bells rang. Elizabeth saw that her sister was nimble and speedy, whereas it seemed that McDaniel was clumsy and fumbling.

Sophia seemed puzzled. "Where are we?" asked Elizabeth, her voice a conspiratorial whisper.

"36 point 42 degrees."

There was a silence. They both were visualising the charts their father had shown them and the latitudes of numerous ports he had drummed into their minds.

Then they simultaneously said, "But surely that's south of Cadiz!"

*   *   *

Receiving new information which is contrary to ones' belief is unpleasant and confusing, and is often rejected to maintain comfort. But there is no comfort: knowledge cannot be unknown. Sophia had checked her quadrant several times, but it was sturdily consistent. She had checked her father's charts which corroborated their latitude.

"What does it mean?"

"It means, Lizzie, that we are not going to Cadiz."

"So where are we going?"

"We don't know; but those who do know are not telling anyone."

"But why are they keeping it a secret?"

"I know not; but believe me that it is not good."

"We must tell Mama, Sophie."

"We must think, Lizzie. We need to find out more information, and Mama knows less than we do. Telling her will just upset her. But we must find some friends from among the crew."

"But how do we know who is - and who is not - in on the secret plot?"

"The captain knows, and it is probably his idea. He must have told the mate and second mate, as they know all the information about where the ship is. But we cannot tell which of the other members are part of it."

"Yes we can, Sophie. The sailor who joined the ship at Lisbon, Jack Wheatear. Assuming that the plot was hatched before the ship left Whitby, he would not have known. And he is a good man."

"We shall ask him. He is in the Mate's watch, so we might be able to find him when he is by himself."

*   *   *

The girls found him, some hours later, alone coiling rope. Elizabeth explained the literal situation as calmly as possible, and Wheatear listened carefully without interrupting her. Then he said, "You are lucky to be born of two good parents."

Sophie, who had restrained herself from interrupting her sister's explanation, said, "Thank you, Mr Wheatear, but what shall we do?"

He replied, "We need to find out all the information we can. I am convinced that your evidence is sound; we have passed Cadiz, and it is unlikely, as we are going due south, that we are going to Gibraltar or the Mediterranean. It is still possible; but if it is, the captain is taking us two sides of a triangle when the third side would not only be the shorter but also the faster as the wind is nor-westerly. There is something very wrong here. I am not familiar with these seas, if we continue to go south, where will we be, Miss Sophia?"

"The Morocco coast, and the next port would be Tangier."

"That is something of a pickle-pie. If we went to Tangier, how long would it take to get there?"

"If she continues south, and then veers east, we shall arrive perhaps in two days. If we sail direct, sooner."

"Then we must act quickly. But we need to know what is going on, so we can be prepared."

It was Elizabeth's turn: "I have noticed that in the last few days the two mates go into the captain's cabin shortly after four bells in the afternoon watch, and stay there some time."

Sophie interjected, "That must be when they discuss their plan. I can listen at the door!"

"Don't be silly, sister. You would be easily seen."

"Our cabin is next door to the captain's. I could break a hole in the wall."

"That is a good idea, Mistress Sophia", said Wheatear. "But again it has to be done in secret. The captain and both mates are on deck some time before noon, and some time afterwards. I could borrow a large drill from the carpenter and make a hole at that time."

"A sound idea, Wheatear; but Sophie is right in that we have to do it. You might be seen, and it would look suspicious. Give me the drill and I shall wrap it in my cloak. We shall make the hole, and I know the best place for it. In the master's cabin there is a low table against the wall on which he keeps his chest, a hole under that would not be visible. From our cabin it would be under our bunks. We would also need a bung to seal the hole for when we are not using it to ensure the captain cannot hear what we say. We would have to be quick with the drilling, so we could take it in turns, couldn't we Sophie?"

It was all agreed; but the conspirators knew that there was little time to find out where the ship was going and what was planned to happen when she arrived there.

Chapter 21

At two of the clock there was a knock on the door of the captain's cabin.

"Enter!" commanded James Boyes, and Samuel Suggett came in followed by Alexander McDaniel. The Captain ensured that both had somewhere to sit and a glass of rum, before he coughed which meant the mates must be quiet and listen.

"Tomorrow, about noon, we shall anchor in sight of Tangier. You, McDaniel, shall row me ashore. We shall take samples of some of the goods we acquired at Whitby: sailcloth, alum, wine and rum. I have names of dealers in all the kinds of trade we shall be selling, so we shouldn't have any problems. However we shall both be armed with two pistols, a cutlass, and a knife each. These Arabs are a devious race, and will try to cheat us, so we need to be careful and assertive. And we must be brave; any outward signs of fear and all will be lost. Is that understood, McDaniel?"

"Yes, sir. I thought the Moors did not drink alcohol. Will they buy wine and rum?"

"We are Christians and we have been known to fail in keeping to the Ten Commandments. We are no better or worse than them in observing our holy laws. Which brings me to the other cargo we are to sell: slaves. I enrolled Joseph on the crew so we could sell him as a slave."

At this point he stopped talking as they heard a squeak. Suggett said, "There be mice in your cabin, Master."

The captain grunted and continued. "We shall have to do some haggling; but we should be able to get around £6 for Joseph. The bitch, though past her prime, is still saleable and strong enough for manual work even when she becomes no longer valuable as a whore. As for her two little daughters..."

There was another squeak. Boyes turned to Suggett and said, "Tomorrow get that cat and put it to work. I want no mice in my cabin. Understood?"

"Yes, Master."

"Where was I?"

"The daughters, Master."

"Oh yes, save the best till last. Young, white, virgins will sell for large sums. It depends on the supply and haggling, but I reckon we could get 15-20 pounds each – maybe more. You will each have 10%, and I shall set aside 5% for emergencies, bribes and other expenses."

"Thank you, Master" – in chorus.

"But it is not going to be easy. Tomorrow will be straightforward. You will be in charge of the ship, Suggett, for most of the day. Tell the crew that McDaniel and I will be making deals with merchants for our cargo – which is, of course, the truth. If anyone asks what the port is, stick with Cadiz. None of the crew is clever enough to know where we are – mostly they have sailed on nothing except on colliers trading between Newcastle and London. Monday will be more difficult as we have to carry the merchandise secretly, so it will be best to make the preparations tomorrow night. The pinnace must be firmly secured under this cabin window. I shall summon Joseph here, where Suggett will be waiting – tie him up and gag him, and lower him out of the window into the pinnace, where McDonald will be. I shall then summon the woman, and we give her the same treatment. Then we shall invite the children into this cabin one at a time. They are just young and silly girls and should be easy to truss up and put in the pinnace with the others. You, Suggett, will remain in the boat and look after them – make sure they don't die or get damaged, or their value will diminish. At first light on Monday Suggett will row me ashore in the pinnace with the bound slaves. You, McDaniel, will be in charge of *Dolphin*. Keep the crew busy, ensure the ship will be ready to sail as soon as we return. Make it as ordinary as normal. Tell them that we are purchasing some victuals for the journey. Is that all understood? I shall be relying on you both: do it well and you will be paid well."

"What shall we say when Joseph and the women do not return?" asked Suggett.

"Say that Joseph had deserted, and that the women had sought protection of a wealthy English merchant. Now, both of you, back to your work. And, Suggett, don't forget the mice!"

*   *   *

Dolphin's sails were furled, and the bower anchor dropped, shortly before noon on Sunday. The shore was not much less than a nautical mile away; buildings could be seen, but no details could be discerned without a telescope, which pleased the Captain as he knew the crew had neither telescope nor quadrant.

He did not know that Sophia and Elizabeth owned both, and that at noon they were secretly measuring latitude and spying with their telescope, while Suggett was doing much the same but more openly.

Elizabeth used the quadrant, and found they were at 35.8 degrees, exactly the latitude of Tangier. Sophie was looking through the spyglass, telling Lizzie what she saw, more loudly than was wise:

"I can see those tall pillars with blobs on the top which Papa used to tell us about; the Moorish monks stand on the top and sing, from time to time."

"Hush, Lizzie. We have to be quiet and careful."

The pinnace was lowered, and the captain and the second mate climbed down into her. McDaniel took the oars and revolved the boat until the prow pointed shoreway, then he set to work pulling the oars firmly in large sweeps. Samuel Suggett stood upon the poop deck watching the pinnace diminish to half a walnut shell. He was happy. The weather was warm but not sweltering, the sea was dark blue marble with swirls of white, and he was in command. Nothing, he assumed, would present difficulties until the evening.

*   *   *

Sophie had been the girl who was listening with her ear pressed to the hole. After the captain's conference was finished she carefully inserted the bung into the hole. She crawled out from under the bunk trembling with fear and anger but managed to tell what she had heard coherently though, to spare her mother and sister, some of the offensive words and all the references to money were not mentioned.

A pause of disbelief faded into misery.

Caroline was the first to break the silence, fearing despair would smother action, "We must first tell Joseph, then Wheatear. I think that the carpenter might also be on our side."

"And," said Elizabeth, blushing slightly, "I think that Hans Nielsen will help us."

The news had spread among the crew, so when Suggett turned from watching the pinnace vanish into the hazy distance, he was surprized to find all the six crew and the three Norrisons standing in a silent group on the deck below him. Instinctively his hand went to his pistol.

"What is the meaning of this? Begone! Go to your stations now!" he shouted with a bravery he did not feel.

Instead of dispersing they climbed up the stairs to the poop.

Suggett allowed them to come up, and this time he adopted a quieter tone:

"Clearly you have some grievance, an *alleged* grievance. Who is going to be the spokesman?"

Jack Wheatear, with grim firmness, "I have agreed to represent the crew."

"I do not think that would be sound, Wheatear. You have been with us a very short time, not sufficient time to know our crew, or how we manage this ship. I do not accept you as a representative for the men."

Caroline stepped forward.

Suggett continued, "Nor you, Mrs Norrison. I mean no disrespect," he bowed his head with a smug smile, "but you are a passenger and a woman. Two sound reasons why you are unable to present the crew's grievance. So if the women and Wheatear step aside I shall be happy to hear a representative from the actual crew."

They obediently shuffled into two groups.

Suggett continued, addressing the men: "This is clearly a great matter you have in mind. Coming uninvited onto this deck is a serious breach of the rules of the sea, and would merit being put in chains for several days. Coming in such numbers is, in effect, a mutiny – and the punishment for that would be very unpleasant. It would certainly mean that the mutineers among you would never work again, and you would have no money to support your wives and families. Fortunately, as the Master and owner of this ship is not aboard, this cannot be an official trial, and I suggest you take time to think of your futures. Willson, you are a man of some experience, tell me what has brought you to this disagreeable position?"

"Well, Sir, it is like this. Erm… There has been talk among the men…a rumour that is… maybe a true one….that…erm…the Captain is planning to sell Joseph as a slave."

"And, Willson, who started this rumour?"

"It was the women, sir, and they did say they were to be sold as slaves as well."

"Women's stories! And did you all believe this? Look," he said, pointing to the city on the horizon, "That is Cadiz.

We may not think highly of the Spanish, but have you ever heard stories and rumours of the Spanish selling people into slavery in their fishmarket?"

"No, Sir. Now you put it that way, it appears rather foolish."

There was a slow edging towards the stairs by some of the crew.

"No! The Mate is lying! That city is not Cadiz. It is Tangier!" Sophie shouted.

Everyone else froze momentarily. Then Suggett regained his composure, and asked,

"How old are you, little girl?"

"I shall soon be thirteen."

"God's beard! A twelve year old girl! I suppose you tell this nursery story with your puppet doll!"

"This is Tangier, not Cadiz. I know that – and so do you."

"No you don't girlie! None of the crew has a quadrant."

"And none of the crew is lying, which is more than can be said of you. The crew may not have a quadrant; but I do."

Sophia knelt down an opened a box which she had carried with her. From it she took an instrument.

"My father's quadrant. I have been taking latitude every noon; and I have to say I know my way round a quadrant better than you do, for all your pompous vanity."

"Your fantasy story about selling people on this ship into slavery is sheer nonsense."

Sophia leapt to her feet. "No it isn't. I heard every word through a hole drilled from our cabin into the captain's. You can see it if you wish, Mister Mate." She turned to the members of the crew, adding, "Anyone can see it, if they wish."

"You may have a quadrant, but it stretches the imagination to say that you, a mere girl, can use it accurately – it is just a toy to you. And as for the alleged selling into slavery, you invented it – no-one else heard it!" Suggett was becoming desperate; he was aware of the murmurs of those present, and the occasional phrases which came out clear: "I believe her", "I've seen her use the quadrant", "Her father was Captain Norrison."

Sophia looked at Suggett with unflinching, unblinking, stony eyes; after what seemed like several minutes she said, "And, Suggett, don't forget the mice!"

Although he remained standing, all the fight seemed to leave Suggett, as a hanged man flops into death.

Sophia knelt down again and extracted from her father's box another item.

"I have another toy for you Mister Mate; and it is charged." She stood up, pulled back the cock to full and released the safety lock, "We have no parson on board, but confess your lies and tell the truth. Or I shall shoot you!"

Suggett's fingers twitched indecisively round his own pistol.

Wheatear shouted, "No, Sophie, 'Thou shalt not kill'!", seizing her gun arm and raising it up. The trigger was pulled, but all that emanated from the barrel was a small

144

puff of grey smoke – it had not been loaded. Suggett fired, and Sophia sank to the floor, spurting blood.

Elizabeth ran to help her sister, pulling off her scarf and holding it tight against her wounded thigh, calling for help.

Caroline, distraught with tears and anger, was punching and slapping Wheatear, crying "You fool! This is all your fault!" and he could think of no reply but, "It's the fifth commandment! The fifth commandment!"

Joseph threw himself at Suggett who fell to the ground, his firearm scuttering across the deck. He sat astride his victim holding him by his shirt collar, and banging his head upon the planking. "A slave am I? Well consider this a slave revolt. If she dies, so do you." Joseph called for rope to tie up the mate, which the carpenter obliged.

*   *   *

Out of chaos came order. Surprisingly. Sophia was on her mother's bed, being looked after by Joseph who had a smattering of skills in this area. There was also a small gathering of onlookers. He had gently examined her left thigh where the ball had entered. He said that it had gone right through the leg, and that this was a good thing. Several of the audience pulled somewhat sceptical expressions, but said nothing. Joseph had insisted the wounds should be cleaned with boiled water and then they should be firmly bound with well-washed bandages. He also said that applying a little rum to the wound and to the patient would be helpful. The good news was that with care she should live; the bad news was that in her thigh the bone was broken and the muscles were torn: it was possible that Sophia would never be able to walk again. "But," he added, "such results are in the hands of God, and the claws of the Devil."

Hierarchies formed themselves. The young, and previously indecisive, Matthew Willson was nominally the Master, though he relied heavily on Hans Nielsen who was the new Mate, and with Joseph as 2nd Mate. The carpenter and the cook continued their functions, but appreciated there would be more work for them to do. This left Wheatear as the rest of the crew.

So much had happened since James Boyes and Alexander McDaniel had rowed away in the pinnace.

Willson, the new captain, stood on the poop deck to address his crew:

"My friends, there is much to do, and it will not be easy; but as friends we shall overcome the difficulties, and as true Christians we shall go the extra –nautical-mile."

This was well received.

"And I am sure that Jack Wheatear will be able to tell us where in the Bible to find the quotation I alluded to."

Jack responded "St Luke's Gospel Chapter Five."

"And which verse?"

"Verse 41!"

This was greeted with cheers and shouts; they felt they were a proper crew again.

"Thank you, Jack. Now what we have done is not a mutiny, we have managed to foil wicked deeds; we have done good things. We are not stealing *Dolphin*; we are borrowing her. We shall sail to Whitby and surrender the ship to the Harbour Master, who will keep it for when or if Mr Boyes comes to claim her. On the way we shall drop anchor in Lisbon, we shall sell what is now in the holds to pay for necessary supplies, and for the crew's pay. I do not think we shall need to dock anywhere else until we reach Whitby. Our prayers are for Sophie Norrison, and for Mrs Norrison and for Elizabeth." Much nodding and sympathetic grunts.

"And we shall benefit from their skills: by the end of our voyage we shall all know how to find latitude and to read charts!"

Again cheers.

"Nielsen and Wheatear, you will be in charge of the rigging. The rest of you to the capstan, we must raise the bower anchor. And when I say 'we' I mean it: I may be your captain for a while; but I shall always play my fiddle. So, look lively lads, and put your backs in it!" In no time everyone was at their posts. Willson tuned his fiddle, and improvised the first verse:

> *What shall we do with a wicked captain?*
> *What shall we do with a wicked captain?*
> *What shall we do with a wicked captain?*
> *Early in the morning?*

Straining on the capstan in time with each other, the sailors responded with one of the many traditional choruses:

> *Put him in the bilge and make him drink it*
> *Put him in the bilge and make him drink it*
> *Put him in the bilge and make him drink it*

Early in the morning....

When the anchor was raised and fixed in its place at the bow, *Dolphin* began to move with growing speed, sailing large to the North West with a quartering wind. The sails were set, and the crew were to be happy sailing homeward bound, hoping against hope that the diminished crew would be able to cope with the fierce Bay of Biscay and the treacherous German Ocean.

Lizzie, co-opted for this important task, upturned the half-hour glass and rang one bell of the First Dog Watch, though Joseph was deputed to keep an eye on her. On the west the sinking sun scattered its magenta light across the waves, and illuminated the diminishing outline of Tangier.

Chapter 22

Freelove dropped anchor off Whitby. John Walker, leaving the mate Solomon King in charge of the ship, was one of the first ashore in the jolly-boat. After a brief discussion with the Harbour Master, John walked down Baxtergate, turned right near Bagdale Hall into Skate Lane and knocked on the door of William and Margaret Backas, which was eventually opened by Hilda, wiping her floury hands on her apron.

"Is your Master at home?"

"Yes, sir. Who is asking?"

"Captain John Walker, junior."

Hilda gave a bow. She did not know him, but his name was well known in the town. She said, "Would you care to come in, Captain?", and she stepped aside.

Walker entered the hall, passing his hat into her care.

"Would you be so good, sir, as to be seated?" Hilda indicated the chair with a sweeping gesture. "I shall see if the Master can see you." She put the visitor's tricorn, upon which she stamped her floury fingerprints, on the hat-stand. Hilda then slowly and sedately stepped to the Chief Constable's study door. As soon as she was inside she was all bustle: "Quick, Master, it is Captain John Walker junior to see you!" Backas removed his home cap, and Hilda replaced it with his wig – after giving it a peremptory brushing with her hand which made it look as if it had been well powdered. Then she helped him out of his gown, and gave him his jacket which was green as seaweed and with shiny brass buttons, and which looked very smart as he only wore it on important occasions. William shuffled out of his slippers and put on his buckled shoes. Hilda removed his caterpillar clothes into another room, returning to see the butterfly Backas who braced himself into a man of importance, and –in the absence of Margaret- he turned to Hilda and asked, "How do I look?"

"Most fine, Master." She smiled, and so did William.

"Show him in, Hilda!"

She went out into the hall, closing the study door behind her.

"The Chief Constable will see you now, Captain." John Walker rose, and followed Hilda across the hall, which was so small that it could be traversed in less than half a dozen strides. Her knock on the door was followed by, "Come in!"

Walker stepped in and Hilda shut the door behind him.

William Backas was sitting behind his desk in a pose he had seen in a painting. He rose, bowed, and held out his hand muttering, "An honour." His guest did much the same, except his mumble was, "The pleasure is all mine." After these niceties, the Chief Constable indicated a chair. Unfortunately at that moment he saw that he had left a plate on his desk with a crumble of cheese and a biscuit on it. Deftly he moved his tricorn hat to cover it, and then sat in the other chair beside the empty fireplace.

"How can I help, Captain?"

"We have just returned from trading at Lisbon."

"I did see that in *The Daily Courant*."

"At Lisbon we met *Dolphin*, master James Boyes."

"Ah! Were the Norrisons aboard?"

"Yes."

"Alive and well?"

"They were alive, yes."

"Thank the Lord above, I must tell Hilda at once!" William was in the act of rising from his seat, when John held up his hand.

"Wait. Who is Hilda?"

"The eldest of the Norrison family. She works here. She opened the door for you."

"I was not aware of this. You can tell Hilda that her family is alive, and there is food enough aboard ship, and that Boyes said that they were sailing to Cadiz."

"But you have doubts?"

"Yes; I dined with Boyes. The Norrisons sat with us but said very little. Boyes claimed that he and Mrs Norrison were engaged and that they were going to get married. She denied this which made Boyes very angry."

"Boyes and Caroline to be married?" exclaimed William. "There were times when I thought that might happen; but that was before there were rumours that he was seeking to take over Ralph Theaker's wicked trade."

"It was clear that she no longer perceived him as a suitable husband and a father to her children. I did not know that Boyes saw himself as a new Provider? Did she?"

"When *Dolphin* sailed, I suspect that he presented himself as a saviour who will protect her and her family from her part in the Provider's Empire, as she had allowed Theaker to hide his contraband in her storeroom."

"Then it is likely that he has moved those contraband goods to one of his own hiding places. I suspect that *Dolphin* will come back here. It is in Whitby that he imagines he will grow his prosperous future. I humbly recommend, Sir, that you have a word with the harbourmaster, so that when *Dolphin* arrives you can take some of your men on board before anyone leaves the ship".

"Thank you for your wise suggestion, Captain, which I shall set in motion. But from what you said, he thinks he will gain from marrying her? What gain is that; the whole family is poor."

"They have the tenement in Atty's Yard," said Walker flatly.

"But surely the value of that would not be sufficient to feed and look after a woman, whom he appears not to like —let alone love— and her...." His voice faded into a mumble because he suddenly realised some of the many possibilities that a man could gain when he came to own a woman and three young children.

After a pause he continued, "Now I know why you came, Captain."

Chapter 23

The swift lancet of the morning sun broke through the shrouding mist to reveal a ship anchored on the Whitby Roads. It was *Dolphin*.

Oliver Armson (the Harbour Master), Christopher Woods (the Collector of Customs), William Backas (the Chief Constable), the constable and three watchmen were rowed out in a coble to the ship.

When they came alongside, Armson called out permission to come aboard which was granted, and a rope ladder was lowered. Armson went up first, then Woods then Backas. The others remained in the boat. Once on board they were greeted by Matthew Willson.

The Harbour Master was in charge of this group, and it was he who did the questioning:

"Where is the captain of this ship?"

"I am the temporary master."

"And your name?"

"Mister Matthew Willson."

"Are you owner of this ship?"

"No. This ship belongs to James Boyes."

"Where is he?"

"So far as I am aware he is in Tangier."

"When did you last see him?"

"On the 22nd of last month, while he was being rowed to Tangier by Alexander McDaniel, the second mate."

"And did they not come back to the ship?"

"We sailed away before they returned. We had reason to believe that they, together with the mate, were planning to harm at least four of the people on board."

"Who were the four people?"

"Mrs Norrison, Elizabeth and Sophia Norrison, and James a free negro sailor."

"Are the Norrisons safe and well?"

"Mrs Norrison and her daughter Elizabeth are well; but Miss Sophia Norrison was shot in her thigh by the mate. She is alive; but needs professional help and care."

"Fetch the Norrisons now. We shall send them ashore." Then he turned to William Backas and said, "Take them ashore with everything that belongs to them, reunite them with Hilda, ensure that Sophia receives the appropriate medical treatment, and find out from them what exactly happened on this ship."

"Certainly, Mr Armson, I shall leave my constable and one of the watchmen on board for you."

"And don't forget to send the coble back for us!" A comment that elicited the first smile of the day.

Armson returned to his interrogation of Willson:

"Who was the mate who shot Miss Sophia Norrison?"

"Samuel Suggett."

"And where is he?"

"We took him prisoner; but he escaped from the ship in Lisbon."

Armson raised a doubtful eyebrow, but said nothing more about Suggett's escape. He moved on to more pragmatic issues.

"You may bring this ship into the inner harbour. Anchor her firmly, but ensure she does not impede other ships. Remove all the sail once they are dry, and then lower the yards and the topmasts. Secure everything as safely and as dry as possible, including property belonging to Messers Boyes, McDaniel and Suggett. Mr Christopher Woods, the Collector of Customs, will of course need to examine the contents of the vessel, and we shall expect that all of you to be honest and helpful in that. Matthew Willson, as temporary master, will be responsible that all members of the crew fulfil these orders. Once they are all finished, Master Willson must find me and give all the keys to me. If the ship or anything in it is not claimed in the next three years from today, then the crew and passengers on this your most recent voyage from Lisbon can claim the ship and all that is within her. Such a claim must be in writing and submitted to me. Any questions?"

"No, sir," replied Willson.

"Once all that is done, then Mr Backas the Chief Constable will wish to interview all of you individually, in order to ascertain what crimes have been committed, how far self-defence mitigates the said crimes, and who if any will face prosecution. You shall all need to be at his office in Skate Lane first thing on Monday morning. Mr Willson will continue as master who will be responsible for all of you to be there on time, and you shall do as he commands until all of you are at the office of Mr Backas."

*   *   *

When William Backas returned home he told Hilda she could have the rest of the day off to be with her family who were at home again in Atty's Yard. He explained that Sophie had been wounded, but he could not bring himself to say that her sister had been shot. Anyway Hilda was in no mood to linger, and sped out of the door and ran all the way home. When she leapt up the stairs and banged on the door, shouting "Mama! Sophie! Lizzie! It is me!" she was tousled and unkempt: her bonnet had blown off and hung round her neck by its ribbon, her shoes were muddy, and although she had held her dress as high as modesty allowed –or even higher as many heads were turned– it was still bespattered from the filth of the road. But none of this mattered as she threw her arms round her mother and Elizabeth, smothering them with kisses. When she saw Sophie lying on the bed, her tears of joy mingled with those of sorrow.

"Oh Sophie dear, what has happened to you? What have they done to you?"

"I was shot in the leg by Samuel Suggett, the mate - a story you will hear later. But do not be sad for me. At first they did think I might die, but I was well nursed and here I am alive. It is possible that I may be able to walk. All is going to be well for us, dear sister."

"I hope that Suggett has been arrested, Sophie. He will hang for this."

"He has disappeared, Lizzie. Let us forget him."

Their mother interjected: "The mate was not the only villain; if that wicked ranter Wheatear had not interfered none of this would have happened, and Sophie would be dancing to see us. There is nothing worse than a man who believes he does the work of God and treasures the Bible above people."

"Mother, what has happened has happened. Time to forget and forgive."

"Sophie, you are a lovely and kind daughter. But as for me, I shall neither forget nor forgive that rascal Wheatear. As it says in the poem: 'This hand can stretch your days, or cut your minutes short'."

Chapter 24

Long before William Backas had interviewed all who had been on the recent voyage in *Dolphin* and had been able to put it all together as a coherent account, varied stories of the events were circulating wildly throughout Whitby. Such rumour mongering was eagerly heard and passed on by all sorts and conditions of those in the town, spreading out like a relentless tide over the local villages and hamlets.

Re-telling by word of mouth can be very accurate; but in this case that was not so. It already had the ingredients of a good yarn yearning for spinning. Like light through a prism the truth was distorted but more colourful. Every ship and boat leaving the harbour was to carry crates of gossip and casks of scandal: how there was a mutiny in which a negro slave threw the Master into the sea, and a lady passenger –dressed as a man– acted as master and steered the *Dolphin* from Tunisia and how she shot several Barbary Pirates who tried to board the ship. How there was a mate shot dead by a young girl who was going to be chopped up and cooked as there was a lack of food aboard, but her life was spared by her sister's pleas for mercy and promises of breaching a keg of rum.

In due course such stories even appeared in London broadsheets: *Valiant Sailor saves Damsels from Life of Degradation* and *She-he Sailors bring the Ship Home*. These were to find their way back to Whitby, barely recognisable.

But, no matter how the truth was obscured, most of those in Whitby were certain that all who arrived in *Dolphin* were heroes and heroines, maybe with one exception (not counting Joseph. Typically he had evaporated from the story.)

*   *   *

Jack Wheatear was known as one of the heroes of *Dolphin*, one of the initiators of the rescue of damsels in distress. But there was some doubt about his actions: Had he prevented Sophia Norrison from killing Samuel Suggett or had he interfered in such a way (and a religious way at that) which had allowed Suggett to shoot her? The effect of Sophia's wound was visible as she tried to live a normal life with a crutch. She was living evidence, and consequently Wheatear was increasingly blamed. There were even rumours that he had done something bad on coronation day; though the nature of it was unspoken, and possibly unknown. When someone who propagated this rumour was asked what exactly the nature of the crime was, they would clasp their hands and give a sideways glance and a knowing nod as if to say "We all know, but I am not going to sully my mouth with anything so shameful." Nearly everyone in Whitby (as elsewhere) was nominally a member of one or another version of Protestantism, mainly of the Church of England; but that did not mean they were eager to hear loud and regular snippets from the Bible voiced in the street. Such convert fanaticism was generally considered to be bad manners.

For Wheatear, being an object of hate was almost as unpleasant as was being an object of adulation. Shields

159

was his next port, and he would be there in a matter of days – maybe to ask Abigail for forgiveness, and to give her some Biblical texts unasked for.

*   *   *

William Backas had spent many long hours putting together all the evidence to complete an account of the 'Dolphin affair', for submission to the Justice of the Peace. He knew it was largely a waste of time as most of the planned crimes were prevented and so there was no point in pursuing any offences except the shooting of Sophia Norrison, and that would probably be futile as the guilty party, Samuel Suggett, was unlikely to be found. The opinion from higher up confirmed this.

Officially the matter was over; but this did not stop Margaret and William Backas discussing it. In the warm late summer afternoon they sat in their small garden and in the smaller part of which was not in the shade. Their stunted apple-tree was scattering its redundant petals, flaunting its miniature fruits which would grow large and tasty. Beneath the tree were some cranesbill, and a smattering of other flowers were spread randomly around the garden: oxeye daisies, cornflowers, dandelions and scabious. A robin hopped round pecking up insects, while an unruly crew of house sparrows flew amongst the apple-tree branches cheeping noisily.

"It was wicked was it not, William, that Boyes suggested that Mrs Norrison should write a letter to Hilda explaining where she was going and then destroy it?"

"Indeed, Margaret, most cruel."

"And allegedly -which usually means certainly- he was planning to sell Caroline and her daughters as slaves."

"That is terrible indeed."

"Why do men treat women so badly?"

"Because of a sinful disposition which corrupted God's original plan for mankind. Sin is not solely men treating women badly, they also wrong their fellow men. Boyes was going to sell Joseph as a slave."

"Joseph is strong, and his race is used to the labours of slavery. He was not going to be sold as a prostitute, as Boyes was planning for Caroline and her two daughters."

"What Boyes planned for Caroline and the young girls was unbelievably wicked. It is a mercy that they were able to foil the plot, particularly with the help of Jack Wheatear."

"I am not so foolish to think all men are wicked and women are all angels. However, it seems that men do more evil than women do."

"I suspect that it is because men have the power and the money to enable them so to do. That is why the *Dolphin* voyage is so wonderful: women foiled a plot that men had planned in order to destroy them."

"At least we shall never see James Boyes again."

Chapter 25

On the Sunday after church, as was appropriate, Mark Hill payed a visit to Mrs Norrison. She was very pleased to see him, particularly as he had sent a joint of beef round the previous day. Although she was something of a heroine in the town, few had come to visit her; it seemed that her fame had whisked her out of the realm of ordinariness, and many of her former friends were socially embarrassed, and knew not how to approach her. And indeed, although she was still attractive, Caroline bore marks of her experiences. It was not long since he was last with her, but Mark noticed the slight drooping of her eyelids, that her eyes had lost much of their sparkle, that her smiles seemed weary, and the occasional tremble of her right hand; but he knew this was the charming woman to whom he had become so close.

Hilda arrived. She was pleased to work in the Backas household, but the Sunday family reunion was for her always the highlight of her week.

Lizzie was much the same as before, but was clearly trying to be a grown-up. Sophie was as vivacious as ever, bubbling over with fun and ideas. She was out of bed, but hobbled slowly with a crutch, her left thigh distorted and swollen. "Oh, Mark, how delightful to see you! You see we are all safe, even Ninetails the cat. She was wonderful, a heroic cat! I think that Addison should write an ode to her. And you, Mark, how you have grown! You are a man, and a handsome one at that."

"Mrs Norrison," said Mark, "it is a pleasure to meet all your daughters. You said you would like me to be your son-in-law, but I could never choose which. But, to important matters: has the cat cleared all the rats from your rooms? And is your warehouse overwhelmed with rats?"

"Ninetails has earned her keep: not a rat in the house now! But to tell the truth I do not think that any of us has been in the cellar since our return." This was a signal for Lizzie to fetch the large key and descend down the stairs. Caroline and Hilda followed with a lantern, but Mark hesitated, "Shall I help Sophie?"

"No, she will do it by herself. She is brave."

At the bottom of the stairs Hilda and Lizzie were chatting about their two quasi-pet rats; Mark looked back out of the corner of his eye and saw Sophie coming slowly, and clearly painfully, down each step. He looked away in respect.

When all were assembled Lizzie declared the official opening of the double-doors. Hilda, holding up the lantern with its dull glimmer of the candlelight, edged in cautiously peering this way and that.

"Look!" cried Sophie, "Look! In the corner there!"

Red eyes reflected the candle flame, but only one pair.

"Only one has survived," said Sophie.

Caroline said, "Rats do not live for long, Sophie. William and Walter will have died long ago. William had a torn ear and Walter had little of his tail so they had both been in fights, they were never going to live long. However, you seem to have found another rat."

And indeed, this rat did not run away nor crouch for attack. Sophie came closer. She spoke quietly not to cause it to run away.

Hilda slowly held up the lantern, "Look, it has a long tail which is stripy. I have never seen markings like that before in a rat. And it also has a damaged ear. It is a very special rat. What shall we call it?"

Sophie said, "It shall be called Wilfred!"

Suddenly they were all happy, hugging each other with unexplained tears. Their lives seemed to have flipped back to as it was before; but the rat ran away and hid.

Mark turned to Caroline, "Now this space is empty, could I use it for my work? Ever since my father's death the business has expanded. I could do with somewhere to put bulky material, empty barrels and suchlike. Naturally, I shall pay rent."

"Certainly you can, Mark, my son-in-law". Caroline's smile had returned.

Mark thought: *I am a man now with a business. I am too old for these young girls, delightful as they are. I want a real woman, I want Caroline.*

*   *   *

Something important he had to do.

The sea was choppy but although the wind was moderately strong it was blowing from the south-south-west: a warm wind and easy to use. Solomon was not in charge of this ship. He was a passenger on a coastal vessel taking people and goods up the coast to Shields. At last he was going to Shields; at last he would see Abigail once more.

After he had disembarked Solomon walked to the Fish Quay where he was certain that he would be able to find out where Dunn the weaver lived, and sure enough he was soon walking up Tanner's Bank looking for a house with a green door and a wooden building in the yard, which –he was informed- "You'd know coz it soonds clicketty-clack, leeke a clog dancen".

Solomon, with pounding heart, knocked on the green door. After a while it was opened by a man in his twenties, but what was most noticeable about him was his mop of flaming orange hair.

He said, "Yes? What do you want?"

"I would like to speak to Abigail Linskill, please."

The man grunted and went inside, shouting "Abbie, it's someone for you!"

"What's their name?"

"I don't know. He didn't say."

"Tell him I'll be down soon."

The man returned to the doorway. He muttered, "She'll be along soon", and then vanished inside again.

Solomon waited. He thought that Abigail must now be nearly sixteen, grown up; he was twenty-two, not a great age difference. He noticed that he was trembling, but wasn't sure whether this was a good thing or a bad. *Without Abigail there is nothing else*.

Then suddenly Abigail was there in the doorway. She was taller than before: more of a woman, less of a child. Her hair was still shimmering gold, a lock of which she had combed to cover some of her smallpox marks. In fact these blemishes were not severe; Solomon thought she was still beautiful, in fact more beautiful. Her green eyes sparkled.

"I know you," she said. "You're Solomon the sailor man!"

"Yes."

"I was talking about you a bit ago with Jack Wheatear."

"With Jack Wheatear?"

"Indeed. What a changed man he is! He said he had seen you when he was trying to find me."

"But he was the man who assaulted you!"

"Yes, but he is not that man now. He is different – a good man, a religious man. He was the hero of the *Dolphin*; did you hear about that?"

"Yes, I did."

"How remiss of me, keeping you standing on the doorstep with us chatting like fishwives."

She ushered him into a comfortable parlour. "Please sit down and I shall show you my fine boy. He's just had his first birthday, but he's very clever."

She left the room, leaving Solomon considerably perplexed; he had expected a rejection, but had hoped for passion. *But this? She is friendly with the man who raped her!*

Abigail returned with her child in her arms. "He's called Jonas". She put him down and he waddled a bit on his chubby legs before suddenly sitting on his padded bottom. "Isn't he clever? He can talk too, he has been able to say 'mama' for some time, but he hasn't said 'papa' yet. Isn't he just wonderful?"

Solomon concurred, though he thought that he looked like any other baby. *But who did the child think was papa?*

He could not eradicate images in his mind: *I was there when this child was conceived.* But what was happening seemed unbelievably banal.

"It is a pity Jack is not here. He said you became good friends when you met at Pickering."

"Mmm. And where is Jack now?"

"He is at sea like you. He stayed here for several weeks which was a joy, as he was here for Jonas' birthday. He left but a fortnight ago. He is contracted as second mate in the Norway trade. My three sailors! Jack, you and my brother Jonathan. Jonathan is also at sea now. My other brother you met just now. He doesn't say much; he lives among the noisy rattle and thump of weaving. He loves it, but I think it is damaging his hearing."

"Jack seems to be doing well."

"Do you like my poesy ring, Solomon? Is it not pretty?"

"Very pretty. Are you getting married? To Jack Wheatear?"

"Yes, of course. Where could there be a better man?"

Sitting in front of you? Solomon simply asked when the marriage was to be.

"Oh, it's all planned; but it is a secret."

"What do your brothers think of your marriage to Jack Wheatear?"

"They don't like it at all. They think I should marry my cousin Esau so the wedding would also make a fine weaving business. Typical men, thinking only of money! Where is their passion, their love?"

"I assure you, Abigail, men have passions, too. And Cupid's arrow strikes just as often and deeply into a man's heart."

"Oh, Sol! You have a secret love! Tell me who it is? Is it someone I know?"

"Ah, Abigail, men can keep such secrets, perhaps better than women can."

"Have you told Jack? If so, I shall certainly wheedle it out of him."

"No, I did not."

"I suppose because you are not so young that your feelings are not so passionate as those of Jack. You must be at least three years older than him."

"Well, Abigail, I suppose there is not much else to say, so I should be leaving."

"But you haven't wished me well."

"I always wish you well; but I had best hurry away before I become too old to walk."

They both rose. When Solomon reached the door, Abigail put her hand upon his shoulder. He turned and looked; her expression had changed to one he could not read. She said, "Just now, Solomon, you commented that men can keep secrets, perhaps even better than women."

"I did, and believe it to be true."

Abigail looked around to make sure no-one else could overhear. "Solomon. What I am about to say is in absolute confidence." He nodded, which was sufficient. She continued, "My father had no son to avenge his downfall and death. I know that, as a Quaker, I should dispel all thoughts of revenge; but it still calls for me. Sometimes a woman must do a man's work in this wicked world. The higher the rise of praise, the greater fall of humiliation. Rest assured, I have no intention of giving my son a father like Jack Wheatear."

After Solomon had left Abigail mused, *I shall have you Solomon, but not yet. There is much to do; much to do that is unpleasant. But a bad deed can make things well.*

Chapter 26

"I have been pondering over something I heard yesterday, Margaret, which I can scarcely believe."

"Now you have my full attention, husband dear."

"I heard it from John Walker junior who heard it from Solomon King, the mate of *Freelove*."

"Whom did Solomon King hear it from?"

"That's the odd thing. King said he heard it from the woman concerned." Margaret was even more intrigued. She liked gossip about other women. Men's lives she thought were often rather dull, and their shortcomings were usually limited and predictable.

"Tell me more."

"You remember Abigail Linskill?"

"Certainly, it was not long since. Her father Jacob died, and Abigail went to live with her aunt and uncle. Sadly both she and her aunt died of smallpox shortly afterwards."

"Yes. But she is not dead after all. King has seen her and spoken to her."

"How can that be? Surely if what King says is true, it is most unusual that no-one has found this out afore."

"I suppose if she did not want people to know that she was alive. It can be quite easy to remain hidden."

"Did King say where she was living?"

"Yes, in Shields."

"I could do some asking about and find some more information."

"No, if she wishes to be thought of as dead, we should leave it that way."

"But she could have committed a crime. She may have been a thief, or even killed someone."

"No, Margaret, I insist. Promise you will remain silent, or I shall not tell you more."

"I promise, William."

"There is a matter of inheritance. Her father was poor, but the house was entailed; it should be hers."

"All the more reason for us to make it known, William."

"No. It must be kept a secret for now, but I shall talk further to John Walker and Solomon King, to see if they can pass the information to her. It is possible that she knows about the inheritance but does not wish to live there."

"I doubt it; if someone is given a house to live in they would be a lunatic not to accept it." After a brief pause she added, "She's not insane is she?"

"I think not; but then King has probably not told the whole truth."

*   *   *

The sulphurous sky shrouded the collier ship like a much-used blanket. She had managed to manoeuvre the much-feared rocks called the Black Middens under the vague outline of the castle of Tynemouth, and out into the German Ocean. It had been a risk to do so with such poor visibility, but the master was also the main owner of the vessel and he was prepared to take risks. There had been problems, and the ship had only managed four runs with

Newcastle coal to London and back whereas he should have achieved seven at least. He did not want the part owners to lose confidence in his ability and withdraw their funding. There was talk that there was going to be a storm, but he thought that was unlikely as the clouds had thinned making the sun visible, and that there was a moderate north-westerly wind. Just in case he whispered a prayer to "God on high whose might and power doth far extend above the cloudy sky". Then just -to make sure- he took off his tricorn hat, waved it thrice in the direction he wished the wind to blow, and then scratched his wig three times beseeching Poseidon to subdue the waves.

On board was an able seaman called Simon Scott. It was clear that he had been worried since he boarded and saw one of the crew members who was young and red-haired. He was certain that this sailor was not only female, but that she was Abigail Linskill pursuing him to wreak vengeance for his part in her father's death. He felt he had to talk to someone, so he approached the mate who was staring vacantly out to sea.

"I beg your pardon, Mr Mate, but I have a worry."

"We are all going to have a worry soon," he replied, "But what is your problem?"

"That sailor over there, sir," pointing to a fresh-faced youth who seemed unremarkable except for his copious hair stuffed clumsily under his woollen hat.

"Why is he problematical?"

"He is a girl, sir."

The mate looked again and said, "No, he's a man. He's called Jonathan Dunn."

"She is disguised."

"I know a girl when I sees one, and clearly you don't, Scott. I think you're a secret Miss Molly, and you want to disguise your perverted lust by trying to persuade me he's female. Believe me, if there was a female masquerading as a male on this ship she would soon be discovered and returned to her family", gratuitously adding, with a leer, "– after the crew had played with her somewhat."

"You cannot be certain, sir. There are many accounts in the newspapers of women dressing as sailors and not being discovered for years."

"Wives' tales and chapbooks more like! No sensible woman would dress as a man and submit herself to the dangers of the sea – not to mention the dangers of the seamen. And the work would be too hard for a woman, she wouldn't last a week."

"Women aren't that weak, sir, my gran could swab the decks, reef the sails, heave the capstan and not break into a sweat."

"I'd give a shilling to see that! Anyway, why would any of these women that you say dress as men want to go to sea? They'd be stupid to think of it!"

"Why do any of us go to sea, sir? To get away from a dull life and to see faraway places. But it is said that women who dress as men mostly do so to be near their sweethearts."

"Windbag words, Scott! Even if that red-haired sailor is a woman, who is his sweetheart? Mayhap that old man over there with more hair in his ears than on his head?"

"Ah, sir," said Simon shaking his head slowly from side to side, "she has no sweetheart on this ship. She is not on this ship for love."

"So why is she here then?"

"For revenge."

There was a silence. Then suddenly the sky was filled with startling light, followed almost instantaneously by a broadside of thunder.

"All hands! All hands!" shouted the mate. The calm wind suddenly swung fiercely easterly. Then the rain fell as if the ship was under a waterfall.

The mate turned to Scott, "Up the main mast and furl the top gallant sail or the ship will overturn, I shall send up help as soon as I can." Simon knew what to do. It was a task which required complete attention, made more difficult by the icy pounding of the rain which chilled fingers and cut vision. When the sail had been gathered up –gloveless hand over gloveless hand– and being secured, Simon cast a quick look to see who his colleague was – he saw it was the young sailor, certain that she was Abigail, whose long red hair was tangling round her face in the eddying wind. The shock caused him to lose his balance and one of his feet slipped from the rope.

"Who are you?" he called, shouting over the moaning of the wind.

"You know who I am," came the shriller response. After a pause it continued, "You will fall."

Whether this was a warning or a curse was not clear; but Simon was struck with terror. His hands slipped from the wet canvas and he fell backwards, one of his feet catching awkwardly in the stayrope which broke his fall. He dangled upside down, held only by the rope twisted round his ankle, a swaying pendulum as the ship pitched and tossed."

"Don't move. I shall come and sort you out."

Simon's voice trembled, and his fear was audible: "No! No! Keep away from me! Stay back!"

The mate and the crew watched as Jonathan Dunn inched along the yard towards Simon, who writhed in panic fear.

A giant wave crashed against the side of the ship which swung and shuddered, the rope holding Simon's ankle released its twisted grasp and he fell, with a moaning cry of despair and flailing arms, forty foot to hit the aft hatch with a dull thud. His body rolled this way and that upon the watery deck with the swaying of the ship, until a massive slap of the sea swept over the vessel taking the chicken coop and Simon's broken carcass overboard.

*   *   *

An especial favourite of the *Dolphin* heroes, particularly (but not entirely) among the young women of the parish, was the 16-year-old Norwegian apprentice sailor Hans Nielsen. He had tousled blonde hair, eyes as blue as a summer sky, a gentle manner rare among sailors, and a Norwegian accent which transformed common North English phrases into charming eloquence.

As to his bodily physique, any who were interested in such a matter had to use their imagination to divine his contours beneath his outward and visible seaman's clothing.

However, three young women, having spent the morning on the shore collecting nereid worms to be used as bait for their fishermen fathers, felt they deserved the afternoon for fun. So they spent some time in the Market Place and then they turned into Church Lane, arm in arm, full of giggles, silliness and ale. Hans Nielsen was coming the other way and found his way blocked. Politely he requested:

"Excuse me, ladies. Can you please let me pass?"

"I knows who you are," said the oldest, grinning. "You was on *Dolphin*."

"I was in *Dolphin*, yes."

Comments were spouted from the other two often without thought:

"He's the foreign one, from Holland,"

"Don't be stupid, he's Danish."

"Perhaps he's a Swede."

"A swede? That's a vegetable!"

"What you called?" asked the oldest, who was marginally the most sensible of the trio.

"My name is Hans. I am Norwegian." This triggered another spate of comments:

"No matter what he is, he's good looking, isn't he girls?"

"I should say so."

"I bet he's got a good body."

"I reckon he's had fun with a lot of women. Don't you, girls? After all, he weren't called 'Hands' for nothing."

"Hans," said Nielsen.

"Ooh, you wants hands, do you? Let's give him hands, girls. What do you think?"

"I bet he's a good kisser!"

Suddenly they were on him. One put her arms round him; another was moving in with pouted lips, and the oldest said, "I bet he's got a big one!" with her hand moving in to test this hypothesis.

Hans struggled free, turned on his heels and ran. They were after him in a flash. He reckoned that although they could run fast he had more stamina that they, so if he ran up the wooden steps up to the Church he could not only leave them behind, but could seek sanctuary.

Hans went into the Church. It seemed very peaceful; the only person there was the vicar, who was making sure that everything was ready for the Sunday services. He turned to Hans and asked if he could do anything to help him.

Hans smiled and said, "I would like to come into your church, if that is all right."

"Of course you can. You don't have to hurry. You are Hans Nielsen, I believe."

"I have come in haste to escape the clutches of sin."

"The Devil is everywhere."

"This was three devils. I think it may be that I am foreign that they troubled me."

"It is difficult to be at peace in a foreign land. Maybe you can derive something from the devils. What did your devils look like?"

"Until they attacked me they looked like any other young women."

"Were you attracted to them at first?"

"Possibly."

"It is perfectly normal to feel such passion when young, but you must move on to a marriage for the rest of your life with the true partner. So forget what is past, no matter how you found it attractive, and move to a better place where you can be more yourself, not yearning for the past. After all, the King, and his father before him, both made that change, leaving behind the mistress of Hanover for the wife of Britain. Though he was not wholly faithful. "

"I did read something of that sort in your newspapers. And of course there is gossip about it."

Hans began to be uneasy about where the conversation was leading. It sounded as if the rector was saying it was acceptable to have sex with women until marriage, and then one had to be faithful to her alone.

"But I have not had any mistresses in Norway, sir."

The vicar laughed, and said, "There is no need to pursue the metaphor to death, Hans. I am glad you have abandoned the old way already. If the change you are going to make has been done by the King and his father, I think you should follow their commitment."

"I see. Yes, I do intend to live and work in Britain."

"Which is why you want to come into our Church. The Anglican Church has always accepted new members. If royalty abandoned Lutherism for Anglicanism, why should not you?"

At last Hans realised that they had been talking at cross purposes. Embarrassed, he at first thought how he could extricate himself from this confusion. Then he thought, *Why not? If I am to live in England I might as well be a member of the Church of England.*

"How is the change from Lutherism to Anglicanism?

"It is only a bishop who can finally make the change. In the meantime come to church, every Sunday, when you are not at sea, starting with the Morning Service tomorrow morning, the churchwarden will show you where to sit. You will also need sessions with me so I can explain the nature of the Church of England."

"How many sessions, and when?"

"You will gain an idea of what Anglicanism is like, when you go to the services. In the sessions I shall tell you about the differences between Lutherism and Anglicanism, and recount some of the history of our religion. Half a dozen such meetings should be sufficient. Then I can confirm that you are suitably willing and knowledgeable to be allowed into the Church of England. Would before Mattins be convenient, at about half past nine on Sunday mornings?"

"That would be fine, sir"

"I look forward to seeing you tomorrow morning, Nielsen."

The vicar did not realise what was going to happen at Sunday's official service of Morning Prayer.

Chapter 27

Mattins was in progress in the Parish Church of St Mary at Whitby on top of the East Cliff. On this particular Sunday the congregation was rather depleted, because of the warm and tempting weather. Some were surprised that Hans Nielsen was in Church; some thought that seeing him was a divine gift to compensate for the laboriously dreary chanting of the familiar *Te Deum Laudamus* by the congregation. Whether they were glad to have reached the end, or whether the final verse had a confident though rather ambiguous reassurance, it was spoken with greater firmness than the former 27 verses:

"O Lord, in thee have I trusted: let me never been confounded."

The congregation was then seated while the vicar declared the banns; a relief after all the standing and kneeling. For some, this was the best part of the service. It was always interesting to see who was marrying whom.

The vicar waited until everyone was quietly settled, then he began:

"I publish the banns of marriage between Jack Wheatear..." At this point there was a certain amount of whispering and muttering. The vicar scowled, scanning the congregation until everyone was once again quiet, before continuing, "Between Jack Wheatear, bachelor of this parish and Abigail Linskill, spinster..." Again the vicar had to stop; this time the noise was so loud that the verger had to bang his staff of office shouting 'Quiet! Quiet!' There was disorder teetering on the edge of

Pandæmonium, and it was some time before order was restored. The vicar's voice was loud and firm: "You *will* be quiet while I read these banns, which are to be delivered without interruption in accordance with the laws of Church and State. Anyone making noise will be removed from the church and may be subject to legal penalties." Utter silence ensued, though, judging by the facial expressions of many, this was with the greatest reluctance.

"I publish the banns of marriage between Jack Wheatear, bachelor of this parish, and Abigail Linskill, spinster of North Shields in the parish of Tynemouth. If any of you know cause or just impediment why these two persons should not be joined together in holy matrimony, ye are to declare it: This is the first time of asking." The vicar gave a sigh of relief; then changing from his official church voice to his ordinary speech, he added "If anyone has any problems about this marriage please come and see me after the service. Now we shall continue with the *Jubilate Deo,* and please sound as though you are 'joyful in the Lord'.

*   *   *

At ten of the clock Abigail knocked on the door of a house which had for her so many memories: memories of great happiness and of unfathomable misery. There had been changes: it looked smarter, cleaner, the shutters were new, and the door had been painted in fashionable blue. This door opened to reveal a young lad of about 15. He looked her up and down and was clearly not impressed,

"What does tha want?"

"I am Miss Linskill, and I have come to discuss business with your master."

He grunted, but stood aside to let her in.

"I'll get t' maister. Do'nt move," was his parting shot as he went grudgingly out of the hall. Surprisingly Esau Linskill appeared shortly from another door, like Pantaloon entering stage right after a zany had been jeered off sinister. But this was serious business, and besides Abigail had never seen a play of any kind.

"Good day, Cousin Abigail. It is a pleasure to see you. Pray come into the drawing room and make yourself comfortable." She did; it was not like it had been when her father had lived here when almost the whole of the ground floor had been one large room with no hall, a single door opening to the outside, and her father's loom and its accoutrements taking up most of it. Esau had clearly had the room partitioned; the drawing room was still fairly spacious though, and the newly panelled walls and the modern chairs made it welcoming.

"Pray be seated, cousin." He gestured towards a comfortable sofa covered in maroon velvet, she gave a token curtsy and sat down, and then he chose to sit in a beautiful but seemingly rather austere chair. He rang a bell and a maid entered, smiled and bobbed. Esau asked Abigail if he could offer her anything, "Some tea, perhaps?" She declined, and the maid disappeared. As soon as they were alone Abigail introduced the topic that both of them knew they must discuss:

"Mr Linskill, it seems strange to be offered hospitality in my own home."

"I understand how you feel, cousin."

"I beg to differ, Mr Linskill. I suspect you have not the slightest idea how I have felt since my father died."

"My apologies, it was a clumsy thing to say."

"And I, sir, also have a clumsy thing to say, namely: this is my house."

"I do not doubt this in principal. But it is complex. You have seen the will?"

"I know what is in the will, but I have not seen it. Not yet." A smile spread over her face, which Esau could not fathom. Abigail continued, "My mother told me that in my father's will the house, free of any debt, would come to me."

"Indeed that is so; but it was thought that you were dead. In the meantime the house came into my possession, as the next closest of kin to your father. And, as you see, I have altered the house, and out back I have enlarged the shed into a thriving weaving manufactory."

"I was not dead, and am not dead. I was not in hiding. I lived openly in Shields and did not change my name. Indeed two young men found me with little difficulty. Whoever you employed to find me did very poor work."

"I am not culpable, as I was told you had died. But we shall have to come to some agreement about the changes; I have invested a lot of money in these premises."

"And who do you think is culpable? Certainly not me. You seem to have accepted what you would like to have been true, rather than making any effort to find out the real truth. And you had no right so to do. However I am

183

happy for you to stay awhile here until you have removed your moveable property, and replaced it with the moveable property owned by my father."

"But much of the old items were discarded or given away. There was nothing much left, except his loom."

"I assume, sir, that an inventory of my father's possessions was taken at the time."

"No, I don't think so. I was not here at the time. There was no money. I gather that anything of value was sold to pay for some of his debts. The rest of the debts were paid by the members of the Whitby Meeting – I suspect out of guilt. Jacob was stubborn, but I gather his fellow Quakers did not treat him well in his final months."

"I shall have to have an attorney, and have a good look at that will."

Esau gave her a shrewd look. *She looks innocent, but mayhap she has already seen conditions of the will; if she has not, then she might fall into a trap of her own making.*

"No need for that, Cousin Abigail. How about us going into a partnership? I think we could make an excellent business between us."

"That sounds a possible idea; but I shall have to consult my future husband."

"Yes, I have heard you were due to be married, and I wish you well. To Jack Wheatear, I think."

"News travels quickly. Unless, cousin, you have been attending service in the local steeple house?"

"Certainly not! I am a good Quaker. But I might like to see you married in the steeple house."

"That is good to hear. I was afraid you might not wish to see me married in church. As you are my second cousin, I hoped you would give me away."

"Elisha Root and Michael Cornelius would not like it." *She knows that being a Quaker is one of the conditions of owning the house and she is trying to lure me into a trap. But why is she marrying in church if she does know this condition? Or why marry at all, as she would lose the name of Linskill?*

"They will forgive you in time, cousin," she said.

*   *   *

On the subsequent Sunday, the parish church of Whitby was almost as packed as was the burial service of George Hill the butcher. The vicar was very pleased to see such a large congregation but could not imagine any reason for it except that his sermons were becoming more popular, especially among young women.

The appearance of Jack Wheatear in church had caused a bit of a flutter; but when the vicar stood up to publish the banns of marriage for the second time between Jack Wheatear and Abigail Linskill, the congregation was eerily steeped in severe silence.

Abigail was not present.

Chapter 28

Wednesday August 20th 1729

Backas gasped, "I know this person!"

"Do you know him sufficiently well to give him a name?"

"Yes. He is Jack Wheatear, a sailor." Then after a pause adding, "He was to be married soon."

There was a lengthy silence, neither knowing what to say. Then Backas dragged his sensitive self back to his professional self.

"Tell me, Mr Hartley, how and when you realised there was a body in the barrel?"

"The barrels had been brought out of the ship, and then they were winched up here. This is a regular delivery, so until then no-one had expected anything was amiss; but our men are skilful. Once a cask is brought up to this platform, our men pull the butts onto their side and roll them to the lant storage over there. One of the men said that this barrel felt different, and called me. I suspected something fraudulent; it is not unknown. I had the rogue barrel rolled out of the way and chocked to make it firm. Then I told one of the men to remove the bung to let some of the liquid into a bucket and then to put a bung back in with some firmness. The lant was red; we knew it was coloured by blood. The men said that they had thought, when rolling the barrel, that it had something solid in it. So we raised the butt, drew out more of the liquid, and brought the barrel here where we opened it as you see."

"And no-one has been able to tamper with it since you supervised the opening of it?"

"Absolutely not. Since I left to fetch you, it has been guarded by the senior foreman and two other men. No-one could have tampered with it."

"So, but for your experienced men, the cask could have been in the lant storage area for what? A week?"

"Or even more. We like to keep a supply in storage. If we run out of lant, the whole process would have to shut down until we get a new supply. We have at least a fortnight's worth in store."

"Thank you for your information, Mr Hartley. Can you please get your men to remove the body and wrap it up in a canvas sheet. I shall need to have advice from people who know more about these things than I do. Pour back the removed liquid and seal up the cask. Then bring both to me. Once the corpse has been professionally examined I shall arrange his burial. Thank you for your help."

"And thank you, Mr Backas. I and a couple of our men shall bring you both the body and the butt in one of our carts. We should be there before dusk."

* * *

Mr Hartley had been as good as his word. Mr Backas had made space in his outhouse, and had erected a trestle table within, upon which the wrapped corpse of Jack Wheatear was laid. The butt, which was placed in the garden, was sealed up and covered in a tarpaulin. The cask still contained a sizeable amount of the blood-stained urine and a dead rodent which had floated to the top once the corpse was removed. Mrs Backas was not pleased with these arrangements, and told her husband so when they went to bed.

The barber-surgeon came round on Thursday morning, at William's request. He had a good look at the body and confirmed that the throat had been cut with a large sharp knife, from the victim's left to right, possibly in a single slice. He conjectured that the murderer had held Wheatear by the hair from behind and then killed him. If so, the nature of the cut would suggest a right-handed person. He opened the body and examined the lungs which had no urine in them, so he was sure that the cut was fatal, and that the victim had not drowned in the liquid, though it looked as if the rat did. The back of the corpse's head had suffered a severe blow, enough to fell a man but not to break his skull. There were no other signs of bruises etcetera, except what might have been the consequence of being rolled in a barrel. So it seemed very likely that Jack's death was sudden. Afterwards he and William Backas tidied up the corpse as well as they could.

Then Mr Backas went along the road and up the stairs to the church where he told the parish clerk that there would be no marriage between Jack Wheatear and Abigail Linskill, but there would have to be a burial instead. He was not looking forward to telling this to the parson whose first reaction would be sorrow at the tragedy, and his second reaction would be that it saved a lot of paperwork, as Abigail had to go through much teaching and verification of sincerity in changing from a Quaker to an Anglican. Financially the vicar would have received five shillings for a marriage by banns and a wedding certificate, whereas a burial was only one shilling and sixpence; but of course such worldly considerations never crossed his mind.

*   *   *

William Backas had learnt that Abigail Linskill was lodging at the Angel Inn, and after going home to collect his wife Margaret, they went there to break the bad news to her. The inn-holder showed them to Abigail's room, and Backas knocked on the door.

"Who is it?"

"Mr and Mrs Backas."

The door opened. "Come in! Come in!" Abigail was all smiles and excitement. "How nice to see you! Come in! Jack has told me about you, Mr Backas. He spoke highly of you, and often said you carried out your duty with sincerity and thoroughness."

"Thank you. Miss Linskill, can I introduce my wife?" Abigail smiled at Margaret and gave a brief curtsy. William continued, "I regret that we bring bad news."

Abigail's face switched from smile to worry, "What? Is there a problem? Has the vicar been taken ill? Has my wedding gown been spoiled?"

"Worse. Your Jack is dead."

Abigail, pale-faced, collapsed. William caught her and carried her to the bed. Margaret sat beside holding her and comforting her with gently murmured consolations.

Abigail sat, flumped, staring into nothingness for an incalculable time. Then she said, "Dead? How dead? An accident?"

"No. I hate to bring such bad news. He was killed."

"Killed? How? By whom?"

"He was murdered. We do not know yet who killed him, but it is my duty to find out."

"But who would want to kill him? He was the kindest man in England."

"I regret to say, Miss Linskill, that in order to discover the villain and insure that he receives the punishment he deserves, I shall have to ask you some questions."

"You said 'he'. Is the murderer a man, then?"

"It is too early to know whether he is a man or a woman. Are you prepared to answer my questions?"

Margaret interrupted, "Abigail, I realise this will be difficult for you. Shall I send for some tea for you?"

"Thank you Mrs Backas. That is a kind thought, but I am strong enough to help in any way I can to bring the murderer of my betrothed to the gallows."

"You did not attend church when your banns were first read," said William, "Why was that?"

"I was in Shields, where I live with my cousins."

"When did you come to Whitby?"

"Last Thursday."

"And you have stayed here since then?"

"No, this is rather expensive. I only came here a couple of days ago. Before, I was at the Neptune in Haggersgate – cheaper, but it did smell rather too much of fish."

"So you were in Whitby last Sunday, but did not attend in church. Why was that?"

"I had heard that there was some unseemly behaviour in the church when our first banns were read. I did not wish to be the cause of disruption in the steeple house – I mean the church."

"Why do you think that the reading of your banns caused such a disturbance?"

"Jack was one of the heroes of the *Dolphin*. You know how people, particularly young woman, make an idol of heroes – even in the church apparently!"

"Are you now a member of the Church of England?"

"Not fully yet."

"Are you going to become a full member?"

"In my present grief, I have not thought whether I shall or not."

"I apologise for upsetting you, Miss Linskill. Just two more questions, if you feel you are in a sufficient state to answer them."

"Ask what you wish, Mr Backas. I am stronger than you might think."

"What made you want to marry Jack Wheatear?"

"That is an easy question. He was handsome, clever, strong, virtuous and kind. Not averse to hard working. He was a hero, and he was the father of my son."

"And why do you think anyone would want to kill him?"

"That is a harder question. Envy, jealousy and other wicked sins, I imagine."

"Thank you, Miss Linskill, you have been very helpful, and we apologise for bringing evil news, and for intruding into your grief. If you recall anything else that you think would be helpful to catch the murderer, you know where to find me."

*   *   *

When they were back home, fed and settled after a long and troubled day, William asked his wife, "What do you think of our visit to Abigail Linskill?"

"It is difficult to say, as people grieve in different ways; but I felt that she already knew that Jack Wheatear was dead, and was keen that we should not know that she did."

"I had a similar feeling, Margaret, as she did not shed a single tear."

"Not everyone cries in that sort of situation. A shock often prevents tears; but I did rather expect that her eyes would well up later - perhaps when she was answering your questions. But there were a number of oddnesses. For example, we were strangers, but she put on a show of unbounded delight. Why? Was she expecting us? Maybe that is how she greets all new people? Maybe, as a Quaker, she has been taught to be friendly."

"I have never met a member of The Society of Friends who greeted me in quite so friendly a fashion."

"Indeed, William. I did feel -though feelings are not always true- that she was putting on a performance for us. Another thing seemed a bit strange. She said something about what Wheatear thought of you. It was something like 'He spoke well of you, and said you were hard working'.

"What is strange about him admiring me?"

Margaret made a little snort. "It is not your merits that are interesting, William, but the way she said them. Her words, I think, were that 'Jack *spoke* highly of you and *said* you were hard working'; one might expect her to say something like 'Jack often *speaks* highly of you, and *says* you are hard working. It was almost as if she knew he was dead."

"That is a clever point, Margaret. But she also made it clear that she was not very eager to become a member of the Church of England. It could be that all this happy family image which she has been propagating was another bit of acting. Maybe she was planning not to marry him after all."

Chapter 29

The body of Jack Wheatear was interred at three o'clock in the afternoon, and the service was intended to be quick with a minimum of people: the vicar, the parish clerk, the grave digger and his assistants. Also William Backas in his role as Chief Constable together with the Justice of the Peace. It was noticed that Abigail Linskill was not there.

However, the news of the murder had circulated swiftly and several had come, rather sheepishly, to see the wicked hero buried in the solid soil; though if asked exactly why they were there it would have been likely that few could give a precise answer.

Jack Wheatear was buried near the grave of George Hill, the butcher, who had a small memorial stone.

A tied bunch of withered flowers lay there.

*   *   *

William told Margaret about the burial. But it was Margaret who moved the conversation into the questions both had been wishing to discuss thoroughly: who killed Jack Wheatear? Why? And what was the significance of the butt of lant?

William replied, "That is what I now have to discover so I can present sufficient evidence before the Justice of the Peace. Then he can set a trial in motion and the perpetrator be hanged. I have my constable and his men, and no doubt we shall find information, evidence, conjecture and other sources of help. But it is you, my dearest Margaret, whose opinion I value most."

"I shall do what I can, husband. But I am sure there are cleverer minds in Whitby."

"Indeed, no doubt there are many in Whitby with swifter minds and keener skills of reasoning than both thee and me; but when I have a problem we often solve it between the two of us."

Margaret paused for a moment, she could see it was meant as a compliment, but she did not like the idea of 'many' people in Whitby being cleverer than her. Then she shrugged that off. "Let us be orderly in our thoughts, William, and take one issue at a time."

"I think that would be a sound plan. What do you think we should consider first?"

"To my mind the most intriguing idea is why the murderer took all that trouble. Why did the villain not just push him over a cliff, or stab him in the dark in a ginnel?"

"I suspect he wanted the victim to suffer, or to get information, or so the victim knows why he is being killed."

"You call the murderer 'he'. Do you assume that he is a man?"

"I suppose I do. Surely it would take a man, and a strong man at that, to concuss the victim and then insert him into the barrel so neatly."

"If the event is as you say then I may have to agree; but there are other ways of getting a man into a barrel."

"How?"

"Persuade him."

"Ah, I see what you mean. We know the murderer had a knife, and the victim is told that he must get into the barrel at knife point."

"Yes; but it can be done in other ways too. You have to bear in mind that most men, especially the young ones, are rather stupid..." William's eyebrows clenched in disapproval, but Margaret was in full flow, "...If you say to one such, 'I bet you cannot get into this barrel' the chances are that he would be in there as quick as a winter storm. Women have more means, such as 'You are so virile, let me see you get into that barrel', 'If you loved me you would get into that barrel', 'If you can get into that barrel within five minutes I shall let you have your way with me', 'I asked John to get into the barrel and he couldn't, I don't suppose you can do this even though you are bigger than him', 'If you don't get into the barrel I shall spread it about that...'"

"Enough, enough, Margaret! You have convinced me. So anyone, male and female, strong or week, old or young could have been the murderer. I was hoping we were going to be able to reduce the number of suspects, but now all the inhabitants of Whitby could have been the culprits."

"Why restrict it just to Whitby?"

William made a groan in jest. "We can reduce the number. The murderer is most likely to have been known to Jack Wheatear, so we must learn more about him and those who knew him. Also the murderer is clever. The elaborate business of a body in a butt of urine is complicated, but it hampers us finding out where he was killed or when. Normally when there is a murder the body is found in the place where it happened and comparatively soon after the deed was done. But we shall have to find out both these things, which won't be easy. Tomorrow I shall go and see Mr Lant. And I would be grateful if you could circulate in the market and any other places where you collect information and find as much as you can about when Jack Wheatear was last seen alive, and whether he had been seen arguing or fighting with anyone. And now, I think, we should turn to happier and more enjoyable pastimes."

"I will not argue against enjoyable pastimes, dearest."

*   *   *

It was a cool late August day when William Backas set forth to find evidence of who killed Jack Wheatear, why and how. If it was not his duty he would have stayed at home, as he was not feeling right. He walked down Skate Lane, turning left down Baxtergate, over the bridge, and then turned right along Church Street. He had regularly walked that distance and further without being out of breath, but now he was gasping and coughing. But he had to persevere. It was not long before the road turned into a lane and that was where he met 'Mister Lant' as he was universally known by virtue of his business. It did not seem to be a business as at first sight it looked like a large field thick with wild flowers and berries, and scattered with vats, ankers, butts, barrels, tuns, hogsheads, firkins and kegs all surrounded by a musty aura of piss. Two carts lay idle and a stalwart horse was steadily cropping the grass. A rather small brick building near the entrance served as home and office for Mister Lant who emerged to greet the Chief Constable.

"Mr Backas, sir, a pleasure; I received your letter. How can I help you?"

"Well, sir, I would be grateful if you could tell me your real name. I cannot call you by your nickname."

"I am so used with saying 'Mister Lant' that I hardly recall my real name. It be David Dunn."

"Thank you, Mr Dunn."

"Pray come inside, sir, where we can discourse in comfort."

Inside they went, to be greeted by a shock of heat from a large fireplace which forced Backas to remove his coat which he hung on the back of the door. He was offered a rather austere chair. When they were both seated, he continued:

"You may have heard, Mr Dunn, that a corpse has been found in a butt of urine."

"Aye, Mr Backas, sir. This news has percolated even to this meagre end of town."

"So as you deal in casks and urine, I naturally come to you."

"Are you going to arrest me, sir?" asked Dunn, smiling.

"No," said Backas, also smiling but which turned into a coughing spasm, "At least not yet. However, I am hoping that you can help me by describing your routine."

"I work alone, as you might know. My wife died some years back. My son used to be my helpmeet, but he's gone to sea. He said it would be a more exciting life, and less stinky; when he first came home he said he were right about the former, but the fo'c'sle smelled worse."

"I can imagine; but if we could return to the business in hand..?"

"Aye, Mister Backas, sir. Mainly I work at night. I have two rounds which I take on each other night, one round town, and t'other round local villages and farms; but never over t'moor. Customers, or their servants, know roughly when I arrive and they pour the buckets of lant collected indoors into their lidded outside vats for me to collect. The lid be right important, sir; if the lant is diluted with water it causes problems in t'alum process. Some put a chalk mark at the rim to avoid neighbours stealing it."

"Is that a problem?"

"Happen. Lant is money, or I couldna have a business. I tip the lant into a measure, which I record in my book. Then I pour it into barrels. When I get back here I empty the night's takings into a butt. Once the butt is full I close it, putting the head in the notches on the staves and hammering down the hoops. I fill about four butts a week. It costs me seven pence ha'penny to buy a butt of lant, fifteen pence to ship it to Boulby mine, and I can usually make a pound a week profit."

"And you have recently shipped some lant to the Boulby alum works?"

"Yes, that be so sir. Eight butts which I took to the quay on Tuesday last, and had them all passed and the documents signed as proper." He added, chuckling,

"Some folk think because I'm the Lant Man I canna sign my own name."

"And then you came back here."

"Straightway. Time is precious. I had to get ready for my night work."

"In the town?" The last word was gasped into a splutter, and it was some time before Backas could formulate the last word coherently.

"No, sir, it was the villages and farms."

"So these premises were empty of horse and man, almost all night?

"Aye, sir, 'twas so: left for the rats, moudiwarps and hedgehogs."

"Have you noticed any of your casks missing recently?"

"Aye, 'tis a problem, sir. As I am away at night, sometimes I think a cask has been stolen, but I have so many it is difficult to say. However, sometimes I return to find lant has been siphoned out of my current supply — I know how much because 'tis all in my book."

"Would it not be a sound idea to employ a man to guard the premises when you are absent?"

"Not worth the money, sir. Some people take it for dyeing, some to re-sell it later. 'Tis all small scale, no actual business would benefit from stealing small amounts."

Dunn's answer had difficulty being heard as Backas was gasping and choking.

When all was quiet again, Dunn said, "I know what you are suffering from, sir, and I have just the thing to cure it. Give me five minutes and then you will be fine."

It was some minutes more than the five promised, during which Backas had no coughing, though his heartbeat was too quick. Dunn said, "This be a right grand infusion which cures your ailments exact. Inhale the vapour till the medicine be cool enough to drink. All the herbs be from my field. That did not fill Backas with much enthusiasm when he thought of Dunn's field regularly dosed with piss and horse dung; however the inhalation was already making him feel better so he later drank all the potion. When Backas was feeling good he continued the conversation:

"Have you had any lant stolen recently?"

"Great likely. A few minor thefts. Mayhap 'tween fifteen to twenty gallon over the last month."

"Any butts stolen?"

"Happen; but not that I know of."

"Are there other ways of collecting lant?"

"Sure you be jesting with me, Mr Backas!"

*   *   *

William Backas made his way home and was fine until he reached Skate Lane when suddenly he felt a desperate urge to get inside the house before he made a disgusting exhibition of himself. He opened the door, and shouted for Hilda who came running. "Quick," he said, "bring two chamber-pots to our bedroom!" He managed to pull off his clothes, hat and wig in a scattered heap, and put on his nightshirt. Hilda brought the receptacles just in time; vomiting and diarrhoea each to its own.

Hilda found Margaret who was wondering what all the noise was about. "Mistress, the Master is very ill. I fear for him. He is in a very poor state. He is in your bedroom."

"Do not panic, Hilda. Let us go together and see what has happened."

They went in to the bedroom. And William was lying pale and still on the bed.

"Is he dead, Mistress?"

"No, he is not, Hilda," said Margaret, "And the first thing to do is to empty the chamber-pots and bring them back clean. And it might be a good idea to be quick as possible." Which she did.

"William, how do you feel?"

"Very weak and fragile."

"What happened?"

"I went to see Mr Lant. But on the way I felt out of breath and suffered from copious coughing, which got worse. He gave me an herbal infusion, and I felt better. Then once I got home I had new symptoms, as you are well aware."

"I shall boil some water for you. When it is cool, drink it when you are thirsty; but don't take anything else. Rest if you can." She stroked his shaved head gently.

After Hilda had renewed the chamber-pots, she came into the kitchen where Margaret was flipping through an old herbal which her mother had given her, it was full of handwritten marginal notes.

"Mistress, is he going to die?"

Chapter 30

"Not if we can help it, Hilda. He suffered from coughing and shortness of breath, and Mr Lant gave him a medicinal drink."

"He tried to poison the Master?"

"I think that unlikely. If he was the murderer of Wheatear, trying to poison the Chief Constable would be drawing attention to himself. Any sensible murderer would lie low."

"Perhaps he misjudged the poison, and expected him to die there and then. Then, begging your pardon Mistress, the Master would be in the next cask."

"Really, Hilda, you go too far! I think it much more likely that he misjudged the medicine and gave the Master too much. I suspect he had used foxglove which, I believe, cured breathlessness and coughing - as my mother's herbal suggests. So, Hilda, less thinking about my husband being dead, and more attention to make him better. No food for some time, obviously. Just boiled water with..."

Hilda interrupted, "Yes, mistress, that is what my mother used to do when we were ill; and if we were vomiting she would make us an infusion of mint..."

"No doubt, Hilda, but ginger root is more effective."

"We have none in the cupboard, mistress. And anyhow that would make the bowels more painful, surely."

"So, chamomile, we have some of that dried."

"Or I could make some applesauce, mistress. I hear that is a good remedy"

"Chamomile, Hilda. And then there is the Master's original ailment to be dealt with."

"My mother gave us thyme."

"But my mother, Hilda, swore by elderflower and honey. Very efficacious. Let us go and see how the poor suffering invalid is struggling on."

They tiptoed quietly into the bedroom. He was lying on his back, snoring loudly, and looking moderately healthy.

"Typical men!" said Margaret, "They have no consideration for our feelings."

Hilda smiled; but said nothing.

*   *   *

Solomon King was frustrated by the docking of *Freelove*. He thought there was no need to sail into Whitby. The carpenter claimed the need to replenish the lacuna in his stores, but Solomon wanted to fit in two more collier runs before the end of the season. However the master, John Walker junior, had the final decision.

Mark Hill, the butcher, came on board in person to find out if Solomon King had appreciated the cask of beef that he had donated as a recompense for the previous confusion. King confirmed that the beef was of the highest quality, an opinion which the cook, and indeed the crew, shared. He said that if the meat retained its excellence, and that the accounting was honest and delivered to him in person, he was happy to initiate a contract, provided that price was acceptable. Mark replied that the current price for flesh meat, of any quality, was twenty-nine shillings and eight pence per hundredweight. He was prepared to sell the best quality – as before- for just the twenty-nine shillings for the next calendar year, after which the price would be adjusted according to the fluctuation of the price of meat. Solomon agreed and the contract was written out twice and signed and dated by both parties.

Solomon King was pleased with Mark Hill's efficient business - almost as much as Mark himself did.

Mark: *Much as I miss my father, he had made many foolish mistakes which, I suspect, he would not have done if my mother was still alive. However, I cannot but admire his self-sacrifice which led to the hanging of Charles Legge, and the scattering in terror of the once-powerful corrupt empire of Ralph Theaker. More importantly it meant the business came to me unencumbered, and I am answerable to no-one. I can make it not just a respected shop, but the best one in Whitby and for miles around. It needs expertise, efficiency and impressive butchery. I shall need an apprentice but I am not aware of any suitable boy who would be sufficiently committed to the trade and who would live with his own family – I wouldn't want a young lad cluttering up my house and shop, and also that would mean that I would have to employ a housekeeper which would cost, and then there would be two strangers infesting my premises and I would have to raise my prices to cover that.*

However…I could kill two rabbits with one shot if I trained Sophia Norrison as my apprentice –she is sufficiently open-minded to accept, and her mother is unlikely to say no. Indeed, Mrs Norrison would probably be pleased with my suggestion and would be very grateful. Then maybe in time Caroline may agree to be my wife...

     *   *   *

While the weather was still keeping friendly, the crew of three colliers assembled round their appropriate ships, which were moored alongside St Ann's Staith in Whitby, all bound for Shields, possibly for their last voyage of the season.

Normally there would be nothing unusual in this: the more experienced seamen would plod away from their homes or lodgings, heads down, holding their sea chests. Their wives, with clinging children, watching them depart, with tears in their eyes at the separation and at the fears that this time their man would not come back. The women wondered why their husbands said so little and why they expressed no feelings; the men wondered why their women made such a fuss, and contained their locked-up fear that they may never see their wives and children again. The young sailors with sweethearts made more of a show of parting with much kissing and embracing; youth feels indestructible. Some of the girls feared they may be pregnant, and hoped that if it were so their man would come back healthy and strong and marry them. But this time things were different; no grunted greetings, head noddings, and shoulder slappings, but more like a continuous swell and mutter of surprise. They were all looking and pointing in the same direction.

But strangely what they were all looking at was nothing.

Chapter 31

The ship *Dolphin*, which had been moored up abandoned and neglected for some months had suddenly disappeared. But business was business, and soon the men were aboard their ships, sorting out their bunks in the fo'c'sle, and preparing for their departure.

The Harbour Master, Oliver Armson, once all the three colliers had been safely beyond the outer harbour, felt he should go to Mr Backas to explain the disappearance of *Dolphin*. Mr Backas had decided to visit the harbourmaster, and they met outside the Golden Lion. It seemed sensible to go in and to discuss this strange occurrence over a pint of the finest.

Armson explained that early in the morning darkness there had been a knocking on his door. It turned out to be none other than James Boyes himself who had come to claim his ship.

"I asked about what he had been doing but he was very reticent about that, except that he had to pay a sizeable amount of money for ransom. There was no doubt that it was his ship, and no doubt that the man who came to claim it was James Boyes. I had no other option except to give him back his ship. I collected the keys and we were both rowed over to *Dolphin*. I was rather surprised to find a full crew of unknown men already on the deck. We completed the relevant documents, and I went home."

"Was there no way you could detain him?"

"No it was all in order. And, as you know, no charges have been made against him. Our hands are tied."

"I have to concur with that. He is a wicked man who intended to do wicked things. It is a shame that he is beyond the reach of the law."

"Samuel Suggett is not beyond the reach of the law, though. He was the man who shot Sophia Norrison. But he was not among the men on the ship, I would have recognised him."

"It is unlikely that he would not have returned with Boyes. Most probably he is not very far away; perhaps Robin Hood's Bay or Sandsend."

"There have been rumours that Boyes and Suggett intend to recreate an organisation like that of Theaker's," said Armson.

"Yes, I have heard that." In fact it was his wife Margaret who told him this, but he did not wish to lose face.

"Unfortunately there are many people who were involved with Theaker who would be happy to join a similar network."

"I think we should talk to Mr Christopher Woods. As Collector of Customs he needs to be involved. Between us we might be able to do serious damage to the violent smuggling trade along this coast."

"An excellent scheme. Perhaps we three could meet at this time in this place each Saturday. And an advantage here we have a view of the harbour. We need to be prepared. Boyes might be planning to unload contraband along the coast, but his ship needs a port."

"Indeed. At least we know what ship he owns, so we can track her. All we have to do is to keep an eye on *The Daily Courant* for *Dolphin* captain Boyes."

*   *   *

At their inaugural weekly Saturday meeting at the Golden Lion the sole topic was the murder of Jack Wheatear. Although it was not professionally relevant to the other two, they were interested, and William Backas was keen to hear the thoughts of intelligent and discreet men.

He gave a thorough account of his conversation with David Dunn. He even included his question about other ways of collecting lant. This evoked much laughter among his colleagues and lightened the darkness of discussing death. However, he did not mention his recent illness, as he thought that the others would consider it a weakness.

Christopher Woods said, "The whole barrel business was clearly a way of obscuring where and when the murder was committed, and therefore we must seek to limit as far as possible the time when Wheatear was killed.

Oliver Armson replied, "Well, I can help there. A ship sailed into the harbour on Tuesday 12th August, needing repair and some stocking of food supplies. I noticed that Jack Wheatear was the only member of the crew to stay ashore; I gathered he disembarked as he was due to marry shortly after. The ship had sustained nothing serious and she sailed out afore noon on the 14th. I remember that as *Freelove* came in on the same day, but she had sustained worse damages and could afford better repairs so she was in harbour for several days."

211

"I saw him at Church on the Sunday after when his banns were published for the second time, which was on the 17th."

"That is excellent, Mr Backas," said Woods, "we at least have a *terminus a quo* but it still leaves several days before the body was found. However I recall that the lant ship left the harbour at about half past seven last Tuesday morning. Eight butts of lant were delivered to the quay the previous evening at about eight o'clock, and I did the paperwork and checked that the barrels were tight. Then I went home. In the morning, that is the 20th at about five o'clock, I was back at the quay and I watched all eight butts being taken aboard."

"Is it usual to leave casks on the quay unattended overnight?" asked Backas.

"Obviously the small casks with valuable contents are locked away. For large low-value cargoes, yes it is common practice to leave them on the wharf. Stealing any of them would be of small profit and if caught it would be not only a criminal offence but also a hanging offence, which is a serious deterrent. And, Mr Backas, your night-watchmen are usually vigilant. I do not recall any such theft being made, do you?"

"No, that is true."

"So we can assume that one of Dunn's urine casks was exchanged for the body in the butt on the quay sometime between about 9.00 at night and 4.00 in the morning. Unless David Dunn himself was the murderer or was unknowingly carrying the corpse in one of his casks."

"I think that is a sound deduction, Mr Woods. So we can be fairly sure that Wheatear was killed sometime after Mattins on Sunday 17th and the absolute latest very early on Friday 20th, assuming it was not aboard the lant ship itself, which seems very unlikely. When the barber-surgeon examined the body, I asked him if he could suggest how long Wheatear had been in the barrel. He said he had examined many corpses which had been in the sea and could say fairly exactly how long they had been immersed; but in this case, because it was lant and not sea-water, and contaminated with the blood, he could not be exact. He suggested anything from a day to five days, but that it was only a guess. However I think that the murderer, unless they were strangely minded, would wish to dispose of the body as quickly as possible."

Armson joined in: "In an ideal situation, Mr Backas, I agree. But the murderer is constrained by limitations. He has to get a barrel, bring Wheatear to it, force the victim into it, then pour in urine —maybe slowly as he explains the reason why he is going to kill him— then stun him, cut his throat, and top up the butt with lant. Then seal it up and exchange it for one of Mr Dunn's within a space of very few hours. He may well have planned to kill Wheatear some days beforehand to ensure it all goes successfully."

"That may well be," responded Backas, "but where would he dispose of Dunn's legitimate butt of urine which he exchanged?"

213

"Which may bring us back to Mr Dunn, as Mr Backas suggested. Was the exchange made in his property? Is it still there?"

"What I judged from visiting Mr Dunn was that his business was a bit disorganised. He is meticulous in the volume he collects from each household, but is quite resigned to the fact that comparatively small amounts of lant are regularly stolen, and that sometimes some of his casks are stolen. He seems to accept these losses provided that they are less than the amount he would have to pay for someone to guard the premises when he is away."

Chapter 32

September slowly slid into October; the number of cold evenings increasing surreptitiously. William and Margaret Backas sat in front of the smouldering coal fire, there were sporadic flames but the heart of the fire was bright red and emanated great warmth. They were drinking cups of mulled wine with fingers of toast. Usually in such circumstances they would be nodding into somnolence; but the murder of Jack Wheatear was always in their minds like lice in a rented bed.

Margaret broke the long silent musings. "William, the more I think about it, the more I am puzzled by the proposed wedding between Wheatear and Abigail Linskill. Although Abigail was apparently going to abandon the Quakers for the Anglicans, she was never seen in church."

"Indeed I agree that the whole wedding seemed strangely unreal; we both felt that when we broke the news to her that Wheatear had been murdered. Since then I have done some research on this matter."

"You never told me."

"That is because I was no wiser at the end."

Margaret was about to make a witticism about William's wisdom at his expense, but refrained. Instead she said, "If you tell me what you found out then maybe we might be able to untangle this knot together."

"A wise idea, dearest. First, about Wheatear. I went to talk to the parish clerk, whose duty is to ensure that everything is in order. He said that Wheatear had told him that he had been baptised in Keysbeck in Farndale, in the

215

parish of Kirby Moorside, in 1709; but he could not produce any certificate. Because this needed to be validated, he had written, on behalf of the vicar, to the incumbent of All Saints Kirby Moorside; but the parish clerk there had replied that there was no decipherable entry in their records of anyone of that name being baptised on or near that time, because a leak in the vestry roof had rendered the relevant pages of the register blotched and illegible. Though he did say that there was a couple called Wheatear who have lived for many years in Keysbeck working a smallholding; but they have never been seen in church, and were considered to be notorious heathens. The vicar accepted the validity of Wheatear's baptism."

"That seems rather dubious."

"I agree. And I think the clerk and the vicar were also of that mind; but what could they do? Being baptised twice would be offensive, so the only other choice would be to accept Wheatear's assertion."

"If the vicar makes that decision, I suppose we have to accept it. But surely, William, a marriage in church is not valid unless both parties have been baptised into the Church of England, and Abigail is a Quaker."

"Indeed, dearest. Which brings us to Abigail Linskill. The clerk had approached the vicar on the behalf of Abigail about having a baptism 'of those of riper years' in order to be married in the parish church. He said that such a baptism required notice, sent to the bishop or the archdeacon, at least a week beforehand by someone who can affirm that she was 'sufficiently instructed in the

216

Principles of the Christian Religion.' Also she would need godparents. She agreed to all this. A few days later Abigail arrived with her cousins Henry and Jonathan Dunn, who had agreed to be her godparents. I suspect, as I am sure the clerk did, that in fact they were Quakers. The vicar was satisfied that she was 'sufficiently instructed' largely because the parish clerk had told him that was the case. I suspect this leniency may have involved a financial donation. This was on the 9th of August. A letter was duly dispatched to the Archdeacon on the next day to confirm that Abigail was an appropriate candidate for adult baptism. As baptisms are normally on Sundays during Mattins, it was assumed that Abigail's would be on Sunday the 22nd when her banns were read for the second time, but she was absent. But many baptisms take place during the week. She could have been baptised the day before the wedding, or she could have had a private baptism in someone's house, though that would have been expensive. But they would have had to grovel to the vicar; he would have been annoyed to be treated in this way."

"So, William, there was no evidence that Wheatear was baptized, and Miss Linskill had not been baptized into the Anglican Church because she had not fulfilled the requirements to do so."

"Indeed, Margaret, so either or both could have gone through the marriage believing it to be valid, and either or both could later complain that the marriage was invalid."

"A clever piece of planning! But did Wheatear know? Or was it just Miss Linskill's plan? After all, if the marriage was invalid, she could claim that she was and always had been a Quaker, and therefore fulfilling her ancestor's will, and owning her father's house."

"But that seems a considerable complexity. It would be simpler for there to be no thought of a marriage. So, if our thinking is correct, why did Jack Wheatear and Abigail Linskill ever plan to get married at all?

The unsolved question hung silently in the air, broken eventually by Margaret:

"Husband, the fire is good; shall we roast some chestnuts thereon?"

"A good thought, dearest."

Chapter 33

In Sunday's Mattins the vicar had prayed for 'Fair Weather': "We humbly beseech thee, that although we for our iniquities have worthily deserved a plague of rain and waters, yet upon our true repentance thou will send us such weather, as that we may receive the fruits of the earth in due season, and learn both by thy punishment to amend our lives." He had repeated this prayer throughout October, but they had not significantly improved the weather, perhaps because at that time of the year rain did little damage to "the fruits of earth in due season", or maybe because there was unrepentant wickedness in Whitby.

William Backas certainly believed that there was wickedness in Whitby. While the vicar was in his prattling box, Backas' thoughts wandered: *Three serious crimes have happened this year: Charles Legge shot George Hill, the butcher, in broad daylight in front of a cloud of witnesses. He had been hanged. But then Sophie was shot by Samuel Suggett the following month; we know who did it but we have not found him yet. And then was the murder of Jack Wheatear; some two months have passed and we are no nearer solving it than a jingle brains will become king of Britain.*

The sermon ended, and Margaret nudged him away from his meditations.

*   *   *

The relationship between a single maid of all work and the lady of the house -especially if the latter had no

219

children- was always something of an embarrassing ambiguity. Sometimes the mistresses had to be *de haut en bas* when orders were given, but often they shared women's work: the cooking, the buying, the washing, the ironing and at those times they are often talking woman to woman rather than mistress to servant. Monday, of course, was washing day when Margaret Backas and Hilda Norrison shut themselves away together in the laundry room which was sometimes very hot, sometimes chilly, but always totally man free. Of course the rough work was Hilda's and Margaret's was more supervisor and organiser; but when needed she would roll up her sleeves and work side by side. Hilda had come to the Backas house when young, and though she had learnt much from her mother, there were still skills she needed to learn and improve. In many ways she was an apprentice, a servant, but without a contract. In many ways they needed each other.

"Tell me, Hilda, how is your sister Sophie?"

"She will never be able to stand straight, and at times she gets agonising pain which affects all up her wounded side. However, she has always been a positive and lively girl and does not bear grudges. In a way I envy her, she is so much nicer than I am."

"You are you, and Sophie is Sophie; everyone has their virtues and vices. You are a great help to me. You will need to pummel the washing in that tub with more firmness."

Hilda did so. Margaret continued:

"Do you think Sophie will ever find a husband? Young men tend to shy away from young girls who are disfigured."

"I think she may be married; it is her character which is so wonderful. But if she is a spinster all her life, I think she will continue to be happy, vivacious and wise."

"Do I suspect from what you say that she has a young man?"

"That is difficult to say, mistress. Do you know Mark Hill the butcher?"

"The one whose father was killed? Yes, I know him. You can empty the tub now, and rinse it; then fill it with fresh water."

"He is a regular visitor, and gives us joints of meat." There was a pause as Hilda obeyed the instructions. That done, she carried on where she left: "He likes Sophie, and jokes are made that they will become a couple; but I think the one he really loves is our mother."

"He must be some score of years younger than your mother; but she is still a good-looking woman."

"I think Mama is flattered; but at present she is obsessed with Jack Wheatear, whom she blames for Sophie's damage. She hates his fanatical religious obsessions. She believes that his intervention on board Dolphin when he took Sophie's arm made her a defenceless target, and was the cause of Sophie's being shot, which might have been fatal. She is adamant that had Wheatear not done that, Suggett would not have pulled the trigger."

"Think you so?"

"I know not. Perhaps he would not have fired; perhaps he would have killed her."

"And your mother is still angry even after Wheatear has been killed in such a hideous manner?"

"It is so. She says she would like to know who killed him as she would like to shake his hand. She regrets that someone else killed Wheatear as she would have liked to do so herself — except it would have been a slower and more painful death."

"I suspect she will forget it in time. Another rinse, please, Hilda."

Another interval.

"Forget it? I think not. Whenever she looks at Sophie she sees Wheatear the cause of Sophie's ugly damage. The irony is that when Sophie looks in the mirror she sees herself."

"Sophie needs to leave the house. Mark Hill is leaving it too late!"

They both laughed, knowing it was not a laughing situation.

*   *   *

Autumn had been kind. In September many mornings had been cool with sea-mist curling into the little alley-ways and yards of Whitby; sometimes the ailing sun had nibbled away at the foggy gloom and by noonday had shone in glory dispensing as much heat as the season allowed. In October sometimes the weather was nondescript for several days on end, sometimes the rain poured out of the sky as if emptied from vast vats and casks; but Nature's foison was bounteous, and not even farmers complained.

Margaret complained; William complained. Month had slid into month; but no-one had solved the murder of Wheatear. Many people had lost interest. An unsolved murder, although gruesome, if it is not solved sadly becomes merely a has-been topic of gossip.

*   *   *

When Sophie was told that Joseph was living alone in squalor in Frank's Yard, she insisted of going to visit him, taking Lizzie with her. It took a bit of time to find his one-room lodging. Joseph was very pleased to see them, though initially he was a bit reticent, embarrassed because of his poor surroundings and his inability to offer them anything to eat or drink. Neither of the girls was concerned about the lack of refreshments, they chattered and smiled as was their wont, and put him at his ease. Sophie praised him for looking after her when she had been shot, adding that without his expert administrations she would almost certainly not be able to walk at all. She said, "I shall ask my mother to invite you to visit us, as she would be very happy to see you again, and our sister Hilda has heard so much about you that she would be delighted to meet you."

"I would enjoy that very much; but I have nothing to give her in return."

"Don't be so silly, Joseph, you have given her a daughter who can walk, such a present is priceless. You told us many stories when we were in *Dolphin*; bring our mother a story – that will please her muchly. Joseph

223

reached out his arms and embraced them both in one big hug, smiling but with tears in his eyes. "Thank you very much for visiting me."

On the way back they were strangely silent, until Lizzie said, "He has but one chair." The only response was a sad nodding.

Before they reached home Sophie's leg was hurting, but she told no-one.

*   *   *

It was later that day that there was a knock on the door of the Backas residence. Hilda answered and there was an exchange of mumbled words which William in his office could not decipher. Hilda left the visitor in the hall and went to inform her master.

"What is it, Hilda?"

"Someone to see you, sir."

"What is his name?"

"He said he would tell you his name."

"Did he say his business?"

"Yes, sir. He said he had come to confess."

Chapter 34

William Backas was non-plussed for some time as lightning thoughts flashed this way and that in his mind. It was not long before he rested once more into reality. "Hilda, give me three minutes while I get ready, and then show the man in." On went the wig, and he discarded the blanket for his formal jacket. He sat at his desk wearing his serious face.

The visitor was shown in by Hilda, who curtsied and then left the room.

"Good day. Please be seated. My name is William Backas, but I suspect you know that."

"I do."

"I gather you have information for me?"

"Yes. I have felt for some time that I should tell what I know."

"And what is your name, and what is it that you know?"

"My apologies, sir. My name is Solomon King."

"I have heard the name."

"My information is about the night of the coronation."

Backas collected a sheet of paper and dipped his quill pen into the inkwell. Ready to record information, he said, "Yes?"

"It concerns Jacob Linskill and his daughter."

"I know this must be difficult to tell what you know, when you have kept it a secret for so long. There is no hurry. Would you like a glass of wine or something?"

"Thank you no, sir. What happened on the night was this. I was younger and stupid. I fell in with a crowd of young men; but I did not know what they were going to do. Wheatear was leading and he had two young men, Thomas Preston and Simon Scott. Kind of henchmen. We went to the house of Linskill the weaver who, as a Quaker, did not show a candle in the window. There was much taunting and insulting, which became unpleasant. Jacob stood his ground, indeed he rather made Wheatear look like a bit of a fool. Jack lost his temper and beat him soundly, knocking him down, but even then didn't stop the kicking. Then the daughter came in from the back room, probably hiding there, she told Wheatear to stop hurting her father. In response he stamped hard on Jacob's right hand, deliberately to disable his working hand. He got Preston and Scott to hold Abigail saying he was going to rape her. At this time I intervened and told him to stop but he hit me with a large stick and I must have been unconscious for a while. When I recovered, I went outside and saw Preston and Scott holding Abigail. I saw the back of Wheatear. His beeches were down seemingly about to deflower her. I seized the stick and hit him from behind and he fell down. Then your constable and the watchmen came. Wheatear, Preston & Scott ran away and your men followed them. I tried to help Abigail and Jacob, but he told me to go away and to forget what had happened, he insisted that I should never say anything about the incident to anyone."

"Which is why you were reluctant to come before?"

"Yes, sir. And as I spend most of my time at sea, I am often unaware of what is happening in the town. I came back later to see them. Jacob's hand was bad, but it was getting better. I understood that he was getting medical help. Abigail was well. As I am telling the truth, I might as well say that I took a liking to the girl."

"Jacob said that he beat Wheatear, and that was why his hand was bad. He was declared out of the Quaker friendship for acts of violence. We didn't believe his account of the event, though all the four told the same story, so there was little we could do."

"When next I came, Jacob was dead, and I was told Abigail had caught smallpox and died. Only much later did I discover that Miss Linskill was alive and had a boy child, the result of her being raped by Wheatear on Coronation Day. And then I learned Abigail and Jack were going to be married."

"Why are you telling me all this?"

"Mainly because I realised that I was maybe the only person who knew what had happened that night and who was prepared to tell the truth. With Jacob dead, I thought my promise to him was no longer binding."

"And because you wanted to marry Abigail? Jealousy perhaps?"

"Maybe."

"Then you realise that I shall have to put you on my list of suspects of who killed Jack Wheatear."

Solomon laughed. "I suppose that must be the case. But their marriage is a strange one. Abigail may think it a sensible thing to marry the father of her child, even

227

though he raped her —which is a capital offence — but it does not seem likely. She said she planned to become an Anglican and abandon her Quaker community? It does not ring true."

"She also forfeits possession of her father's home, now occupied by Esau Linskill."

"I did not know that, sir. But it makes the marriage even stranger."

"Do you have an idea about why they planned to marry?"

"For Wheatear it would be unlikely that he would to be brought to trial for rape once he had married Abigail. Also he would have a family: a wife and son all at once.."

"What would Abigail have to gain?"

"Her son would have a father. But not the best of fathers in my opinion, sir."

There was a pause, then Mr Backas responded, "In my experience as a Chief Constable, women who have been raped often think they are somehow to blame. Perhaps she believes that Wheatear is the best she deserves."

"I feel no-one deserves Jack Wheatear."

"I understand that you visited Miss Linskill before her banns of marriage were read in church. In what state of mind did you think she was?"

"It seems, sir, you are well informed. She was very cheerful about her marriage and her son; but it was not the Abigail I knew. On reflection I think she was behaving like a poor stage actor saying the words by rote."

"She was hiding her misery, you think?"

"Maybe. She seemed to be rather stoical. But she was always strong-minded. If I were her I would probably pretend to be happy, and then strike."

"How strike?"

"If it were me I would kill Wheatear, but I doubt that would be Abigail's nature to do so."

"But if she did wish to kill him, but could not do it by herself, would you help her?"

"I would be very tempted, Mr Backas."

*   *   *

The Saturday meeting at the Golden Lion had become fixed, as it was good for each to keep the others up to date in their interlocking areas of knowledge. Particularly William Backas was eager to find Samuel Suggett and see him hanged, which meant tracking down the ship *Dolphin*, with Boyes or Suggett as masters. He usually made a point of arriving first, therefore, so he could look through The *Daily Courant*, which the publican provided for his customers along with superb ale and a sizeable fire. It was partly pride, and partly his eagerness to capture the villain that he scanned the Ship News in the paper. He longed for the day when Oliver Armson and Christopher Woods arrived and he would be able to wave the newspaper at them and say "I have found it!"

In the event, when the others came in he simply showed them the relevant entry:

For Sale by the CANDLE,

At Lloyd's Coffee-House in Lombard Street

On Friday, 24th instant, at Twelve o'Clock at Noon, precisely,

The good ship *Dolphin*,

an exceeding fine sailer, square Stern, Whitby built, Burden 280 Tons more or less, with exceeding good dimension, well found, now lying at Limehouse Hole, James Boyes, Commander.

Inventories to be had on board, and at the Place of Sale. To be sold by

Francis Featherstone, Broker.

"Well," said William, as soon as they were all settled on a fireside seat with a pint of ale, "He is up to something. I doubt if he has given up being a ship owner."

"He will buy a new one," added Christopher, "and we shall not know which ship is his, as he will certainly not be master of her, at least when he is in any port or coastline where he is known. I suspect the trail has gone cold."

For some time they sat in silence; thinking, drinking, and basking in the fire's warmth. It was some time before any of them spoke:

"He has out-thought us," Oliver sighed. Then he continued, "It is like a game of chess, and we can only hope that he has made his first move, and that eventually we shall win. In the meantime there is only one thing we can do."

He clicked his fingers, "Landlord, three more pints!"

*   *   *

Winter is inevitable, sooner or later; but hope deludes us that it will not be yet. So when William Backas drew back the curtains and opened the shutters he was surprised to see leafy ice patterns on the window panes. He admired the beauty of them but even more he disliked the icy cold which created them. He turned to his wife who was still in bed and said, "Now it is November, winter has come."

"It should have waited a few more days. Come back to bed."

As it was one of those rare occasions when William had little to do, he was back under the sheets with amazing celerity.

A shorter silence, then Margaret said:

"It looks like being a cold and miserable day, husband."

"I know a way of making it warm and enjoyable, dearest."

"I think that would be a very agreeable idea, my love."

Chapter 35

John Walker senior went over to the fireplace, picked up the poker and gave the somnolent fire a few fierce jabs. Flames erupted shrouded in smoke and surrounded by brilliant sparks which soon died and floated up the chimney. He put another log on the fire.

He had invited his son for a discussion.

"My dear son, I would like to talk to thee about Solomon King. I have a special respect for Solomon King, who was once my apprentice and who since then has shown that he could be a fo'c'sle seamen and an effective mate. Some sailors stay fixed as mates for years, sometime for their entire career. Owners of ships tend to command their own ships and then pass the position on to one of their sons. If they wish to find a suitable captain for one of their ships they would be likely to choose someone who had already successfully been a master in another ship. So, in order to promote his career, I would like thee to surrender briefly your captaincy of *Freelove* for the next year's season."

"He is a fine seaman, no doubt Father."

"It would be sensible, as I have said, to appoint Solomon King as master of *Freelove* for this next year, this is not simply to develop his skills, though he could probably become an excellent ship master when thou wishest to retire from going to sea. The treaty with Spain has at last been signed, so a number of ports could be open and profitable. However, the Spanish are, as recent events have shown, not entirely trustworthy. So it would be wise to send King in advance to spy out the land."

"The Spanish market could well be prosperous. It needs researching. I am sure that Solomon King could fulfil this role wisely and perceptively."

"I am glad thou and I agree on this."

"Certainly, Father."

"And, as next season thou shalt not be sailing about round Spain, thou shalt have time for social activities."

"Social activities, Father?"

"I think it is time thou shouldst be married."

"Married?"

"Yes, John. Do you think that I have not noticed thee looking at Dorothy Frost at our Meetings, and I hear of the cunning ways that thou arrangest secular meetings with her in the street."

John blushed. "Father, Haggersgate is near Flowergate, so it is likely that we should meet from time to time. Besides she is two years older than I am."

"So, thou art sufficiently interested in her to ascertain her age? I do not think that her father would object if thou spoke to him about thy wish to marry her. She is young enough to have many children, but do not prevaricate. The family is prosperous, and will provide a handsome dowry. Her mother's family is well connected in the Quaker community."

"This is largely patriarchal chatter, Father. All this talk of money, children and connections."

"All this is very important. Have I missed something out?"

"Of course you have, Father: She is kind, thoughtful, witty and charming. She is beautiful, her hair...I see, Father. You have tricked me into saying these things."

"Thou hast my blessing, son, and a marriage within the year would be good for all. First, I shall speak to Mr Frost."

"Thank you, Father."

Thus it was that Solomon King became master of *Freelove.*

*   *   *

William and Margaret Backas sat in front of the fire, a single candle burned, the shutters closed, the curtains drawn. Outside, the gloom had turned to darkness and the stars were brilliant. It was a cold evening.

Margaret looked at William and he nodded. He put down his folio of documents about the workhouse, and she speared her knitting needles into a ball of blue wool. Their thoughts were put into words, "An early night, dearest?"

"Yes, husband."

"I'll see to the fire and then be up," said William handing her the candlestick.

Chapter 36

There had been some mild December days, and most ship-owners had taken advantage of the weather to ensure their ships were suitably stripped down and repaired in their winter anchorage. Then, unheralded, the wind switched from south-westerly to north-east, bringing swirling snowflakes followed by pounding, bouncing hail. Large jade green waves were threshed into white spume which crested over the harbour walls. No-one would venture out of their homes on such a day, unless it was imperative.

Now that his career was developing well, and consequently he had a greater income Sol paid off his rent agreement for his leaky room in Gaskin Bank, and moved to a more salubrious and weatherproof suite of rooms in Church Street. It was much more spacious and comfortable and was somewhere that he could invite people to visit, without them worrying that they might be attacked and robbed on the way.

Solomon King had woken early in his new lodgings. He usually did so when on land as he found sleep was sporadic without the pitch and yaw of a ship, the sounds of creaking timber and cordage, and the snap of wind on canvas. After completing his ablutions, he dressed in his new smart clothes, as befits a ship's master. White breeches with polished pewter buckles below the knee. A clean linen shirt with elaborate cuffs. Silver buckles on his new shoes. A new plum-red coat, with superfluous buttons on the wrists to show he did not roll up his sleeves and do manual work. And a fine cloak to keep the cold at bay.

While he was admiring himself in the mirror, there was a knock on the door. He was surprised that anyone would visit at this hour and in this weather. He also felt a bit ashamed to be found dressed above his station, as he was not yet *de facto* master of the ship. He was more surprised when he opened the door and found two girls.

"Quick, come in!" he said, hurrying them –and a shot of hailstones– inside. Then closing the door behind them.

Once they had brushed their coats and stamped their snow-clad shoes, one said, "Good morning, Mr King."

"Good morning, Mr King," said the other.

"You have the advantage of me, ladies. Who are you?"

"I am Sophia Norrison, and this is Elizabeth, my sister."

"I have heard of you. What is it that you want of me, so early in the morning?"

"We want you to grant us two favours – one each."

"In which case, rather that standing in the hall, you had better come in." He led them in and invited them to sit down, they bobbed and then sat. Mr King gave a polite nod, sat down, and inquired, "What is your wish Miss Sophia?"

"You will have heard of the ship *Dolphin*?"

"Indeed; I think everyone in Yorkshire has heard of it."

"Can you name all the people on the ship who brought her back to Whitby?"

"This is a strange favour."

"This is a prelude to the favour. Humour me please Mr King."

"You two and your mother, of course. Matthew Willson, whom I knew as an apprentice; he acted as master and brought the ship home. The late Jack Wheatear, who could forget him? Hans Nielsen, an apprentice from Norway. I do not recall the names of the cook and the carpenter. Have I missed anyone out?"

"Yes."

"Let me think a moment." A pause. "Ah, yes. Joseph who has no surname."

"You see, Mr King, many people forget Joseph. I do not forget because he looked after me when I was shot in the leg. Had he not known how to treat my wound and had he not known how to nurse me I probably would have died in *Dolphin*. I would have expected that such a hero would always be employed, even as a common sailor. All his employment since *Dolphin* were two short-term coastal sailings."

"And he is poor?"

"Yes."

"And you have no money to give him?"

"Even if I did have money, I would not give it to him. He is a young man, skilled in his trade. He is a proud man; he wants work, not charity. But he is a negro, and his father was a slave, a freed slave. Owners and masters do not appoint such men, even if they are skilled. Usually the seamen themselves do not mind working with men of any colour, whatever their father did, provided they know what they are doing and do it well."

"And your favour is?"

"It is known that you have recently been appointed as master of *Freelove* - as your clothes confirm. If you have not yet appointed a mate, my favour is that you appoint him as such under you in *Freelove*."

"You are a good advocate, and your favour is for someone else which is commendable."

"It feels as if you are about to say 'but', Mr King."

"You are right. But I shall not make a judgement until I have heard what Miss Elizabeth will ask as her favour."

"My favour," said Lizzie, "is that if you grant Sophie's favour, you do not mention that we have had anything to do with it."

"That is a good request."

"Will you grant our favours?" asked Sophie.

"I will grant your favours, but on certain conditions. First, I shall ask around to see if he is suitable. Second, that I shall interview him to see how knowledgeable he is for the post in question. Thirdly, that I shall discuss the decision with John Walker, the owner of the ship. And fourthly, that he gets himself a surname. Agreed?

"Certainly. Your favours are already a quarter fulfilled. Joseph has a surname; he is Joseph Fox."

"I am glad to hear it. You are brave to come to visit to see me in such vile weather."

"And thank you for listening to us as adults."

"Yes," said Lizzie, "And I think your coat is splendid, sir. A stylish cut and a magnificent colour."

Sophie said goodbye and virtually dragged Lizzie out of the building. "Really, Lizzie, you are so childish sometimes. Why on earth did you comment on his clothes? What will he think of you?"

Solomon stood in front of the mirror, and murmured to himself: "Yes, it is a gorgeous colour, and beautifully cut."

Chapter 37

The early months of 1730 were dreary, miserable and cold. The merchant ships crowded into Whitby's inner harbour, many with their sails, masts and yards taken down and they looked like a cluster of hulks which would never sail again. In fact they were being repaired and restocked for the new season. Eager and ready for a new year, fair weather, and prosperity.

The weeks passed and William Backas was frustrated. His day-to-day work was done and done well, but always tantalising him in his mind was the murder of Wheatear. He seemed to be making no progress. The Justice of the Peace said that this was one of many cases where there simply was not sufficient evidence, and therefore it must be abandoned. He evidenced the case of Suggett who was known to be criminal but had apparently disappeared, and of James Boyes who had allegedly done many criminal things but could not be arrested because there was no evidence.

William was not going to give up; but how? He looked out of the window as the sun, orange like an egg yolk, spread its half-hearted light over the crisp snow of the garden. He thought, *Why cannot murderers wearing distinctive footwear trample clearly in the snow as they go from the place of crime to their home, or better in mud which then freezes?*

*　　　　　*　　　　　*

William was no more cheerful when he went up to the marital bed.

Once they were both abed, Margaret sat up, fluffed the pillows and drew the eiderdown up to her chin.

"I have some important information, William."

There was a long silence but for the rattle of the window panes.

"Indeed?"

"Indeed. There is a ship registered at Burlington, named *Prosperous*."

"And Queen Anne is dead. This too is no great news, Margaret; there are three vessels called *Prosperous* in Whitby, and probably as many at Burlington. But how did you come by this information?"

"In the usual way, my dear."

"Which usually means that there is more than a fifty per centum chance of there being some truth in the rumour. However it should be easily checked." Then he added, "Your expression suggests there is more."

"Oh yes. There is more."

"No teasing, dearest."

"The owner is registered as a Mr James Boyes. The master is Mr Guest."

*   *   *

"So Boyes is back! Ah, that is news indeed; let's drink to it!" Oliver Armson and Christopher Woods agreed with Backas' suggestion and drank heartily.

The information about James Boyes' vessel *Prosperous*, captain Guest, had recently been confirmed by the Burlington harbour master. They all agreed that they should keep this ship under close surveillance in the light of the ever-increasing rumour that Boyes was planning to replace Ralph Theaker as the *Provider*. The demand for illicit goods was strong and constant. Since Theaker had been driven out, he had left a vacuum. The customers were likely to trade with people they know and can trust, and Boyes was well-known in Whitby. The *Dolphin* episode if anything had enhanced his reputation as someone who sailed close to the wind and was not caught.

The outcome was that Woods, Armson and Backas drafted a letter to be sent to all the harbour masters along the coast between Yarmouth and Newcastle encouraging them to be vigilant, and to send any information about James Boyes, the ship *Prosperous*, the captain Guest, and find out the names of as many of the crew as possible.

Business over, they sat back, got out their clay pipes which they filled and lit, and ordered another round of drinks. Relaxing in a semi-torpid state of silent pleasure they felt all was momentarily well. Occasionally a brief conversation slipped out.

Suddenly the noisy chatter in the main bar went totally silent. This happened rarely, and the trio were shaken back to alertness. It was the kind of response which might happen if a Frenchman had dared to enter their pub. The eerie quietude seemed to last for ever, broken at last by a woman's voice:

"Where is Mr Backas?"

"In the backroom, Madam, over there; but they may not wish to be disturbed,"

"Fiddlesticks!"

Mrs Backas swept into the back room, closing the door behind her.

"I am sorry to interrupt your meeting gentlemen."

Mr Woods sprang to his feet, fetched a chair for Margaret to sit on, and made her feel comfortable. "How can we help, Mrs Backas?"

"Thankyou Mr Woods, but I have come in the hope that I can help your group."

She now had all their attentions.

"I understand that although Boyes has returned you have nothing with which to convict him?"

They all nodded.

"But Suggett has committed a crime; though he cannot be found?"

Mr Armson replied, "Yes, that is true, Mrs Backas. He has either died or is in a different country or is hidden right here. We have been looking for him, but if he is in disguise or in a good hiding-place it is a very good one."

"And do you agree that he is a clever and cunning man who may take a pleasure in appearing so disguised that you cannot see him? That he likes to taunt you and play games?"

"Yes, I think he is just that sort of man. But that does not help us catch him?"

"I may be wrong. It may be just a coincidence; but sometimes people who play such games often go too far."

"To what are you implying, Mrs Backas?"

"Could he be Mr Guest?"

"Guest is taller and fatter than Suggett, he has a scar on his face, his hair is of a different colour and he dresses

243

his hair in a totally different way. He also wears totally different kind of clothes. So many differences."

"All of which can be created. But consider he plays games. If you jumble the letters of his name G, U, E, S, T you can make S, U, G, E, T: Suget. I think he has played a game too many."

William stood up, "That is marvellous, Margaret; you are so clever!"

Mr Armson also stood up. "That is very clever; and if we look at him more closely we may well see that he is Suggett. But my suggestion is that if he is our man, we must not in any way let him know that he has been discovered for the time being. He may lead us to greater crimes."

Everyone agreed, and the meeting was over.

William held Margaret's hand all the way home. He was so pleased that he had a wife who was clever, and who would be brave enough to enter a bar full of men. "You were wonderful, Margaret. I was so proud," he said. Margaret squeezed his hand, and they went home in silence; but smiling.

Chapter 38

Solomon King was now the master of *Freelove*, and had appointed Joseph Fox as mate. Already King had shown wisdom by waiting until early March at Shields until the weather was likely to be good, and not take serious risks. She was laden with coal in the fore hold, several barrels of smoked herrings in the aft hold, and four six-pounder cannon with shot and powder carefully stowed in the great cabin. She was ready to sail.

King's future career depended on how well he fulfilled the exploratory voyage to Spanish ports. Whatever he was thinking or feeling he must be seen and to be obeyed as if he were a captain with at least a dozen years of experience, so he stood on the poop deck and eagle-like surveyed all that was done as the ship was towed out of the harbour. The seagulls were unusually silent, calmly gliding effortlessly on the spiralling thermals. It seemed a good omen. When *Freelove* was loosed out in open sea, she caught the freshening south-easterly wind and scudded smoothly across a gentle ocean.

The first port was the Hythe at Colchester. The coal was sold at a good price, and the corn was purchased cheaply. All hands were set to cleaning the coal dust out the fore hold, so the corn could be taken on board. Also cloth was taken aboard, as well as water and food. Thus provisioned, *Freelove* sailed away to Spain. Being at sea was what Solomon loved, and sailing into Spanish ports that they had not visited before was a challenging prospect, a mingling of excitement and fear.

*　　　*　　　*

"I hear," said Margaret "that opinion agrees that Wheatear was killed by one of Abigail Linskill's family, as revenge for his raping her, and his being instrumental in the death of her father which has resulted in many unpleasant consequences."

"It is a possibility," replied William "Jonathan Dunn seems to be a likely candidate. It seems that he possibly killed Simon Scott. Henry Dunn is a weaver and would benefit if Abigail did not lose her father's house by marrying Jack Wheatear. Henry and Abigail could make a thriving company, they are both very skilled. But this is far from being proved as yet. We must not leap to the end."

"It has also been said that Abigail herself was the killer. Few could understand why she chose to marry him; but it makes sense if she lured him into believing she loved him and then when he felt secure, killed him. And she killed him slowly in that barrel. He deserved it; rape is a capital offence and he has escaped the law."

"Jack Wheatear was a bad man in his youth, but he repented that wicked life."

"William, I am ashamed of you, you are even beginning to sound like Wheatear. We are talking about a thirteen-year-old girl, innocent of the wickedness in the world, who was raped, and who was the first cause of her father's death. Wheatear robbed her of her innocence, and two years later she would certainly be motivated and capable of murdering him."

"It says in the Gospel of St Luke- 'if he repent, forgive him'."

"Just quoting a few verses from the Bible, and saying 'I repent' does not wipe out what has been done. God is not stupid, and he is not going to be deceived, by just a few words. If I were The Lord Chancellor of England, I would pardon anyone who murdered a rapist, and if I were God himself I would send anyone who raped a mere child to Hell where demons would have his member slivered as thin as a butcher cuts ham!"

"I am not supporting rapists, my dear, whatever the age of their victims. But murder is murder and anyone who kills another person, even if they know he is a rapist, is still a murderer and must face the legal consequences."

"I think all women who are raped should be allowed to kill their rapist. Men think they are better than women, they take advantages. Men in the street look at us in that way they have, in their foetid imagination unstringing our corsets and raising our skirts. It's no good pulling that face, William, I still get those looks! Indeed, women much older than me are subject to such unwarranted attention."

"You sound as if you are insulted if they look, and insulted if they don't."

"What a typical manly response! You men, you have no idea what women's lives are like and what we have to put up with. We are owned by our fathers when young, and by our husbands when we marry.

"I don't think of you as being owned by men, Margaret."

"That is not the point, William. Even in this modern allegedly enlightened age women are not understood by men."

"And I suppose women understand men?"

"Of course we do. We can read them as if reading a book, my dear husband."

Chapter 39

Shields; early morning. William Backas had sailed up from Whitby in a coastal ship, which had a cheap cabin for ordinary passengers, and a more salubrious one for wealthier ones. It was the latter that Backas had used; his salary was modest, but he could claim expenses. He disembarked, and it was not much after that when he found himself standing in front of the house in Tanner's Bank, listening to the noise of the looms in the adjacent wooden shed.

Backas knocked on the house's green door which was speedily opened by Abigail Linskill herself. She greeted him heartily, saying that she had received his letter and, as agreed, had chosen a time when both her cousins were at home. She then led him into the main room and introduced them, namely: Henry, a weaver and the older brother, and Jonathan, the younger and a sailor. Abigail then invited Mr Backas to sit down on the finest chair in the room which he did, sweeping his coat tails aside with habitual nonchalance. The two brothers, who had sprung to their feet when the visitor entered, sat down again after which Abigail was seated, being the lowest of status in the room. Backas began:

"Thank you all for allowing me to come and talk to you. I come in my official role as the Chief Constable of Whitby, and I do so in the hope of finding some information which will lead me to the identity of the murderer of Jack Wheatear. I realise that this be difficult and intrusive, especially for you, Miss Linskill,

249

who hoped for a marriage and found a funeral. Are you all willing to answer questions in front of us all? I would be happy to do so in private if you so wish."

This was answered by mumbled assent and nodding of heads.

"In that case I would like you to be the first, Mr Henry Dunn. If that is agreeable?"

"Aye, I am happy to go first, sir."

"I would like to clarify your family a little. Your mother had two first cousins. One who married Jacob Linskill and the other married an attorney in Pickering?"

"Indeed, sir. Both of them now dead, alas. Our mother was right fond of them. By the by, our mother says sorry, but she cannot come."

"Her absence is not a problem. Abigail wrote in her letter that your mother would probably not be present."

"And our father died years back, he were a ship's carpenter. Lived in Whitby."

"Are you related to David Dunn, lant man of Whitby?"

"So I've been told, sir, but distant."

"Have you met him?"

"Nay, not that I know."

"You are a weaver?

"Aye, sir. And many in my family afore: granddad, greet-granddad and his dad, who met George Fox."

"Are all your family Quakers and weavers?"

"Aye, in me Mam's line, all did."

"You may not wish to answer this question, but what did you think about Abigail marrying Jack Wheatear?"

"We have nay secrets, one from t'other. I told her strait, I did. I said, 'Abigail you're a canny lass, you're a bonny lass and you're a Quaker and a weaver. And as for Jack he's nowt but a greet feckless lump. And if you marry him, you'll lose your father's house'."

Abigail's face was impassive, unreadable. Backas continued:

"Thank you, Mr Dunn. Now Mr Jonathan, can I ask you some questions?"

"Aye, that you can, sir."

"Do you agree your brother's opinion about Abigail's proposed marriage?"

"That I do. But me being a seaman not a weaver, I have no worry about Abigail marrying one. Apart from that, my brother is reet. Wheatear is not part of the Quaker community, and he treated our sister horribly, I find it difficult to forgive that. I know nowt about bairns, but so far Jonas seems to be like most others: cannot really talk, cannot really walk, cannot piss and shit in the right time or place, and wakes us with his bubblin in the night. He'll grow up; then if he is like Abigail I shall be pleased; but I worry that he may grow up like his father, so the less he saw his father the better. I didn't like the idea of the wedding, and I am glad he be dead."

Abigail remained immobile, apart from sporadic eye-blinks.

"I gather you sailed in a collier a few months back which was caught in a storm, and you left the ship at Whitby. During that voyage a sailor died."

"Aye, he fell from the top yard. He panicked. I tried to rescue him, but I could not get near enough. Such things happen in storms."

"Can you remember his name?"

"I think he was called Scott. Stephen Scott, I believe."

"Simon Scott."

"Aye, that was him."

"Did you see much of him?"

"He was on the same watch as me. But I kept well away from him, he blathered on about nonsense. He seemed to think I was a woman, another reason why I kept away from him." Jonathan delivered this comment with a smirk.

"Why did you leave the ship in Whitby, when you originally signed on to sail to London?"

"The ship needed repair after the storm; I could find a bunk on another ship before she was seaworthy again. Also I did not trust the judgement of the captain."

William nodded, the turned towards Abigail.

"The man who died on this ship was called Simon Scott. Miss Linskill, have you heard that name before?"

"Yes," said Abigail so quietly it was almost a whisper.

"Am I right in thinking, Miss Linskill, that he together with Thomas Preston were, on coronation night, those who held you while Wheatear abused you?"

"Yes. At the time I did not know who they were, I learnt their names later from your constable and the night-watchmen."

"Abigail, your cousin Henry said you and your two cousins have no secrets one from another. Is that the truth?"

"Yes, sir."

"So you would have told them what Simon Scott did?"

"What they did, yes. I may not have mentioned their names, though. I was not with my two cousins here until sometime after the event."

"Do you not think it is a strange coincidence that Thomas Preston and Simon Scott who aided Wheatear in his crime against you are now dead, and that now Jack Wheatear himself is also dead?"

"A coincidence, maybe; but not a strange one. Surely, Mister Backas, in your work you must have come across many coincidences that are random and have no significance. Preston and Scott are dead; they were sailors, and sailors die at sea."

"That is true. Miss Linskill. Back to the subject: is it true that Solomon King was also there when Wheatear, Preston and Scott abused you?"

"Yes, sir, he was."

"And what did he do?"

"He tried to save me from being raped."

"Were you pleased with him?"

"He was brave, and tried to save my father and myself; he was badly hurt. Then your constable and his men saved us from worse."

"What is your relationship with Mr King?"

"We are friendly."

"Just friendly?"

"Yes."

"Have you ever thought of marrying him?"

"No. Well, maybe. When he visited us when my father was still living I had a brief childish ardour for him, and I sensed he felt much the same for me. It faded, and I put it away with my other childish things."

"Do you think Mr King wishes to marry you?"

"I doubt it. He has never spoken to me about that."

"Would you be surprised if he asked to marry you?"

"Surprised, yes. As I said, we are just friends."

"If he asked you to marry him would you be pleased?"

"Mr Backas, you go too far with your questions. I have only recently buried the man I was to marry!"

"My apologies, Miss Linskill. But I would still like to ask some more questions."

"I suppose that is what you have come for."

"Is he such a good friend that he would help you whatever you asked of him? Like help you with some heavy work?"

"I can see where these questions are going. You mean might I ask Solomon to roll a large heavy cask?"

"Would you?"

"I don't know. I have never been in such a situation. And I cannot envisage I would ever have the need or the whimsy to ask such a question."

"So Solomon is just a friend, even though he rescued you on coronation night?"

"No doubt that was his intention, but he failed as he was not strong enough. And if he had succeeded I would not now have my lovely son Jonas. As it says in the Bible,

'Out of the strong, came forth sweetness'. Jonas is my sweetness. Henry made a toy loom for him which he plays with all the time, a born weaver. Of course, Jonas' surname is Linskill, and he will keep that name no matter whoever I marry. So my father's house is mine, but Jonas will inherit it after me, no matter whom I marry."

William Backas realised he would get nothing more from that line of questioning. So he moved on: "Miss Linskill, can you please tell me why you planned to marry Jack Wheatear?"

"At first, I hated him and his two colleagues. But over time I became more understanding. They had been young, drunk and foolish. As a Quaker I read the Bible, and I ponder in quietude the significance of the words within, and allow my inner light to shine so I see what is meant more clearly. I was reading the story of Jesus on the cross. I cannot say which book and verse (Jack would have known) but it was the crucifixion —an abuse far worse than what I had suffered- and Jesus said, 'Forgive them, for they know not what they do.' And then all the hatred and anger ebbed away from me, and I felt happy and freed. Have you read Bunyan's *Pilgrim's Progress* where Christian gave three leaps for joy? I felt like that. Then I met Jack who had experienced something similar. And he was so good to me, and I felt happy to be with him. He also told good stories, and he would make me laugh."

William Backas was touched; but wondered if she too told good stories.

Chapter 40

In the absence of her husband, Margaret Backas decided it was time to clear from the back yard the hideously grim tarpaulin-covered butt. Every time she was in one of the back rooms she could see this *memento mori* in which Jack Wheatear had been killed. She had frequently asked William to have it removed, but he always said that it might be important as evidence when the murderer comes to trial. Margaret said that one barrel of lant was much like another and that he was being nibetty-pick, and that he was never in the back rooms so he never had to see it.

So she asked Hilda to send a message to the Lantman that the butt was for sale. Margaret said that Hilda could keep the money, which spurred her on in her task, even though Margaret was not the owner of it. Dunn arrived with his cart at midday; Hilda took him round to the back, and removed the tarpaulin from the cask.

"Is this the butt that Wheatear was killed in, Miss?"

"Yes, sir, it is. The very same."

"There is no true lant therein?"

"There is a fair amount of lant - all of which is mixed with blood."

"I can't sell that; but I'll pay you for the butt."

"Can't sell it? Are you making fun of me?"

"What do you mean, Miss?"

"That cask, with its blood-stained lant, is worth a fortune at St Hilda's Fair. You can sell the carmine urine in little bottles, not only as gruesome mementoes, but they would probably also be able to cure unpleasant diseases such as scrofula, gout or the French disease. You know more than I do about medicinal cures. As for the butt you could auction it at the Fair as well; I would imagine that some people would pay quite a few shillings to own the very cask that Wheatear was murdered in."

Dunn's eyes lit up with avarice. The price that they agreed on revealed that Hilda was a shrewd bargainer, and it was far, far higher than Margaret would have achieved. Dunn spat in his grimy hand and held it out for Hilda to do likewise; she spurned this physical settlement, feeling she had suffered enough unpleasantness for one day.

Dunn trundled the butt to the road where his patient horse, easing her hoofs in turn, stood otherwise in calm resignation harnessed to the waggon against which at the rear were two planks for Dunn to roll up the barrel. Whether Dunn's eagerness had caused him to be careless, or whether some passing urchin had tampered with one of the planks, or the butt's staves were faulty, or the hoops had not been sufficiently firmly replaced, was not clear; but the cask veered off the battens falling heavily into the road where it splintered asunder. Dunn was transfixed, but Hilda snatched the horse's water bucket and managed to save a significant amount of the valuable liquor, by which time Dunn had managed to accrue some more vessels. That was something, but most of the liquid had gushed onto the road and disappeared, washing down already clogged gutters.

Surprisingly for Hilda, a very dishevelled and very dead rat was thrust out of the cask among the torrent of tinted piss. She gathered it up in a piece of cloth and took it into the garden. She washed her hands at the pump before going in and finding Mrs Backus who was reading a book.

"Mistress?"

"What is it Hilda?"

Hilda told the events, including the fact that the butt had broken and a dead rat had been spilled out, and ending with a plea that she could have permission to bury the rat in the garden.

Mrs Backas was somewhat puzzled. "Why would you want to bury in the garden a dead rat that has been festering in a cask of lant for several months?"

"I forgot to say, Mistress, that this rat is a special one, a kind of pet in our family. He has a damaged ear and a long stripy tail, and is called Wilfred."

"Of course you can, Hilda; but probably it would be better not to tell the master. He may not like the idea of a dead rat in the garden."

"Thank you, Mistress."

When Mr Backas returned he didn't even notice that the butt had gone.

*   *   *

The following Sunday was Easter Day, so William Backas assumed that, once home after the church service, it would not be correct to labour over the workhouse documents. Instead he sat with Margaret and recounted to her his interrogation at Shields of Abigail Linskill and her two cousins Henry and Jonathan Dunn and their responses as accurately as he could - which was considerable. When he was finished he asked for her opinions.

"My first thought, William, was that I wondered why you had not interviewed them individually; but as the discussion continued it became clear to me why you did. Like players, they had all learnt their parts, and most of the time they kept fairly rigorously to the script. It was also interesting how they reacted to your questions. Of the three of them, Henry seemed to be the most honest. My second point concerns the idea that Abigail's son Jonas would inherit Jacob Linskill's house because he played with a toy loom. That was ludicrous. Any attorney would make nonsense of such a claim, which she must surely know. I also wondered why Jonathan Dunn admitted that he was in the same collier as Simon Scott. He made it sound like honesty; but —as you told it— it came across as trying to pre-empt existing evidence. There is no point lying about something you can easily be checked. Lastly, I was not convinced by his reason to sail in the collier when the weather was so vile; if he needed the money why did he not sail on to London, which is what he signed on for? I was not convinced by his reason for leaving the ship at Whitby."

"Thank you for your thoughts, Margaret, you have been very helpful. You are right about the evidence that he was aboard. Mr Armson, the harbour-master, recorded who was on the ship and who left the ship at Whitby as there had been a death aboard and there might be an investigation as to whether it was accidental or no. All the rest of the crew stayed on the ship, only Dunn left her.

Chapter 41

Although they were both Quakers, John Walker Junior had married Dorothy Frost on Friday 17th July 1730 at the beautiful Wren-built Anglican church of St Benet's, Paul's Wharf in London.

It cost them both, and they were declared 'no longer in fellowship' by the Whitby Quaker Meeting. Quaker marriage was not accepted as legal at that time, which meant that in law a wife was a mistress and their children were illegitimate. This could create legal problems, for example if a Quaker died intestate their estate would not go to their children."

John Walker and his wife Dorothy had settled into their house in Haggersgate which had been given as a dowry by her parents who lived next door. It was a spacious building on four floors. The top landing, with windows appropriately small, provided suitable accommodation for servants and for apprentices. It divided into two parts, one for the male, and one for the female servants, with each part having its own separate staircase. The ground floor included a hall, John's study, the dining room, the kitchen and the scullery. The first floor was the withdrawing room, the main bedroom, and the necessarium. The second floor had a guest room; the rest was reserved in the hope of children. There was a cellar where food was kept cool, where beer could be brewed and a row of barrels were ready to be filled, leaving space enough for any small cargoes.

Dorothy at first had brought a maid from her parents' home to help her with all the cleaning and organisation. Between them there was much hard work, but it meant that they became friends as they never had before and there was a lot of laughing and giggling. In the first week at home there seemed to be a cart arriving at the door every few hours with furniture old and new, casks, cases, boxes of documents to fill up John's study, and wedding presents.

After the first week was over there were a number of visits, some social, some commercial. John had a few apprentices, but as he had not been able to accommodate any of them at his father's house in Flowergate, the apprentices either had to live with their parents during the winter or he had to find them accommodation, neither of which was practical or effective. When his parents had moved to Grope Lane, there was a little more room for them, though his brother and his sister still stayed in the house. Now he had his own home he could have his own apprentices *in situ* and he could teach them properly. Word went about that John Walker junior was looking for apprentices.

A housekeeper was also needed; the requirement was that she should be mature, but not old, and worldly wise. It was understood that she would, amongst her other duties, look after the apprentices and keep them in order when they were in the house. Also when Dorothy had children, she would help care for them. The one chosen was Mary Hardwick, 23, daughter of a ship's carpenter who was currently in the Walker ship *Freelove*, with Solomon King as master.

There was also a vacancy for a maidservant. Of those who applied, Dorothy chose Elizabeth Norrison, who was only 13, but Dorothy and John were also young, and were keen to have staff that had not already developed fixed ideas about this kind of work, so they could train them as they wished.

*   *   *

Margaret and Hilda were doing the ironing; or, more precisely, Margaret was overseeing the work. Hilda did not really need to be supervised, but both of them enjoyed the opportunity to have a woman-to-woman talk. How else could they find out what was going on, considering how inept men were at exchanging information:

"How fares your sister Lizzie?"

"She has gone to work as a maid in John Walker's house."

"The old one or the young one?"

"The young one, who recently married."

"I imagine she has found a good billet there."

"She is happy there; she is learning much."

"Has she any particular friend?"

"Oh yes, mistress, there is a Norwegian sailor, one who was on the *Dolphin*."

"I have heard of him. I think he is called Nielsen."

"Hans Nielsen, though he is often referred to as 'Niel Handsome' in jest, as he is very good looking."

"I hope it goes well with her; often good-looking men can be trouble, especially if they are considered to be a hero."

"Oh, mistress, Lizzie is a very sensible young woman." She paused and then added, "Well, maybe *somewhat* sensible."

"And what about yourself, Hilda? Is there any young man on the horizon?

Hilda blushed, squirmed a bit, raising her shoulders and with eyes downcast. This all for a moment, a brief moment. Then she was upright, her chin raised her eyes wide and fixed on Margaret's, and her whole face suffused with smile. "Well....There may just be a young man who is interested."

"And who is he?"

"Matthew Willson."

"I don't think I have heard of him."

Hilda frowned. "You should have heard of him, mistress. He was one of the heroes of the *Dolphin*. After the ship was taken by the crew he became the master."

"You are right, Hilda, I should have known. But it is often the way that if a group of people do something heroic, only two or three of them receive the acclamation. For example poor Joseph, also a *Dolphin* hero was, I am told, living in poverty. On the other hand it may be a benefit not to be famous." Hilda nodded sagely, then Margaret continued, "Are you going to become married?"

"Gracious, no mistress!" she shrieked, momentarily hiding her face with her apron. Then, "It is early days. I do not know what he feels for me. I have not even told my mother. I would not have told you if you had not raised the matter."

"You think that he may be fond of you?"

"Several times when we have passed in the street, he smiled at me raising his hat and wishing me good day."

"Did you smile back?"

"Indeed, mistress. Why would I not?"

"Is that as far as it went?"

"Only this last Saturday when you sent me to the market to make some purchases, he was there. He came over to me and offered to carry the parcels. How could I refuse? He walked me all the way back, and we talked a lot. He said he would like to meet me again."

"And?"

"I said that I would like that."

*   *   *

Elizabeth was in the cellar being trained in how to use the smoothing iron for different kinds of fabric. Dorothy Walker was watching but it was all a bit dull, and she took the opportunity to give Elizabeth advice about how to behave when the apprentices come to live in the household; namely, she should keep away from them if possible. She should be polite but wary; as young men who had experienced all-male shiplife for most of a year were likely to be untrustworthy. Lizzie was a sensible girl in many ways, and appreciated her mistress's reticent caution. She put the iron down on the trivet and listened as Dorothy read out the names of the apprentices who would descend on the house at the end of the ships' sailing season. When she said 'Hans Nielsen', Elizabeth gasped and suddenly felt very drained and shivery. Suppressing her outward symptoms as best she could, she put on a blank expression; but she could not control the colour of her face nor could she control her heart-rate. Dorothy noticed nothing, largely because there was a knocking on the door.

Amidst of all this domestic business, Elisha Root and Michael Cornelius rapped on the door. John opened it himself, knowing that Elizabeth was in the cellar with Dorothy. John was not going to allow anything to spoil his honey month, so he greeted his visitors with smiling happiness.

Elisha said, "Not only hast thou forfeited friendship by marrying in a steeple house, but also it hath come to our attention that when thy ship *Freelove* sailed, she had four cannon aboard. That is against one of the fundamental rules for Quakers: that we should be pacifists - no violence, no fighting and no involvement in warfare. Thou must repent of these wicked errors, and it may be a long and humble time before the Meeting can accept thee back into our friendship."

John readily accepted that he had done both deeds which were against the Quaker ethos, and he accepted that the offences would mean that he would be unfriended perhaps for some time. It was a stunning surprise; Elisha, who had expected a lengthy argument, was speechless. John showed them to the door. Elisha left in silence; Cornelius was also silent, but with the greatest difficulty of managing neither to smile nor to giggle.

Chapter 42

Walker junior was so busy that he failed to notice the arrival of *Freelove*, and he was a bit surprised when Elizabeth knocked on his study door to say that Mr Solomon King was in the hall, awaiting audience. Walker was delighted and ushered King into his study, asking

"What is the news, Solomon?"

Then he realised they were both standing.

"Sit down, sit down, sir. *Freelove* is a beautiful ship is she not? What is the prospect of trade with Spain?"

Solomon sat, smiling and gesturing with lowering of his hands to indicate that John was talking too much and too quickly. When Walker calmed down, sat down and was silent, Solomon spoke: "I learned on the quay that you are living here now," he said, "and that you are married to Dorothy Frost. Allow me to congratulate you, and wish you much happiness."

"Thank you. I like being married. You should try it some time. My father told me that you were rather fond of Abigail Linskill."

Solomon smiled, but said, "I do not think he should have told you that. Yes, many years ago that was the case."

"Not that many years ago. You are still young and she is now available."

He smiled again, raising his shoulders in a shrug and moving his head from side to side, which seemed to say 'maybe'. But he changed the subject.

"About Spain. I shall put all the information on paper for you, sir. In brief, Spain is very varied, and the present peace may not last very long, but there is trade to be done there. Hence my advice: one more year trading with Spain."

"And in the meantime?"

"We should be able to fit in three coal runs before the end of the season."

"You have done well, and I appreciate your competence. Next year of course, I shall reclaim my beloved *Freelove*. However, I have spoken with a ship owner who is looking for a good master for her for next year. I shall recommend you for that post, if that is agreeable."

"Very agreeable, sir."

*   *   *

The atmosphere of the Golden Lion Saturday Club varied from week to week, though the ale was constant. This day was somewhat gloomy.

They had all read the *Daily Courant* which had recorded the arrival at Deal of *Prosperous,* master Guest. Unfortunately since then there have been several vessels called *Prosperous* which had left Deal, but none had Guest as master; worse than that, there were no ships at all which had left with Guest as master. *Prosperous*, master Guest, seemed to have vanished.

"Maybe his *Prosperous* is yet to leave Deal," suggested Woods. "She may be leaving as we speak."

"Unlikely, Christopher," replied Armson, "Though it is a pleasing thought. It is expensive to linger in a port as there are dues to be paid, and the ship is not earning money. In short Gentlemen, I think that Guest has defeated us, again."

"I think not," replied Backas. "We all know that the Ship News in *Daily Courant* enables people to track a particular vessel: owners and part-owners, merchants, and those who have husbands, relatives or children aboard. But it is not an infallible text. There are many reasons why a particular ship may not be recorded: for example, laziness, incompetence, bribery, foggy weather or the name was misread. If any of these applied then sooner or later the ship and master's name would appear somewhere else. This has not happened, so we can be fairly sure that the ship's name and the master's name have deliberately been changed."

"Yes," interposed Woods, "that is precisely what Armson said."

"Agreed; but what we can deduce is that, most probably, the ship's name was changed, or painted over, and either the captain's name was falsely given or there was a new master. However, Boyes has comparatively recently sold a ship and bought another one, so it is unlikely that he would buy yet another so soon. Similarly he places considerable trust in Guest as master. Again it would be foolish to change captains at this stage. I think that *Prosperous* sailed out of Deal —at dead of night or with obscured name- and that the master was probably Suggett."

"That seems likely, William," said Armson, with something of a sneer in his tone, "but not helpful. You are saying that we are looking for a ship whose name and master are unknown to us!"

"You are right," replied Backas, "It is certain that we are in the territory of supposition. But it would be a near certainty that Suggett, whom Boyes trusts, has been given some task to undertake, possibly some smuggling enterprise, as that is his line of business. It also seems likely that Suggett would keep his Guest alias out of pride, and because he would have no reason to think that anyone is aware that he is Guest. If this is the case, where would you sail to buy contraband good, which is conveniently near Deal?"

Christopher Woods smiled, as he experienced a eureka moment, "I would imagine it must be The United Provinces where he could accumulate a fine collection of items for smuggling."

"Indeed. And where do you think he would sell his contraband? It would have to be somewhere he knows, somewhere he has contacts, and somewhere he knows there is an effective process of taking the items ashore and distributing them speedily."

To which Woods and Armson cried out in unison, "Robin Hood's Bay!"

After a few happy minutes, Woods said, "Of course, it could be Sandsend."

"Or Ravenscar," added Armson.

"Or Runswick," added Woods.

"Or even Whitby," added Armson.

"All right," said Woods, "There may be a large landing of contraband goods, which may be on this coast, but we have not the slightest idea where or when it may take place. It is possible that *Prosperous'* new name was a Dutch one.

Armson had the last word: "Without this knowledge, we do not have the facilities to cover all the likely places and times,"

Nothing else could be said of this problem, so more ale was needed.

*   *   *

In the following week the meeting at The Golden Lion was even more disheartened, and assembled in silence.

After a long period Woods drank the rest of his ale, belched and then said, "We are stretched already. We do not have enough men or money to deter, let alone terminate, smuggling on our coast. For example, we only have one Riding Officer. Last year the Inspector of the East Coast Ports, came up to investigate smuggling on this coast between Tees Mouth to Old Peak, visiting all the ports in our range. He submitted a report."

"What was said in the report?" asked Backas.

"He said it was 'a fine and comely coast', but that smuggling was endemic and one of the worst was Robin Hood's Bay 'where running of goods is commonplace'."

"So nothing we don't know already?"

"You're right. Any of us could have written the report without him troubling to make the journey."

"Typical of government reports!"

"It wasn't all bad, though, William. The area that we are responsible has been reduced to the coast between Redcar and Old Peak. It is an improvement, perhaps; but it doesn't solve our problem, namely we don't have enough men. We have asked our member of parliament to endeavour to persuade the powers that be to move a militia unit to encamp near our coast to reduce this tax avoidance. The response was that it was felt that an armed force attacking our own countrymen smacked too much like state internal police forces that are found in tyrannical countries such as Russia, Prussia and France."

There was little else they could do except fill their tankards and their pipes.

*   *   *

After a few weeks of comparatively pleasant late autumnal weather, Whitby and most of the North-East coast was sliced by sickles of icy sleet and struck by fierce and changeable winds which snatched tiles from rooves, blew rancid detritus down the streets like grapeshot, and imprisoned those who could stay indoors. Those whose work forced them into this turmoil stumbled through it, wrapped up hunched and huddled, keeping close to the buildings, lurching from one grasped solid object to the next and praying that the mountainous waves rearing up over the waterside would not seize and pound them into a spumy death. Fishermen stayed at home as their cobles and keelboats heaved and clattered, tugging at their quaysides ropes. The night brought no release and little sleep. On late November the wind subsided, but the temperature dropped, the rain turned to hail which bounced prettily but viciously on the hardened ground, and the whole sky seemed one massive cloud of gloom.

At midday, the sun was still a pale disc which could be watched with open eyes.

Several vessels had been expected in Whitby harbour. Oliver Armson stood on the quay waiting for ships to come, even a battered wreck was good news. Along the quayside were several silent groups of women, their shawls wrapped round them, their bonnets tied firmly under their chins, their eyes trying to pierce the greyness, huddling together for shreds of warmth.

Fortunately all the ships that were expected, and some that were not, arrived – many in a poor state. Luckily, although many of the sailors -and all of the ships- were bruised and battered, there were no fatalities.

It was Nature's signal that the shipping season was over.

*   *   *

It was becoming something of a habit. At the end of the working week Mark Hill would choose a piece of meat or poultry and have his boy take it round to Mrs Norrison in Atty's Yard. Then Caroline would send Sophie round to invite Mark to dine with them on Sunday after Mattins, no matter what the weather was like.

At first Caroline had tried to fashion this meal as a serious gathering, and sought to develop serious discussions about the vicar's latest sermon. Unfortunately Mark often fell asleep in church during the sermons, considering it as a well-deserved and undisturbed rest after a busy week. Sophie was frivolous such as remarking how often the vicar said 'erm' during his sermon. Hilda was the only one who was prepared to treat the sermon seriously, but then she would ask a question like 'How can God be three in one?' which not only failed to generate interesting conversation, but rather resulted in an embarrassed silence. Caroline had given up turning these meals into something worthy and educational, which was a great improvement.

This was especially the case as Joseph Fox had been invited for the first time. Sophie and Lizzie knew him already and liked him enormously, and Caroline had admired his work in *Dolphin*; but it did not take long for both Caroline and Hilda to share their enthusiasm. He was clever and witty, and could tell a good story. They didn't think much of his singing though, as it grated on their ears and did not sound like music at all.

Joseph was very pleased to inform the company that Solomon King, master of John Walker Junior's ship *Freelove*, had chosen him as mate, and that they had sailed round the coast of Spain, trading. He said it was a great responsibility, but he enjoyed it. Joseph had asked Mr King why he had been chosen for the post, to which he answered that it was by his talent alone. Joseph thought that was very flattering, though he said that someone influential had probably put in a good word for him.

At an appropriate moment, that was when all had finished, wiped their lips and placed their napkins on the table, Mark said to Caroline, "Mrs Norrison, would it be acceptable if Sophia became an apprentice to me? She is strong so there would be no problem about her cutting up flesh; but she would have to learn all the cuts of meat etcetera. I would not expect payment, as in the near future she would be cheaper than my hiring a young qualified butcher. I think all young women should be skilled enough to earn a living, especially when..."

Caroline cut short this sentence, sensing what he would say. "I think that is a kind and helpful idea. But it is Sophie's decision to make, not mine."

They all looked at Sophie who nodded politely towards Mark. She said, "Mr Hill, I appreciate your offer. Your mention of chopping up carcasses is perhaps that you have been made aware that I am skilled in dealing with implements of violence." There was a pause before the rest realised what she was alluding to, then there were smiles and titters. She continued, "And I would be happy to be your apprentice, provided the contract is clear and acceptable." More smiles and approval nodding of heads. "But," Sophie continued, "if this, Mark, is a clumsy way of asking if I would like to marry you, then you will have to produce something far, far better!"

All were happy.

Joseph insisted on clearing the platters and helping with the washing up; tasks which he always thought was the norm for him.

Chapter 43

Solomon had just finished his breakfast when there was knock on the door which he opened. There stood a man of about forty, dressed in a rather ordinary manner, but smart. He was slightly stooped, but he had a cheerful demeanour. He touched his hat politely and said, "Am I by any chance addressing Mister Solomon King?"

"I am. And who are you?"

"I am the senior clerk for the attorney in Baxtergate.

"And the purpose of this visit?"

"My master has sent me to see if you were able to come with me to his office."

"Now?"

"If it please you. My master was to say that it was a matter of some importance."

"Wait there and I shall be with you shortly," said Solomon, shutting the door. He pondered for a while wondering what was appropriate attire for discussing 'a matter of some importance' with an attorney. He eventually decided there was no point in changing his clothes, he simply put on his hat, scarf and outdoor coat. Thus dressed, he left the house.

Part of him thought it may be a trick, but the clerk was still there, and still cheerful. The latter said, "We shall be walking, if that is acceptable with you."

Solomon King nodded, and drew tight his thick coat. There seemed to be no point in having a conversation, as their words would be shredded by a vast agglomeration of seagulls tearing the sky with their noisy hunger.

Solomon was soon in Baxtergate, soon at the house, soon inside the house, soon gone through the polite necessities, and soon sitting opposite the attorney.

"Mr King, have you been in touch with your father recently?"

"No, I have not been close since the death of my mother. I believe he has subsequently married, and I presume he has other children."

"I regret to tell you that your father died last Thursday at his home in Guisborough."

"How did he die?"

"It was a sudden heart failure. He must have died quickly."

"Thank you for letting me know," said Solomon, rising as to leave.

"One moment, sir, there is the matter of the will."

"What will?"

"Your Father's will. As you are mentioned in the will, I am duty bound to read it to you."

"If you must."

The attorney started reading the will, "Whereas it is the duty of every Person to consider how transitory and uncertain is this Life, and that it is appointed for all Men are to die..."

"Is this a will or a sermon? I thought wills were composed largely of standard phrases."

"Usually, yes; this is rather unusual; but just be patient, please, Mr King."

Solomon shrugged his shoulders as a grudging 'yes'.

"..moved with these Considerations, I, Francis King, merchant, of Guisborough, being in good Health of Body and sound Mind, do make and declare this my last Will and Testament in Manner and Form following as touching and concerning such Means and Estate of what Nature or Kind soever, which it hath pleased Almighty God of his Mercy and Goodness to bestow upon me..."

Solomon interrupted once more: "God Almighty had nothing to do with bestowing goods on my father; mainly it was acquired by greed and sharp practice."

"Please, Mr King, please let me continue."

"My apologies; but my father never liked me, and I did not like him. All this is getting round to me being appointed as executor of a will which bequeaths all he had to his wife and children. But go on; you have your work to do."

"I do hereby constitute and appoint my Son, Solomon King, as sole Executor of this my last Will and Testament..."

Solomon was about to say something at this juncture, but decided to remain quiet.

"...to take the Burden of said Office concerning all that I shall die possessed of or invested or shall belong unto me at the time of my decease wheresoever and howsoever in any manner of wise the debts by me owing and my Funeral Expenses being thereout paid..."

Solomon put his head in his hands. This seemingly endless incomprehensible document appeared to suggest that his father had gambled all his money away or spent it on loose women, and that Solomon was going to have to pay off the debts.

"...I give and bequeath unto my aforementioned son all my Money, Mortgages, Bonds, Bills, Notes, Ships, Shipping and Parts of Shipping Profits and all other of my Estate of what Nature Kind or Nature or Quality soever." The attorney added that the rest was just a matter of the signatures of the witnesses of this document."

"But what does it all mean?"

"It means that you are his closest relative. He did not marry again, and has no other children than yourself. In short it means you are going to be one of the richest men in Whitby."

Solomon remained silent for some time, then he shook his head slowly from side to side, and muttered, "Oh dear."

*　　　*　　　*

When Sophie awoke with the dawn, she noticed a letter had been slipped under the front door. It was addressed to her, but she did not recognise the handwriting. Intrigued, she opened it. It was brief:

Miss Sophie Norrison

It has come to my attention that there is going to be a very large delivery of contraband goods at Robin Hood's Bay on Christmas Eve at dawn. If the weather is too fierce it will be that afternoon, or dawn on Christmas Day. It has been organised by Mr Boyes. You will need to tell the appropriate authorities.

A brown thing

Chapter 44

She was even more intrigued after having read and reread the letter. She was surprised that Ralph Theaker's henchman, if indeed it was from him, knew what he was known as; but then she realised that he would know everything to do with James Boyce. Then she wondered why it was addressed to her. After much thought she realised that they knew that she would pass it on to appropriate authorities and not just throw it away, but also he wanted it to be read by someone who was not a member of the appropriate authorities, but also would not pour the information into the river of gossip.

*   *   *

Sophie Norrison had given William Backas the note which she had received and he had passed copies round to his colleagues before the regular meeting in the Golden Lion. They all knew that 'the brown thing' had been a man in the gang of Ralph Theaker, the Provider. They also knew that there were rumours that Boyes and Suggett were seeking to take over Theaker's criminal network.

"So," asked Backas, after the three had filled their tankards and made themselves comfortable as a sign that the Golden Lion Meeting had begun, "How are we to interpret this letter?"

Christopher Woods said, "Well, as Collector of Customs, I would like it to be an accurate piece of information which will enable us to capture a lot of criminals delivering and receiving contraband goods."

"But it is information from Theaker's gang. Are they trustworthy?" asked Backas.

"In this instance, I think yes. We are being used, it is true; but when criminals fight criminals we can often benefit."

Oliver Armson joined in the discussion, "It may be a double trick, Woods. If you put all your best men, and both your Revenue sloop and your cutter, in and around Robin Hood's Bay, Ralph Theaker and his probably well-armed gang could be landing enormous illicit material in another likely landing place. They could perhaps even be landing in Whitby, as a kind of invasion. If so William Backas with his constable and watchmen will hardly be able to stop them. My job as the harbourmaster does not entail my repelling a sizeable influx of feral criminals with their pistols and cutlasses. And if Backas and I survived such an event we would be to blame, and probably lose our jobs."

"I think you are exaggerating, Oliver. I still believe, although it is a gamble, that we have an opportunity that shall in all probability never occur again. And that we ought to plan it like a battle; the greater danger is not that they will be smuggling ashore large quantities of illicit goods. In all honesty that is something we in the Revenue deal with fairly regularly, though maybe not on this scale. The real danger is that we find them off Robin Hood's Bay, and they defeat us."

"My vote is with you, Christopher. Law and order is my job, as you have pointed out. We should get together and make a plan. Oliver, this is more our business than yours, and as you have doubts we will not involve you in the details – so you can have a clear conscience if it fails."

This time, their meeting finished abruptly at this point. No last round of ale.

*   *   *

That afternoon William Backas and Christopher Woods visited Solomon King at his new residence in Baxtergate, where they were well received.

Once the formalities were over, and they were all sitting in a pleasing and tastefully decorated drawing room, Solomon asked them the substance of their visit.

Backas said, "Everything we wish to talk to you about this afternoon is a strictly confidential."

"I am intrigued. But why are you telling me?"

"Mr Woods and I thought of you because we know you to be honest, loyal, trustworthy, and have the facilities to help us."

"I liked the adjectives," retorted Solomon with a smile, "but it seems that there may be a sting in the tail."

"You are right. It is of major importance and there is little time. Will you help?"

"In theory yes; but you will have to tell me what it is, and I reserve the right to say no."

"We wish to hire a ship, ideally a fine ship which is at present overwintering here, and we are aware that you know which might be the most suitable for a task."

"I know many good vessels. I have sailed as master in John Walker junior's ship *Freelove* this year, and know her well, but the terrible weather prevented her taking a late

282

collier run —or even two. The owners would appreciate additional fees. She is a solid and spacious vessel, some 300 tons. I am very pleased with her. What would you do with her?"

"We wish to hire the ship, maybe with you as Commander, and a reliable and honest crew. We only need a few days, but there will be dangers."

"Only a few days; I assume that implies you wish the ship to sail locally."

"Yes. We are fairly certain that there is going to be a large quantity of contraband to be delivered on Wednesday in Robin Hood's Bay. We wish to capture that and as many men and boats involved in this crime."

"This is very short notice. Presumably you anticipate some fighting?"

"We would like it to have at least two six-pounders, and a swivel mounted gun on the poop. Additionally I and some of Woods' revenue men shall also be on board."

"That is a heavy request, Mr Backas. *Freelove* is owned by a Quaker who has already been unfriended for carrying guns on his ship. Finding other ships for this task will almost certainly be difficult, or more likely impossible, to prepare in time."

At this point Christopher Woods took over the conversation: "This is likely to be one of the largest blows we can strike against the smugglers, and would set back this crime for some time."

"I know that the crew would be happy to sail again, and to earn some more money before the winter sets in hard. And we are all keen to reduce smuggling; after all, no-one likes tax dodgers. But I do not want to cause Mr Walker any trouble. Come back tomorrow, and I may have a plan. What is the opposition like?"

"We have no idea what the delivery ship will be like, probably of 200 tons or more. She may have a swivel gun, but it will be unlikely for her to have cannon. Probably most of the crew will be armed with muskets, pistols and swords. She may be flying a Dutch flag. Once the ship is moored and the fishing boats from Robin Hood's Bay, believing everything is safe for them, have collected their first round of cargo, that is when the action begins. *Freelove*, (provided we can hire her), which has been lurking out of sight near Homerell Hole with my revenue cutter. We shall have a spy on the cliff who will be our eyes. They will wave a white flag when the ship has arrived, for us to prepare. When a red flag is waved we shall move in. I shall head for the shore, and *Freelove* will head for the anchored vessel. Your function is to make them let me and others come aboard the ship, so we can apprehend smugglers and to seize contraband goods."

"A risky enterprise, Mr Woods, but a necessary one. It might even be rather exciting. I will do my best; but Mr Walker may refuse. I do not want to make more of a rift between his family and the Society of Friends. Be prepared for a refusal."

*   *   *

Margaret and William spent many hours going over and over the evidence, thinking and rethinking, seeking the identity of the murderer, or murderers, of Jack Wheatear.

"William, there are still whispers that the murderer was Abigail and that she not only killed Wheatear, but also, disguised as a man under the name of her cousin Jonathan Dunn, killed Simon Scott. She was playing a cunning game to kill the villains responsible for her rape, and thereby for ruining her life."

"You are the queen of rumours, my dear, many of which are rich in truth: but I hardly think that Abigail sailed, let alone killed anyone, in a ship when she was still feeding her baby son."

Margaret looked crest-fallen, but rallied: "I believe that Abigail wanted all three of them dead. We know not how Thomas Preston died. Maybe she persuaded her cousin Jacob to kill Simon Scott. She certainly did not wish to marry Jack Wheatear, for all that she says. Maybe she cut his throat while he was helpless in the butt of urine."

"By herself?"

"Maybe. But I grant it would be easier if she had a helper."

"Who had you in mind?"

"Maybe one of her cousins: Jonathan Dunn, or even Henry."

"Or even another woman?" Margaret ignored this, thinking William was having a jest at her expense – which was not the case. William moved on:

"Maybe Solomon King?"

"Why him?"

"He and Abigail were very much in love. It was you, Margaret, who told me so."

"Yes, they were; but that was a long time ago – a youthful obsession. Did she not deny having any interest in Solomon when you went to question her?"

"I'm not sure. I think their mutual attraction grew into love. I suspect each loves the other. Solomon may well have been willing to kill Wheatear for Abigail even if he thought she did not love him. But I think Solomon may well love Abigail, but dared not show it. If that is the case he should take advice from the poem:

> Then Cupid whispered in my ear,
> 'Use more prevailing charms;
> You modest whining fool, draw near,
> And clasp her in your arms.'

It was written by a vicar, so it must be good advice."

"Dearest William, you should have taken that advice from the poetical vicar when we first came together. I thought you would never show any real interest, and when you did I had to wait for aeons of time before you asked me."

"I am glad I did ask you. I thought you must surely have many admirers who would have made much better husbands than me. That is why it took me so long to summon up my courage. I had known that I wanted you as a wife within a month of meeting you!"

"As late as that? I knew the second time we met, before the week was out."

William clasped her in his arms and gave her a loving kiss. Then he said, "My dear Margaret, I love you so much."

"I am glad you do." Margaret blushed, and then smiled - not a casual smile but one that suffused her whole face. Her voice now soft as an embrace, "My dearest, I believe that we shall soon be parents."

It took a few seconds for William to realise what she had said, then he hugged her once more and kissed her. "Oh, darling, this is great news. I am so happy. You must take care, and not do any heavy work; let Hilda do it all. You must lie down often and rest..."

Margaret cut him short, "William, William, be calm! It is not certain and, even if it is, it will be several months yet."

"I am sure you will have a child, dearest, and I hope that he will be a boy."

"And I hope she will be a girl; but, my love, such matters are in the hands of God."

"Amen. And I hope God chooses properly."

Chapter 45

William Backas and Christopher Woods arrived, in a state of febrile agitation, at Solomon King's house. They were led into his study, where they all sat down.

King held up a document. He said, "I was always rather suspicious of attorneys, but never again. Today I have bought *Freelove* from John Walker and all the other owners."

"How have you managed to do that?" asked Backas.

"And how did you manage to do it so quickly?" asked Woods.

King held up another document. "In a fortnight I am going to sell *Freelove* to John Walker and all the other owners. By that time she must be in the condition when I bought her."

King held up another document. "This grants you jointly a lease of *Freelove* for ten days. By that time she must be in the condition when I leased her to you jointly. I shall expect the money to be paid either until you have claimed and received your various expenses or within six months whichever is the earlier. If there is any fighting in this enterprise, it shall be when I own the ship, so any Quaker owners will not be involved. John Walker did not ask, and was not told, what we are going to use her for. I shall be the master. The mate is Joseph Fox, he is already endeavouring to collect the same crew as sailed in her last month. It would be churlish to pay them just for one day, so I have settled on what I believe is a suitable payment for a dangerous enterprise, which is made clear in in this document. All you have to do is sign here."

The documents were read and signed by Christopher Woods, Collector of Customs, and William Backas, Chief Constable.

*   *   *

In the evening Margaret and William settled down before a roaring fire. Normally when there was a warm fire William would have nodded off, but his mind was too busy. Margaret was not doing any knitting because she was hoping for a child, but did not want to make any baby clothes until it was certain - as that would be tempting providence. So she decided that if she couldn't knit anything for her little girl, she wouldn't knit anything; nor, for that matter, would she do any darning or sewing. Hilda could do all that.

William said, "I cannot wipe out the murder of Wheatear from my mind. Ideas are tossed around in my brain like a five-man boat in a storm. I think that we might be able to clarify the matter if we together go through all the possible people who could have done this deed."

"I agree. I still think that the most likely person is Abigail. What woman would marry her rapist?"

"What rapist would become a religious fanatic? These things happen."

"And why has she not already claimed her father's house? I suspect that she was waiting until Wheatear was out of the way. She never for a moment intended to marry him, it was all a charade. All that stuff about her boy Jonas inheriting the house was about as true as a

289

mountebank's puffing his medicine at a fair. And talking of inheritance, Abigail might have heard that Solomon King was going to be very rich as soon as his father's will had passed probate."

"Wheatear was dead, Margaret, before anyone knew Solomon was going to be wealthy. Even Solomon didn't know. But as a ship master he would be fairly prosperous."

"She had quite a fancy for him at one time; and he would be a better husband. Killing Wheatear would leave the way for her to marry King."

"All she had to do was to cancel the wedding."

"Maybe she realised at the last minute, and felt she couldn't go back on a promise. It may seem unlikely; but I have heard of many people who would rather kill than to be the butt of jests and to be enveloped in embarrassment and shame."

"Even if that was so, Margaret, I do not think that she was so full of anger against Wheatear, as the method of killing suggests."

"A woman's love can transmogrify into hate very quickly."

"Would she be able to do all the heavy work with the butt?"

"I don't see why she couldn't, William. There are numerous lads on the street who will roll a cask for a penny or two, that is not unusual. But to assuage your doubts, let us assume for now that she could have had a partner in the murder."

"Are you thinking of her family? They were too reticent and too glib when I interviewed them. They seemed to be hiding something."

"I was particularly thinking of Jonathan who possibly killed Simon Scott."

"There is no evidence that he was murdered at all."

"But it is rather suspicious that both of them were on the same ship."

"Coincidences do happen."

"But events which are not coincidences happen more often."

William then moved the discussion on: "Who else do you think could be a likely murderer?"

"Solomon King. He intervened in Wheatear's violence and rape; it must be galling to him that he was unable to prevent a pregnancy. He had been very fond of Abigail for some years, so when King heard that she was going to marry Wheatear, he must have been overwhelmed with jealousy and anger."

"And King would certainly have been able to have committed this rather complicated murder. But we must not just look for evidence relating to Wheatear's crimes on coronation day."

"No. His so-called conversion was a nightmare. His endless unquenchable spouting of quotations from the Bible was by itself enough motive for killing him."

"And he hardly ever attributed the texts correctly. But I was thinking more about his time in *Dolphin*."

"They say that he would not have been in Dolphin if he had not annoyed his fellow seamen in *Freelove* with his tedious Bible reading out loud, so he was transferred to *Dolphin* at Lisbon."

"That's right, Margaret; but I can't really imagine a gang of sailors, irritated by his Bible thumping, gathering together after they had disembarked to commit the complicated murder we are faced with. They would be much more likely simply to chuck him overboard at sea."

"The plan of Boyes, Suggett and McDaniel to sell into slavery Caroline Norrison, her two lovely little daughters and the freed man Joseph, was a heinous crime. All those affected must have felt not only anger but eagerness for revenge."

"And frightened. We know that Boyes is not far away…"

Margaret cut in: "And Suggett, who is masquerading as Guest, which I worked out."

"You did, and very clever too. Both these could have killed Wheatear, the so-called hero of *Dolphin*. And no-one knows where McDaniel is. He was last seen at Lisbon, but now he could be living next door."

"Living next door to us?" This jest lowered the tension for a while.

"Nice wit, Margaret. But back to serious thinking."

"The real heroes of *Dolphin* are the Norrison girls. They are sadly overlooked, which is typical: the men take all the credit."

"To a certain extent. I hear that Elizabeth has not been overlooked by Hans Nielsen."

"That is not the same, and you know it!"

"Yes, that was trivial. But several of the men have been overlooked. People who are not acknowledged when they have done good deeds can become jealous and angry. Once someone's self-esteem has been damaged they can become very dangerous."

"Are you suggesting that one of the good crew, who saved the women, and brought the ship safely home, could be murderers?"

"Yes, either individually or in a pair, or more, the carpenter, the cook, James Fox the sailor, were, or felt they were, neglected in praise for the part they played. They could restore their pride by killing Wheatear who is not only seen as a hero by many, but as a bungling fool by others."

"You mean Mrs Norrison? She thought he was worse than a bungling fool."

"Indeed. She makes no attempt to hide her view that if Wheatear had not interfered with his burbling about commandments Suggett would not have fired at Sophie, wounding her leg. She believes it was Providence alone that prevented her from being killed."

"And she has said several times that she hates Wheatear and, if she finds the opportunity, she would want to shoot him or stab him, and she would do it as pleasure, as what he deserves."

"High drama, Margaret; she should go on the stage. She is not going to kill anyone. I have eliminated her from the list of suspects."

"That seems obtuse, William. Why in Hades have you chosen to take her off the list? Surely she must be near the top of the list?"

"For two reasons. First, because most murderers are unlikely to spread their intentions in such a profligate way, like a careless farmer sowing seed. People who say they are going to kill someone rarely do. And secondly, because it is not a woman's way of killing. They are more likely to use poison or, if in a spontaneous rage, anything to hand, for example a poker, a knife, or a saucepan."

"What is all this nonsense, William? Is murder a matter of taste or discrimination? If someone is planning a murder, but wears a dress rather than a pair of breeches, then they have to reach for the poison rather than the pistol? Does it apply to all women? Do aristocratic women, the middling sort, and the lower classes have different fashions and reach for different poisons depending on their rank? Do aristocratic murderers kill with dainty hairpins? It is too ridiculous. Women, in anger and hate, may well say they will murder someone, and they may do it or not. That is a difference between women and men because women are open and honest and say what they feel. Men usually hide their feelings, if they have any. So don't you say what women will or won't do, because women are more complex than men. So, William, if the killer of Wheatear is a man, he is more likely to be captured than if she was a woman."

"No doubt true, Margaret; but I was just referring to a list of the weapons used by male and female murderers which I read in the papers. They would be as true, I suppose, as any such information which is printed in a newspaper. Yes, a female or a male murderer can kill with virtually any implement that has been used in the history of murders."

"I am glad you realised that I was right. If Caroline Norrison is the killer, she could have had an accomplice."

"Any suggestions?" asked William.

"Any young men who are keen on her daughters."

"Which would be Hans Nielsen and Mark Hill. However, I think the liaison between Elizabeth and Nielsen has not been long. It would not be a good move for a girl to say, 'Will you help me kill someone?' when she should be saying something more like, 'I think you are so handsome' or 'Kiss me'. It would be a very risky test of devotion. Mark might kill someone for Sophie, but she is a very determined young lady, and if she wanted someone killed she would insist on doing it herself. Not only would she not ask Mark to help her kill Wheatear, but she would not tell him what she was going to do, because he would not wish her to take the risk of being caught, and would seek to deter her. And she would certainly not wish him to kill anyone for her sake."

"What about Joseph Fox?" asked Margaret, "He has not been treated well; he could be a willing partner in murder."

"I don't see any reason why he would want to kill Wheatear, particularly in that gruesome way. He hardly knew him."

"And what about the Quakers? People seem to think that all the Christians except the Quakers have the privilege of killing people? "Thou shalt not kill" is as binding to Anglicans as to Quakers. In fact I happen to know that there are issues in the Whitby Quaker Meeting."

"Are there, Margaret?"

"The Quaker movement is comparatively new, much less than a hundred years old. It is important for the Quakers to ensure the movement will survive. What were all those years of suffering, imprisonment and persecution if the sect collapses before it celebrates its centenary? Part of the Whitby Quaker Meeting is to stick with the old rigorous rules, shutting themselves from the world. Elisha Root heads this group. The other part is more flexible, more involved in the larger world, choosing to live in the 18th and not the 17th century. Michael Cornelius heads this group. The split is visible. The proposed marriage between Jack Wheatear and Abigail Linskill was to be in Whitby, it was a farce, and puts the Society of Friends in a difficult position. A Quaker woman plans to marry in an Anglican Church, she was prepared to be baptized, but does not attend the publishing of her banns, her family pose as godparents, but they were still Quakers. The whole thing is ludicrous. The easiest way to put a stop to this on-going ridicule of Quakerism was to dispose of the proposed Anglican husband."

"You mean that Elisha Root killed Wheatear?"

"It is a possibility, William. Root might have thought that the death of an Anglican rapist might be sufficient to collect the Quaker sheep back into the sheepfold."

"So we have covered all the likely people, though we might have missed a few."

"For example David Dunn, the Lantman, could easily have killed Wheatear in the way he was killed."

"But what motive had he to do so?"

Margaret ignored this question and continued: "We must not forget James Boyes, Samuel Suggett and Alexander McDonald. Their plans were foiled, and Wheatear had an important part in that. Any or all of them have a motive to kill Wheatear, and the method of the killing would be just the sort of death they would choose for him. We have no knowledge of where they are, which is rather frightening, as they would no doubt wish to kill others involved in spoiling their Tangier plan."

"And I am sure that Wheatear managed to accumulate quite a number of enemies in his wild early years."

"But are we any closer to being certain whom the murderer was after all these months? Have we any evidence sufficient to send the criminal to the gallows?"

"In a word, Margaret, 'no'. But in a sentence: Would you like a glass of Portuguese wine?"

"Yes, William, I would. You certainly know how to please a woman."

Chapter 46

The early morning was cold with a sharp but moderate north-easterly wind. The sky was strangely lucent, like a blue velvet cloak gently smothering the last lurking stars. The revenue cutter had arrived at the rendezvous earlier than planned, only to find that *Freelove* was already there: anchored and showing no light. It was quiet but for the mild wind jostling the rigging and the soothing waves rippling on the craggy shore. Imperceptibly the indigo night faded into another dawn. The mates were scanning the now visible cliff top. No white flag. Time passed very slowly, and nothing happened. Was there no flag-man on the cliff? Was no contraband ship coming? Were smugglers unloading illegal goods at Sandsend, laughing at how easily Christopher Woods had fallen for their trick?

Then a white flag. Anchors were raised; men climbed up on the yards ready to unfurl the sails; muskets, pistols and cannon were loaded and primed. Then the red flag. The sails snapped in the wind and the ship and the cutter moved slowly at first and then gathered speed. Rounding Ness Point, there was a vessel visible in the pre-sunrise light, and there were the cobles; some loading, some full making for the harbour. *Freelove* sailed straight for the anchored vessel while the revenue cutter sped to the harbour, the helpful north-easterly blowing their sails to their full portliness. Solomon King, through his telescope, identified the vessel as flying the Dutch flag. *Freelove* was within half a mile before everyone on the brig realised what was happening and even then there was confusion aboard. The crew on *Freelove* were well ordered, and knew what to do; on the command her topsails and topgallants were furled to reduce speed. When within hailing distance King addressed the captain of the allegedly Dutch vessel through his speaking tube, "What is your name captain? I am Captain King, working for the British Revenue. Stay where you are, assemble all your crew on the deck, and put down all your weapons."

The reply was "Ik ben Nederlands. Ik spreek geen Engels."

"That is a pity, Captain. I shall give you ten minutes to learn English. In the meantime I shall show you what will happen if you don't."

Freelove had slowly been sailing the length of the port side of the brig. Once the first cannon drew ahead of her bow, the command was given to fire the starboard fore cannon. The explosion was immense; both ships rocked, blinding flame spurted from the muzzle, and all was then engulfed by insulating smoke. The ball, having made its point, splashed harmlessly into the sea.

Freelove was wearing round the bow, and then slowly moved starboard to starboard.

"How is your English?" asked King.

"I am Captain Jan Mellar. This is a Dutch ship, *Windhond*, and an English ship has no right to threaten and attack a Dutch ship. Our two countries are not at war."

"Your ship is in British territorial waters, and you are doing illegal trading."

"Our trading is quite legal."

"Do not waste my time, Captain Mellar. If you are doing honest trading you have nothing to fear. You must do what I ordered you to do, and quickly. Otherwise I shall blow your little ship into a flotsam of splinters and death. Begrijp je dat?"

"Yes, Captain. I do it."

"I am coming aboard with a number of other men. Do not try anything foolish. If you do, the retaliation will be horrendous."

Freelove's boat was lowered, and William Backas, Solomon King and several armed revenue men climbed down into it, along with seaman Matthew Willson to do the rowing. Those left on board were vigilant and armed. The atmosphere was tense.

Once on board, it seemed that Captain Mellar had done what he was asked. There was a line of men, and a pile of arms. Backas insisted on inspecting the crew, and demanded that their captain told him each man's name and what function they fulfilled on the vessel, all of which he noted. He also insisted on seeing each man's hands. After the inspection he said to the captain, "Is this your vessel?"

"Ja, I am the main owner."

"There are other shareholders?"

"Ja."

"I shall need a list of all the ship-owners."

"Nee, kapitein. I cannot do this; it is private information."

"You will do it. There is no alternative."

Captain Mellar paled, and gulped with misery. Backas continued, "This vessel is about 250 tons?"

"Ja."

"And you have 10 men, including yourself; the ones standing here?"

"Ja."

"Yourself, the mate, the cook and the carpenter, six seamen and no apprentices?"

"That is right."

"That is not right, Captain Mellar. I know what a seaman's hands looks like. You only have four seamen here."

"Four seamen is enough on a fluyt of this size."

"You are wrong, sir. Now bring up all the men and boys who are on this ship. Go in person. As for the mate, I want to see the ship's manifest, and no excuses."

While the master and the mate were absent, William Backas ordered that the eight men should have their hands tied behind their backs. Shortly after, Captain Mellar returned with two other men. They had seaman's hands, and were also tied up. All the ten men were marched into the captain's cabin with two armed revenue men and the door was locked from the outside.

William Backas received the manifest, and went down to the hold with the master, the mate, Solomon King and an armed escort of three revenue men. Solomon turned to Captain Mellar and said, "We know there are illicit goods here, and that some were already discharged to boats for Robin Hood's Bay. We are going to take this ship into Whitby harbour where it will be rigorously searched by the order of Mr Woods the Collector of Customs. And when I say rigorously, I mean it. We shall take this vessel apart plank by plank; not a louse, not a limpet will escape our notice. If, after that, you and your fellow owners wish to collect the pile of timber and nails which will be what is left of your brig, and reassemble it into your fluyt you will be welcome to remove it before it is incinerated. So it will be wise to tell not only the truth but the whole truth. We wish to know exactly what you carried, from whom you bought it, to all those you intended to sell."

"I will tell you all the truth."

"I am not impressed with your truth. You have lied already about the people on this vessel."

"They just came on board. I was not informed. I know them not, sir."

"But you can count. Ten men become twelve quite quickly. I shall want a list of the people on board."

"Yes, sir, the mate have a list of the crew."

"I shall want a *complete* list of the people on board."

"Yes sir."

"How many of the crew are British?"

"All except myself, sir."

"And there are no more than the twelve people I have seen?"

"Yes, sir."

*   *   *

Elisha Root and Michael Cornelius had been invited to call upon John and Dorothy Walker at their house in Haggersgate at noon on 23 December, and it was exactly at this time that Cornelius knocked on the door. They were ushered in by Elizabeth Norrison who took their coats, hats, scarves and gloves and then led them into the drawing room, where they were greeted and seated by John Walker.

Root was all smiles; he and Cornelius both assumed that there would be a submissive repentance by John for marrying Dorothy in a 'steeple house'. They expected that there would be some public act of penitence in the Quaker Meeting House and then they could be officially returned into membership. It was not to be so.

"Friends," began John, "I have received this document from the Chief Constable. I would like you to peruse it, and then tell me what you think." He handed them the affirmation by Solomon King of his witness to the events at the house of Jacob Linskill on 11 October 1727.

Root was the first to read it. His facial expression, which had betrayed a supercilious smirk, merged into a quizzical formation of eyebrows, then to suppressed anger, then to fear. When he passed the document to Cornelius his face was blank but his hand was shaking. Cornelius read it more quickly, there was briefly a raised eyebrow, but mainly he nodded his head up and down.

It was Cornelius who broke the uncomfortable silence. "It was ill done. He was a Friend, from a family of Friends. He was in need, and we passed him by."

"Nonsense, Friend Michael, he brought it upon himself. Did he not refuse the medical aid he was offered?"

"After we had rejected him, Elisha. He had always been a good Friend; we should have given him the benefit of the doubt."

"Doubt? There was no doubt in what he had told us. Did he not say that he hit Wheatear and that was the cause his hand was so bruised?"

"He did, and we believed him. Wheatear had minimal bruising, whereas Friend Jacob's hand suffered from mighty crushing. Anyone could see, if they spent a moment's time to find the truth."

"So, Friend Jacob told a lie. Friends are committed to tell the truth, so we believed him."

"He lied because he had been humiliated. He was guilty of pride; but we were guilty of the sin of a lack of charity, the sin of omission, the sin of thoughtlessness, the sin of seeing only the mote in his eye. In short we have offended against the basic tenet of our faith, that all people are our friends, brothers and sisters to whom we must show love."

"Thou art taking too much upon thyself Friend Michael. There are rules in every congregation of people, be they a religion or a family. Friend Jacob broke the rule. He showed no love and no truth and in doing so he put himself outside our membership."

John Walker, aware of the intended slight to himself in the phrase 'outside our membership', broke into the dialogue: "We are all guilty of many sins. We turned away from Jacob's daughter Abigail, as if the iniquities of the father should be visited upon the daughter. Did our Meeting take any pains to discover what became of her?

We were too eager to go down the wide road and believe that she was dead. And what has our Meeting done for her since we discovered that she was alive and that the Pickering Meeting had cared for her and nurtured her and her baby to a healthy state? Why is Abigail not in possession of her father's house when we all know, in truth, that it is indisputably hers? Has the reason that the Meeting has been slothful in this matter in any way been influenced by the money donated to the Meeting by Esau Linskill?"

Root leapt to his feet, his anger preventing him from forming coherent words. Cornelius rose more gracefully, placing a hand upon Root's shoulder, smiling gently. "Thank you very much, Mr Walker, we are grateful that you have showed us this document. We shall pass this information on to the Meeting which will, no doubt, act appropriately. As Jesus himself said, "Ye shall know the truth, and the truth shall make you free." He bowed, and then, with a firmer grip on Root, steered him out of the room, and out of the house.

Chapter 47

Christopher Woods was pleased. Everything seemed to have gone well. His lugger had showed good speed, and he had disembarked some of his armed men who had taken control of the harbour of Robin Hood's Bay. Albeit three cobles had reached land before them and by the time the revenue men had arrived there was no sign of any contraband goods. The lugger then went out and captured two cobles full of smuggled goods, arrested the men involved, and took possession of their boats. They approached another, but they had thrown their haul overboard so there was no evidence. Some of the cobles headed down the coast where they were met by the revenue sloop, which had been waiting for them at Stoup Beck. Another two cobles were captured. The rest rowed out to sea, scattering their cargo as they went. The two revenue vessels headed for Whitby with their prizes in tow.

Christopher Woods could see that *Freelove* was similarly bringing in their captured ship, and assumed that all was well. It had been one of the finest defeats of such a smuggling invasion, and he, Christopher Woods, the Collector of Customs at Whitby, was the victor.

His vessels arrived, the goods and the culprits taken to the Customs House. The men arrested and gave their names; there was little point in trying to deceive as they were well known, and many were related to -or members of- the prolific Bay Town families of Harrison, Storm,

Moorsom and Richardson. The fines were fixed, and the boats were seized to be sawn in half.

A splendid day's work.

Then *Freelove* arrived. Joseph Fox had checked the bows and the stern where the name Windhond had been carelessly painted on crude pieces of planking. With a crowbar he had prized these name plates away in each case revealing the name *Providence*.

Later Province's gangplank was out, and a sizeable amount of cargo, almost all of it illicit, was taken on carts to the Custom House warehouse alongside that which was taken from the cobles, and kept under guard.

The crew list of *Providence* was largely fiction. There were twelve men aboard her. The captain's name probably was Mellar; but on the crew list were the names for a mate, carpenter, cook, and six seamen. Backas imagined they were all false names. And there were two extra men unaccounted for. When the crew were interviewed they could give the name of the master, but not the names of any of their fellow shipmates.

Backas decided that all the men on Providence including the mate should be made to stand in a row, with their hands tied behind their backs. There was much muttering and complaining as the day was cold, and seemingly colder because of the north-easterly wind blowing from Norway with nothing in between but the German Ocean.

Backas' plan produced an immediate result when the crew of *Freelove* went to inspect the row of Providence men. Joseph Fox and Hans Nielsen immediately identified

Alexander McDaniel who had been the second mate in *Dolphin*. Joseph's first instinct on seeing a man who was complicit in attempting to sell him into slavery was to use his fists and beat him again and again until he no longer looked like a man but more like something one might find in the bilges. He was restrained however by his honour of not hitting a man who was tied.

The news of what had happened that day spread rapidly and soon there was a long queue waiting to have a look at these pirates on parade. Some wished to identify some of the men, some to abuse them and spit on them, some to check that their husband was not there, some out of simple curiosity. The latter was the reason why Sophie Norrison and her mother came to view. The stream of people moved on slowly, but eventually they were on the gangplank, where they could hear the voices of the spectators and of the prisoners. One voice was clear in a moment of more subdued chatter, "God's beard! How long are they going to keep us standing here? I need something to eat, not to mention somewhere to shit!"

Sophie felt her whole body shiver. She whispered to her mother, "It's him." Her mother had noticed nothing, but was arguing with an irritating woman behind her who was trying to push past.

Eventually they could see the row of men. Sophie was perplexed. She knew he must be there, but she could not see him. Slowly she moved down the row, looking carefully at their faces, knowing that much else can be changed. Then she saw what she expected, though it was still a surprise. She looked into his eyes. If one looks into the eyes of someone who intends to kill you, you do not forget it.

She called out, "This man is Samuel Suggett, mate of *Dolphin*, who tried to sell my mother, my sister and myself into slavery!"

Chapter 48

There had been a sharp freeze overnight and the whole town looked as if it had been sprinkled with flour. The houses were almost as cold in as out. The lucky ones –the rich, the titled, and the families of the middling sort– could turn over in bed, pull up the eiderdown and cuddle their spouse, lover or pillow, knowing their housemaid will have been up earlier to light the fire in the drawing room and to bring the range to life in the chilled kitchen. The lesser folk did what they did most days: get out of bed early, dress, wash - though if the morning was wintery chilly this was done as quickly as possible.

Then, when all this was done, the most frequently spoken sentence was, "'Tis the first day of Christmas!" and this served to make the shivering-cold day special, and made people happier even when they had little to be happy about.

In the church people filled their pews, looking about and smiling, nodding and showing off their best clothes. After several gloomy days, light shone through the east window making it sparkle. A special day. Even the sermon was unusually good, though it offended some; it was fairly lengthy as usual, but the meat of the homily was enshrined in these parts:

"The first to go and see baby Jesus were the shepherds; men who had no status, no education,   but they were skilled men looking after the sheep. Every country needs such skilled men, be they   shepherds, weavers, butchers, carpenters and sailors and many more. The Magi were the educated men; but still had to ask the way."

"At Christmas we must think of parents and children. Joseph gave Jesus skills to earn a living; but it would have been Mary who taught him how to live. Jesus was a man of sorrows, but when he was little he was as any child with two good parents who cared for him: cheerful, playful, sometimes tearful, but finally with the values and morals needed to go out into the world."

After the Christmas service, the Norrison family came together for their Yuletide meal. Two days earlier Mark Hill had sent Sophie, who was working in his butcher's shop, round with a fat goose, which had been cooking in the oven while Caroline was at the church.

Hilda, as on a Sunday, was freed from duties after Mattins. As she was leaving the church, she was accosted by Mark Hill. "I am glad to meet you," he said, "I have been hoping to have a private conversation with you." Hilda was perplexed, and rather worried, by this introduction, but she said nothing. "You are a wise and perceptive woman, so I would hope you could give me advice."

"I do not think I am very wise; but ask and I shall attempt to answer."

"I shall not wind my way through snaking ginnels, but stride down the straight road. But I insist that what I am about to say, you must keep as a secret."

"As hidden as if it were locked in the parish chest."

"I am in love with your mother, and have been for some time. I know that she is older than me; but what chance do you think I have of her marrying me?"

"This takes me by surprise, and I think my mother would react in a similar manner at first. There is no doubt that she is very fond of you, and regards you as a good friend; and friendship I think is a firm foundation for marriage. But love too, is crucial. It has been some time since Papa died but she still loves him. Sophie says that Mama simply loves recalling the days when Papa was alive, and I think she may be right. Sophie is wiser than me –as her name implies."

"But you are more sound in your thinking."

"In answer to your question, I can only say that it might be possible. When our father was alive, although we were not rich, he made us think that we were without poverty and misery. He made a life that was fun, and he encouraged –albeit in play– to learn useful trades; but they were boys' trades. We lived in a magic world, a dream, and I think Mama still tries to live in that dream. We were brought up in a world where women and men could both love and be loved, and can do anything they want to do. When he died, we were poor, and Papa's world 'melted into air, into thin air'. Whoever heard of a woman as master of a ship? Lizzie and I are just maids, mop-squeezers. And what future will we have if we don't have a husband? Fortunately Lizzie has a young man who loves her; and I am friendly –more than friendly I hope – with a man who may be a possible husband. It is a wise man who sees what lies beneath a woman's outer appearance, and sees the person within. It is only Sophie who believes Papa's dream and thinks her future can be made by herself. I am pleased you have taken her on as an apprentice, but –without offence to you, Mark– who has seen a female butcher, especially a lame one? About as much chance of a woman owning a fleet of merchant ships, or a banking house! I love and envy Sophie's optimism; but am sad when I think that her world, Papa's world, does not exist."

"And Caroline?"

"She is still in Papa's world. When we daughters leave home, I suspect things will change. She may fall helplessly, as if down a well, into her past. On the other hand, she may build her own life. In either case she will need someone, someone like you. Can you wait that long?"

"I think of her as the only woman I want to marry, and I think of you girls –in some way– as my daughters. We have such fun together."

"We do, Mark. And I would like you to marry Mama; but you would have to be patient, and even then you may have to shake her out of her past."

*   *   *

Caroline had made the house look pleasing by decorating it all green with holly, ivy and mistletoe, tokens of the longer days and the advent of spring.

In addition to Mark, the Norrison family had two other guests: Hans Nielsen and Joseph Fox. Joseph was pleased to be there, but Hans was a bit shy at first as he had not been to Atty's Yard before, and was somewhat overwhelmed in a household of women. He was pleased that Joseph was there, who had been colleagues for some time. Mark took to Hans and soon they were good friends; indeed so much so that Lizzie began to be jealous of the time Hans was spending with Mark when he should be with her. But how could any of them be cross with Mark as he had brought a half-anker of fine red wine as a present. Soon the spigot had been hammered in and all were happily merry, celebrating the beginning of the Christmas season. Mark and Hans were commissioned to set light to the Yule Log after which they all squeezed in round the table, with Lizzie on one side of Hans and Sophie on the other, who in turn was next to Mark, then Caroline, Joseph and Hannah.

Lizzie issued a broadside of questions about Norway:

"What do you eat for Christmas in Norway?"

"We do not call it Christmas, we call it *Jul*."

"What fun! We also call it Yule."

"*Jul*. Norway is a poor country, ruled by Denmark; but we are a proud people and we are -how you say?- unificated?"

"Unified."

"Yes, unified. Not like in this country, I think."

"Yes, but what do you eat at Yule?"

"*Jul*. Like I say, we are poor. We eat what we can find, and this changes with the regions."

"You live near Bergen, don't you? That is a great port."

"But we live over a day's walk from Bergen. My family have a small farm, very steep hills. On *Jul* we eat *lutefisk*."

"*Lutefisk*. Is that some kind of fish?"

"*Ja da*, yes indeed, cod fish."

"Just cod for Christmas?"

"*Nei;* we have cheese, shrimps, cold meat, and other smoked fish. And berries."

"What berries?"

"*Multerbaer*; it is a wild berry. I am told the English say 'the berries of the clouds'. We make of it jam and to flavour strong drink. There is also *tyttebaer*. Please do not laugh at me."

"I am sorry Hans. Go on, please."

"*Tyttebaer.* It is called 'berry of the heather'. It too is wild. We go out and collect them; it is quite a... How you say?"

"Quite a labour?"

"*Nei*. When all the families go out to pick the berries together."

"Tradition?"

"Yes, that is so. Do you not go searching for berries?"

"We do; but not all together."

"You English do little together it appears to me."

"Maybe," said Lizzie and put her hand on Hans' thigh. He did not appear to notice.

"Us Norwegians we are all together. In that way we shall be free."

"We are already free. We are together when it is needed."

Mark, who had been listening to the conversation, butted in, "For example, when we have to fight the French."

"And the Spanish," added Sophie.

"The Dutch, too," said Hilda.

They all laughed.

And Hans kissed Lizzie.

*   *   *

The feast of the Norrisons grew merrier and more reckless as the food and the half-anker of fine red wine diminished.

Sophie was asked, not for the first time, how she had identified Samuel Suggett.

"He was heavily disguised and no-one else was able to identify him. He had padded himself out, had shoes with thickened soles so he looked taller, his hair –which was dyed dark brown- had been allowed to grow long and he tied it at the back of his head like a horse's tail. He was clever. He even altered his speech, with a Northumberland accent rather than his native Yorkshire one."

"How did you manage to see through all that?"

"Well, Joseph, the first thing I noticed was his familiar phrase 'God's beard!', and because he uttered that phrase habitually he forgot to give it a new accent. Even then it was difficult to see him beneath the disguise. It was when I looked him in the face that I recognised him, even though he had given himself a scar on his left cheek. There I was face to face with Samuel Suggett who was prepared to sell most of the people in this room into slavery."

A shudder of revulsion went round the room.

"Father's pistol, which I used to frighten him, was not loaded; but Suggett intended to kill me. As it was the shot struck my leg, and I am lucky, largely thanks to Joseph, that I survived. I would like to know how many of us here would have been prepared to kill Suggett. Please, a show of hands."

Caroline's hand was up in a flash, then one after another the rest of the arms were raised.

"So," said Sophie, "We are all potential murderers. None of us will actually have to kill Suggett, he has been arrested and he will certainly be condemned to death, so you can lower your hands. However, Jack Wheatear was killed, not by accident or a spontaneous response, but by careful planning. We have already admitted we can kill if we have sufficient motive. Maybe the murderer is sitting in this very room at this very moment.

*   *   *

Solomon King, alone at Christmas in his new large house, reassured himself that the killing of Jack Wheatear was a good deed – no more a sin than it was to kill a rat.

He has used Abigail and transformed a lively and delightful little girl into a drab and banal woman. I waited all those years in the hope that I would one day be worthy of her hand in marriage, only to find that she has been reduced to this. How could she even think of marrying Wheatear?

His angry thoughts darted around like lightning; but, like lightning, they swiftly faded.

Maybe...

Maybe, Abigail felt she had been degraded and, as a woman with a bastard child, was not fit to marry anyone else? She is a strong woman: she was sent away by her father, rejected by her uncle the attorney, and gave birth among strangers. The real Abigail may have been battered and subdued, but not destroyed. The Friends in Pickering saw to that. She has talent; she is clever and fairly shrewd. She is not without love. She does love her son: when she plays with him she comes to life, when she talks of little Jonas her eyes sparkle in just the same way as I remember her. She is truly a good mother, a Mary, as the vicar said.

We would make a good couple. My mother used to say, "Solomon be wise. Marry a strong woman, sensible and intelligent. Looks may fade; but a woman of character is always beautiful."

He smiled, thinking that this Christmas may be the start of a new life.

Chapter 49

The constable visited William Backas' house in the morning.

William had a bit of a fuzzy head. "What brings you here?" he said; then remembering his manners, "Will you come in?"

"No, sir. I can see you're busy. It is just to let you know there is bad news. A dead body was dragged out of the harbour late last night. It is believed it happened shortly after the crew of *Providence* left the vessel on Christmas Eve."

"I would have thought that you and your night-watchmen would have attended the evacuation of the crew to prevent riot and murder."

"We would have done so, sir, as you say. But we had been given a tip off that there was going to be an unpleasant criminal action in Cliff Lane. So we went there for the protection of the inhabitants of Whitby."

"Cliff Lane?"

"Yes, sir."

"Did you recall that two years ago on Coronation Day you and your men were advised to go to Cliff Lane and while you were there crimes were committed at the house of Jacob Linskill's house?"

"Yes, sir, now you mention it."

"A coincidence?"

"Of course, sir. Life is full of co-incidences, is it not sir?"

"I see. Do we know who the dead man was?"

"Yes, sir, he was identified as Alexander McDaniel, a Scotsman, who had been second mate in *Dolphin* working for James Boyes. I suspect some bystanders may have beaten him up and thrown him into the sea."

*   *   *

Margaret Backas and Hilda Norrison were sitting in the kitchen. They were drinking tea which they felt they deserved, as they had cleaned the whole room, and sorted out all the bottles and jars.

They chatted about this and that. They had just exhausted a discussion about ways of dressing a bonnet, when Margaret said, "Tell me, Hilda, when you said you had a pet rat did you keep it in a cage?"

"No, Mistress. It goes back to when we were children. We were a bit scared of the rats in the basement, so our mother said we should give them names and talk to them. There were two who were special; they didn't scuttle off like the others. And it worked: we gave them names and talked to them. We weren't frightened and sometimes we fed them. The rats never became tame, but they recognised we were not a threat to them, and they kept out other rats. There were several generations of rats all of which we named. It was just a bit of childish silliness really."

"And now you are grown up you have someone of another species to look after."

"You are referring in Matthew Willson?"

"Of course. I hear he is to be a mate this year."

"Yes, we are both very pleased about that."

"It is said that when seamen become mates, is the time when they have sufficient pay to think about marrying."

Hilda blushed, Margaret continued, "Has he said anything yet?"

"Nothing decisive yet; but we have an understanding."

"He is welcome to come here to visit you - provided we are given notice."

"Thank you, Mistress."

"On the condition of course that he brings his fiddle."

*   *   *

The weekly meeting in the Golden Lion was buoyant. The Customs warehouse was full of contraband goods. Many of the smugglers of Robin Hood's Bay had been caught, identified, fined and had their boats sawn in half. *Freelove* was pivotal in the success, and had been returned to her original owners. It had been a significant blow to the smuggling trade. Even the Inspector of the East Coast Ports had sent a letter that verged on praise.

Though Windhond was clearly *Providence*, it would have been difficult to prove that she had not been bought in Holland. The captain was really Dutch, so it would be difficult to bring him to trial in Britain, and even more difficult to prove he was guilty. However, Christopher Woods' team, as had been threatened, were so thorough in searching *Providence* for hidden contraband that she needed serious repairs. That would supply some of Whitby's ships carpenters with work for the whole winter.

"Another good thing," said Backas, "is that we have Samuel Suggett in custody, safely in the lockup. Alexander McDaniel's drowned body was identified when it was washed up on the sand; officially an accident, but unofficially he was thrown into sea by persons unknown. Some of the other men were identified and fined. All the crew had their details recorded. Then they were set free. We shall know who to keep an eye on."

The Golden Lion trio had never been so cheerful, even though they had drunk no ale. Christopher Woods had asked some of the regular patrons to roll a hogshead of wine from the customs warehouse to the inn. "After all," said Woods, "it is important that we test what is in the barrel. We need to know that it is not only wine, but that it is French wine. And for that purpose, the more experts the better."

The fact that the collapse of James Boyes' contraband network meant that Theaker would attempt to take over once more would be a problem for later.

"After all Nature abhors a vacuum," said Armson.

"Was that Isaac Newton?"

"I think you'll find, William, that it was Aristotle.

"I think it unlikely that Aristotle spoke English."

"That's enough, you two. For now, the wine tasting is important."

"And neither Oliver nor I is going to argue with your hogshead, Christopher."

*　　　　　*　　　　　*

Margaret Backus, now that she was aware that she was probably likely to be a mother, felt different and began to see the world differently. The vicar's Christmas sermon made her realise that Mary was a mother who had given birth to a baby and was to look after him and nurture him, as mothers do, and he survived to manhood. She thought of the wonder of motherhood and the fear that her child might die young, as so many do.

She wanted to go out, even though it was cold, away from the home so she could think. After all, the home would all be changed with a child. She felt drawn to the ruins of the abbey - a place which had been for centuries a home which had no children. And so near to the abbey was the church where people were married and had children who were baptized, who in turn married, had children and died. She scanned across the field of buried people; she was not sure whether she felt happy or sad, but she was now part of that endless chain of life and death. She was there for some time, pensive.

Looking back to the abbey she saw a figure that she first thought was a monk; but it was a real person, apparently - like her- deep in thought. The outline of the figure was obscured by the sea mist, though eerily lit up by the setting sun. She turned and went home.

*   *   *

"Where have you been?" asked William when Margaret came in, her coat covered in rime, but apparently unaware of the cold.

"Just up East Cliff for a walk."

William removed her coat and scarf, and led her towards a comfortable chair in front of a welcoming fire. He said nothing, as he knew it would not be necessary.

After some time, Margaret said, "I walked up to East Cliff for exercise; there was a young man there pacing up and down and clearly brooding over a broken heart."

"You have been reading love poems, too, Margaret. For all we know he was probably worrying about being short of money."

"Sometimes I think you have no soul, William."

"My soul works well, even though I am paid to deal with the nastier side of human nature."

Chapter 50

"Where's the barrel?" asked William Backas.

"So, you have noticed its absence at last?"

"I noticed a long time since, but chose not to comment." His reply sounded weak, even to himself.

"It was sold to Mr Lant. Hilda sorted it all out, so I said she could keep the money."

"Hmm. I suppose it is not really going to yield up who killed Wheatear. You do know the butt was not ours to sell? But then I don't suppose anyone is going to claim it, and its contents."

"Not now, anyway, as it was broken when Mr Lant was rolling it onto his cart. Its contents spilled out down the street, apart from the rat."

"Apart from the rat?"

"Yes, Hilda buried it in the garden. She recognised the drowned rat, it was some kind of childish game in her house. You don't mind her burying the rat, do you?"

"No, if it pleased Hilda so to do. It may improve the soil. But no more of her rats buried in the garden – it's not a rat cemetery."

*   *   *

Abigail Linskill visited her second-cousin Esau Linskill in the house that was once her father's in Flowergate.

After the initial politenesses, Esau said, "Cousin Abigail, may I say how sad I was when I heard that your husband had been killed. A great tragedy."

"Cousin Esau, I believe that you are sad because you thought that my marriage to Jack Wheatear would mean that you could steal my inheritance."

"You are very rude and abrupt, cousin."

"I mean to be so. Many months have passed since my father died, and this house should have come to me then. It is about time you moved out with all your properties herein."

"That will take time, as I have told you before."

"The more time you live in my house, the more will be your rent."

"Let us consider again the idea I suggested when last we met, namely that we have a partnership. It could be very profitable, between us we could defeat those who are setting up small canvas manufactories."

"What you say is possible. However the business would have to be called 'Abigail and Esau Linskill', I would be the chief owner with 60% of the shares, and you back pay me for your residence in this house of mine for two years."

"How about forgetting the rent and you have 50% of the shares?"

"Forgetting the rent and 55% ownership. Final offer."

"Agreed. You drive a hard bargain, but that is good in business. I shall find an attorney to make up the contract, and then we shall both sign it."

They shook hands on it.

"In addition, Abigail, how would you like to marry me?"

"It is worth considering."

"It would mean the business had to be called 'Esau and Abigail Linskill'.

"If I were to agree to marry you I would accept that name of the firm; but I would have to have a greater percentage of the shares, in my own name!"

*   *   *

By coincidence or maybe design, William Backas met Sophie as she was on her way home from the butchery.

"Good evening, Miss Sophia Norrison."

"Good evening, Mr Backas. It is good that the chill in the weather is much diminished."

"Indeed, but I have been wishing to talk to you for some time."

"Is there a problem?"

"No, indeed. I would just like to ask you a few questions."

"Ask away, sir."

"I gather that the butcher's shop in which you are an apprentice, has overcome the problems caused by George Hill being involved in Ralph Theaker, 'The Provider'?"

"Indeed, sir. Mr George's son Mark has not only restored his father's business to the level it was before, but it has gone beyond that measure."

"And did Mark Hill offer to provide the various meats for the wedding feast for Abigail Linskill and Jack Wheatear?"

"Yes, he did indeed. He invited Jack round to our basement, and showed him some fine poultry and excellent beef at a very generous price. I wanted the feast to be in our house but my mother would not allow that as

327

she hated Wheatear, so they hired out the back room in the Fleece where their kitchen staff were to do the cooking. It is sad that it all happened as it did."

"On a different topic, did you know that Hilda had buried her rat in our garden?"

"Yes, she mentioned it. You were kind to let her do so."

*   *   *

A letter had been delivered. It read:

"I know what you have done, and how, and why you have done it. I shall tell no-one your name; but others are not far from knowing what I know. You know what you must do; a trial and a hanging will be the opposite of what your intentions were."

Wilfred

Chapter 51

So many ships were laid up for the winter that it was barely possible to see from one side of the river to the other for the congestion of vessels. Even so, not all Whitby-owned collier brigs over-wintered in Whitby; many stayed in Shields so they could start the coal run as soon as the weather permitted.

Not all of the vessels had returned by the first day of Christmas.

The wives of sailors had a difficult and insecure life. Every time their husband's ship was due, they waited (if they had time so to do) on the quay, their shawls wrapped tight and with questions piercing their minds: Is he still alive? Is he wounded? How much money has he brought home? This last question being especially important when it was the ship's last voyage of the year. That money must last for two months, apart from any casual winter work either could find. A seaman, married and with children, who squandered his money in London - or other ports– on tobacco, alcohol and/or gambling endangered the comfort, health and even the life of his dependant family. If he spent money on whores he could carry back even more horrific tragedy to the family.

At first light on the fifth day of Christmas one particular woman stood alone on the East Cliff near the churchyard, seemingly not noticing the bitter wind. She held a bundle so wrapped up that it was impossible to know what was in it, though the way she rocked it back and forth made it clear that it was a small baby. She was waiting for her husband, master for the first time of a 200 ton ship. It was the first time this ship had sailed across the fierce Atlantic; her cargo was bricks to Virginia and to bring back tobacco and rum.

As the sun rose higher she did not notice how the frosted grass turned slowly green as the sunlight swallowed up the shadows and warmed the frozen earth. Her eyes were fixed on the sea, straining to see a vessel loom out of the invisible distance.

She sang plaintively, perhaps to her child, the old song, as if it were a charm or canticle:

You gentlemen of England, that live at home at ease,
Full little do you think upon the dangers of the seas;
Give ear unto the mariners, and they will plainly show,
All the cares and fears when stormy winds do blow.

After an immeasurable time other wives and sweethearts whose men were in the same vessel were assembling on the quayside also waiting. It was warmer there, and each of them had a shawl of similar shapes, but of different pattern and colours. They chattered to pass the time and subdue their fears. Although they could not see the master's wife standing on the cliff, they knew she was there, and that she would come down to the harbour to tell them the news when she had seen the ship.

She identified her husband's ship before most of the other watching women could have even noticed there was a vessel on the horizon.

"Oh Charlie," she cried aloud, "you have come back to me! May God have kept you well!"

Then she became aware of a fierce noise on Abbey Lane. Turning round she saw a pale horse galloping, snorting with panic fear, its eyes red and large. It was bound to the shafts of a waggon which was lurching wildly. It was impossible to know whether the man whose hands were frantically clenched on the reins was recklessly urging the thrashing horse to go faster or desperately trying to restrain it. Suddenly the trinity of horse, man and waggon veered off the road insanely speeding towards the precipitous cliff. Mary, fearing this was the last horseman of the apocalypse bringing death, ran to the cemetery wall for safety, crouching low, clutching her swaddled child. The hurtling vision pounded and rattled over the grass, passing her by. Then the stallion realised he was racing towards the cliff edge, and stopped, bracing his forelegs against the grassy tussocks, but still sliding slowly. The cart had no such means of halting and its momentum caused it to swivel round the panting beast, scudding sideways. A wheel broke free and rolled over the cliff and the waggon came to a halt, half-hanging over the edge.

All was quiet except the horse's breathing. The silence was broken by a creak, a crack, a groan and then the edge of the cliff broke away in a rumbling clatter, taking waggon, man and horse over the precipice crashing, breaking and splintering on the rocks below. The fierce waves washed over the rocks time and again, each time taking more of the detritus only to spew it up onto the scaur for the gulls.

*   *   *

After breakfast William Backas said, "I know who murdered Wheatear."

"Do you?" replied Margaret. "Tell me how this came about."

"The murderer was clearly someone who hated his victim. I believe that they wanted the victim to suffer and to realise why he was suffering. Unfortunately there are several suspects who might have wanted to do this, as we have discussed before. It is possible that what killed Wheatear was being hit on the head, he was not drowned, so the murderer could simply have killed him and put the corpse in a butt of lant; but he did not. What killed him was having his throat cut. I think the murderer hit the victim on the head to stun him, and then he was put in the butt. This was no easy matter. Either the cask could be laid on its side, the limp body inserted and then the cask was uprighted, or the stunned body was lifted and lowered into the vertical butt. The latter would be more difficult, I think, though some liquid in the base would have steadied the cask. A woman could have done the first…"

"Are you suggesting a woman could not do the second?"

"No, Margaret, I am not; but I do not think it was a woman. It is quite possible, though, that the victim was, for an unknown reason, persuaded to climb into the barrel himself."

"I agree."

"Good. So there was a stunned body wedged in a cask, and that was when most of the urine was poured in.

FRIEND OR FOE

Wheatear became conscious. This was the moment the murderer probably enjoyed, as his victim was constrained and powerless with his knees up to his chest, forced to listen to his crimes and wonder what would be his punishment, while the murderer poured in bucket after bucket of lant."

"You are making a tale of this, William."

"A conjecture; but I think it must be close to what actually happened. The murderer then cut Wheatear's throat, put the lid on the cask and sealed it with the hoops."

"So far, it is something out of a revenge melodrama upon the stage."

"The murderer may have had that in mind. There were, I think, two reasons for this elaborate killing: first, for the victim to be immersed in urine was an act of degradation and humiliation; and secondly, to disguise when and where the murder took place, by ensuring that the butt with the body therein was exchanged for one of David Dunn's casks of lant which were carried away to Boulby Alum Works. A bold plan and a risky one; but it meant that we had no idea where Wheatear was killed, and only a vague idea when. It was entirely down to the skill of one of the men at the Boulby Alum Works that the butt was identified as unusual, otherwise the dead Wheatear might not have been discovered for at least a week, maybe a fortnight."

"Yes, this we already know."

"Indeed. But we know that it is unlikely that the murder was done outside in a public place as it was a lengthy process, so it must have been done somewhere which was private, and almost certainly to which the victim could be lured. The murderer would have obtained a butt and he would have stolen lant -probably from Mr David Dunn- in comparatively small amounts over time which he would later pour into his cask, I reckon that he must have needed something in the order of fifty gallons of piss at least. It all would have taken time. In addition the exchange of casks was a problem: taking a butt (which is a sizeable cask) with a body inside and then exchanging it for another on the quay which is open to the gaze of all is reckless, no matter how late at night it was done. Our murderer is a planner. He would not risk being seen exchanging casks."

"So how would he manage to exchange the casks?"

"He changed them at David Dunn's yard. Dunn has a fixed routine when he goes round at night collecting lant, so it was easy for the murderer -when Dunn was absent- to take the butt with the corpse inside and exchange it for one of those which Dunn had put aside for taking to the quay to be loaded for Boulby Alum Works. So, unwittingly, David Dunn took the corpse in the cask to the quay."

"That's clever."

"But the murderer would have to own, or have access to, a horse-drawn wagon. He would also need a sizeable space to which he had sole access. So we are talking about a trader of sorts, probably whose business requires a heavy implement and a large sharp knife which would cut Wheatear's throat easily."

"So who do you think was this villain?"

"The butcher Mark Hill. He has a waggon, he has space in his premises, but also he has the sole use of the storage room which belongs to Caroline Norrison."

"Would she know what he was doing, do you think?"

"It would be very unlikely. He often worked in there storing barrels of meat for ships etcetera; there would be nothing out of the ordinary about Mark being in her warehouse, which he rented, so there was no reason why anyone else would be there."

"Might he have done it with Caroline as an accomplice? She would enjoy that!"

"First he carefully planned what he did; he would not want another person involved, certainly not Caroline as the whole point was to make her happy. He was very fond of Mrs Norrison, and he would not wish her to be implicated. His motive for murder was —almost certainly— to kill Wheatear because of the sorrow he brought to Mrs Norrison by allowing Suggett to shoot Sophia during the mutiny on *Dolphin*. She had often said that she would not be happy until Wheatear was dead."

"But how could Wheatear be lured? They were not friends, I think."

"That was at first a problem. The probable series of events was thus: Mark had been planning this for some time, collecting lant from a number of sources over several weeks or months. He had several casks of his own which he kept in the basement warehouse, and there was a door at the back which opened onto a ginnel, which ensured his coming and going could be unseen. For the murder he needed two casks, one in which the lant was collected and the other, the butt, into which the victim would be killed and transported. He was, no doubt, rather worried about how he would lure Jack into his warehouse, but then he had a portion of luck: Jack Wheatear was to marry Abigail Linskill. Food would be needed for the wedding feast. Mark, offering a cheap price no doubt, tempted Wheatear to see some special hams, game and meat joints, luring him into the warehouse. An added advantage was that, as Caroline hated him, Wheatear would have come in from the ginnel, taking care that he was not seen. While he was inspecting the food, Mark hit him from behind with his butcher's mallet, enough to stun but not to kill. When Wheatear recovered he was helpless in the butt with urine being poured in slowly. Mark probably went through all Wheatear's sins, from the rape of Abigail when she was just a child to his maiming Sophie for life in *Dolphin*, and then he cut his throat."

Margaret, who had listened long enough, decided it was her turn:

"Your description is impressive, William, but in truth the murder could have been perpetrated by anyone who hated Wheatear —and there was a great deal of them— who had access to a private storeroom. Anyway, as it has taken you such a long time to piece together the events so far, that Mark -or whoever was the murderer- has had ample time to clean up and remove all the evidence."

"It is true that the solving of this crime has lagged like a lame donkey."

"Indeed, you have taken furlongs of your time on this attempt to solve the problem; time which you should have spent on overseeing the organisation of the workhouse."

"I plead guilty to the latter."

"So you cannot arrest Mark Hill, or anyone?"

"No, I *can* arrest Mark Hill. This is where Hilda and you made the decisive link."

Margaret knew by his expression and the way he spoke that this was no jest. All she could think of saying was "Me? And Hilda?"

"It was actually Hilda who found the evidence."

"How? What? *Hilda*?"

"Hilda identified the rat in the vat, because of his uniquely striped tail, as the semi-tamed rodent which she and her sisters had whimsically treated almost as a pet, and which she buried in our garden."

"But how did I solve the mystery, William?"

"By telling me, my dearest. At one point the rat, who lived in the Norrison basement, had climbed into the butt, no doubt scavenging for food, but slipped into the lant. The rat swam, but could not scramble up the side, became exhausted and drowned. The rat linked the murdered Wheatear in the barrel with Caroline Norrison's basement which Mark Hill rented."

"So you can arrest Mark Hill?"

"Yes, but there is no hurry. First I think we should thank Hilda for her part in the success of the solving the mystery, without whom..."

"And me."

"Yes, and you, without whom the murderer would almost certainly escaped the gallows. Please call Hilda, my dearest, from whatever she is doing."

"I regret that you will have to wait," said Margaret. "She is not in the house. I said that when she had washed the breakfast things she could go out into the town. It is rumoured that there has been a terrible accident on the scaur."

"Has a ship run ashore? I heard that one was due early today. We must go and find out what has happened."

"No, William. It is important that we wait for Hilda."

Indeed, Hilda returned shortly after this, she had run all the way and was out of breath.

"Hilda," said William Backas, who was confused and anxious, "has a ship been wrecked?"

"No, sir...not a ship...All well..." she gasped, "But...disaster on East Cliff...Man...Horse and cart...fell...over...dead."

"Who, girl, who?"

"Know not...sir...ran here."

Mrs Backas guided Hilda to a chair. "Sit down and recover yourself, my child." She brought her a glass of water. "When you are recovered you can tell Mr Backas all about Wilfred."

"Wilfred?" said William.

There was a knocking on the door. Hilda tried to get up, but Mrs Backas prevented her. "You recover yourself. I shall open the door."

It was the constable. "Good day, Mrs Backas. Is your husband in?"

"Yes, he is. Come in and follow me."

William Backas, who was beginning to feel that he was sliding into confusion, was glad to see him, hoping that he could restore coherence.

"It is good to see you," said Backas. Please be seated and tell me exactly what has happened?"

"Early this morning a horse and cart with its driver travelling at much speed veered off Abbey Lane on East Cliff and all went over the precipice. This was seen by a woman. She was there looking out for her husband's ship."

"Do you know who it was who died in this terrible accident?"

"The body was badly mutilated and when the corpse was washed up on the shore he was scarcely recognisable. However a few people were prepared to certify on oath that the body was that of Mr Hill."

"Mr Mark Hill, the butcher?"

"The very same, sir."

"Very well. Take a description of the event from the woman who saw the accident, and from anyone else who saw or heard anything of relevance. All the information, of course, you must put in writing and have verified by the witnesses. Similarly with those who could identify the body as Mark Hill. Bring them to me as soon as possible, so I can pass it onto the coroner. Then, if the coroner agrees, make an agreement with the vicar concerning burial. I am not aware that he had any close relatives, but

I would like you to see if there are any. We shall need to know if he made a will."

"Yes, sir. I shall do all these as speedily as I can, sir."

"And do you know a Wilfred who might be involved?"

"A Wilfred, sir? Involved? How? Surely this is a case of misadventure, sir?"

"That is for the coroner to decide; but it does look as if that will be the decision."

After the constable had left to fulfil all his tasks, William sat down and said, "Well, Margaret, we shall certainly never be able to arrest Mark Hill, and watch him hang in York."

Then he turned to Hilda, and said, "You have done well. Without your observation we would never have been able to solve the murder."

"Thank you, sir." Hilda curtsied and blushed.

"But who on earth is Wilfred?"

Margaret intervened, "Didn't I tell you, William, that Wilfred was the name the Norrison girls gave to the stripy-tailed rat?"

Although in the midst of tragedy, all three burst into laughter.

After their merriment subdued, Margaret said, "So, Mark knew that he had been found out in some way, and committed suicide."

"As to whether Mark's death was suicide or misadventure is for the coroner to decide. And as we have no means of knowing if he thought he had been found out, there is no point discussing the matter any further. It appears certain that he was the murderer. Even though his motive seems to have been altruistic, murder is murder - a crime against the state and a sin against God. But as the evidence will never be brought to trial, we cannot say anything about it." William looked meaningfully at both women, though more gently to Hilda.

"So any information about the identity of the rat and its significance must not go beyond this room. I insist. So it will never be heard of as common gossip in the market. Is that clear?"

Both women nodded their heads.

"This doesn't mean to say that I am not enormously proud of both of you and all you have done to solve a difficult murder. And by the way, Hilda, is the rat still buried in the garden?

"Yes, sir. I hope you don't mind."

"The best place for him. Wilfred's grave must not be disturbed."

Chapter 52

William Backas kept back the evidence of Wilfred rat's distinctive striped tail and damaged ear. He knew who the murderer was, but there was no point in sharing this certainty, because Mark Hill was dead and it is not possible to condemn a corpse. Only five people knew of Wilfred the rat's evidence, and they agreed to keep quiet. Caroline Norrison was not told, as it was evident that no benefit would come of her knowing it.

Mark's motive was to kill Jack Wheatear and thereby bring some peace of mind to Caroline Norrison. It was not revenge for Abigail's rape, so the deaths of Simon Scott and Thomas Preston were not related to the murder. The sad fact is that accidents of this kind were not uncommon on board ship. Not all unexplained deaths are murders.

Although Mark's intention was to stay alive, his aim was strangely achieved. Caroline had been obsessed with the unprovable idea that Sophie's wound was caused by Wheatear's intervention, and indeed that it was only by good luck that she was not killed. The death of Wheatear was the end of her monomania. Clearly it was Samuel Suggett who actually shot Sophie, but Caroline showed no interest in his arrest.

Obviously the murder of Jack Wheatear, and the grisly means of his killing, excited the town of Whitby, and beyond. But with nothing concrete, no trial, and no execution at York prison ensured that over time interest lapsed. There was little in the newspapers, and no broadsheet ballads. Gossip is ephemeral.

However, the dramatic death of Mark Hill, the fall over the cliff, the mangled body of man and horse which had been clearly witnessed by a woman who saw it as an apocalyptic warning was by many believed as just that. It certainly excited the press, and the ballad mongers went wild printing sheets with titles such as *'Whitby's Apocalypse', 'The White Horse of Death, Doom and Destruction: A Warning to Wealthy Shipowners', 'The Barghest Hound Chases a Horse and Cart to their Doom',* and *'Is this the End of the World?'* With such dramatic and daemonic yarns to spin, the death of a sailor in a butt of urine was comparatively dull. No-one seemed to link the two events.

The circumstances of the arrest of Suggett, his plan to sell a woman and her children into slavery (no mention of Joseph Fox), his trial and his execution certainly did arouse the newspapers, and broadsheets were printed telling the story of his crimes and his public hanging at York in gruesome detail. But lacking the thrill of religion, superstition, and divine punishment, Suggett's story did not equal that of Hill's.

*   *   *

William and Margaret Backas, after a supper of beef pie and blancmange with some fine Portuguese red wine, had settled themselves comfortably round the coal fire.

Margaret had told William that she was knitting a new pair of socks for him, but actually she was knitting baby clothes.

William knew what she was doing.

Margaret said, "Dearest, what are you reading? More about your obligations as Chief Constable?"

"Yes, my love, a deal of tedious documents about the building of the workhouse." In fact what he was reading was a treatise about childbirth.

Margaret knew that he was not reading documents concerning the workhouse; but patiently knitted until William fell asleep and the pamphlet which he had been reading slipped gently from his hands to the floor. Helpfulness and curiosity drove her to put down her knitting and to pick up the booklet. She perused it briefly.

William woke with a jolt. It took a few seconds to realise what had happened. He smiled, "Aha, my dear wife, you have been reading about the workhouse, have you?"

Margaret laughed and said, "Indeed so, William. After all it is something that will affect me deeply."

William sprung to his feet and embraced her. "I felt I needed to learn something of what childbirth is like. I was not taught any of this as a child; instead I was taught too much Latin."

"That is good, William, my lovely husband. You often surprise me, which I like. But be reassured that the midwife is excellent and she is spoken well of by many mothers. What shall we call our child? I rather like Alice, Susanna or maybe Isabel. What do you think, dearest?"

"After much thinking, I rather like the name Christopher."

*   *   *

Mark Hill's will had been written and signed on 29th December, and was delivered to the attorney-at-law in Baxtergate. It was pleasingly brief:

"I, Mark Hill, butcher, of Whitby, being of healthy body and sound mind, bequeath everything I possess at the time of my death, after all of my debts are paid, to Sophia, frequently referred to as Sophie, Norrison. I appoint as my executor Solomon King of Whitby."

It was signed by himself and witnessed by his two friendly, but competitive, neighbouring butchers.

Acknowledgements

I cannot recall a time when I did not read murder stories, so I have to acknowledge that ocean of crime writers, dead and alive, who have given me so much pleasure and guidance. As a maritime historian, with particular interest in the 18th century and Whitby, I thought it would be fun to write a murder mystery; I was particularly inspired so to do by the Crime Writers' *Bodies from The Library* at The British Museum. However, writing fiction is very different to non-fiction writing, and I have learnt much from many people, not all of whom can be mentioned here alas, but I must name Janet Lawrence, William Shaw and Susan Moody particularly.

My family deserves thanks, also. My wife Susan has edited many drafts, spotting and filling the lacunae and bringing order to the inchoate. Claudia has ploughed through the rough text to clear it of clods and errors, and Eleanor and Philippa have been enormously supportive.

But particular gratitude is due to Mike Linane who has been a kind, thorough and patient mentor for me, spending so much time with great generosity.

Made in the USA
San Bernardino, CA
10 March 2018